Sally Piper is a former nurse and lived in the UK for nine years before returning to Brisbane to complete a Postgraduate Diploma and Master's Degree in Creative Writing at QUT, where she was supervised by Kristina Olsson. She had a story selected in the first *One Book Many Brisbanes* anthology in 2006. *Grace's Table* was shortlisted in the 2011 Queensland Premier's Literary Awards – Emerging Queensland Author category. She has had short stories, poetry and non-fiction articles published in Australia and the UK, appearing in writing journals, literary magazines and *The Weekend Australian*. She currently lives in Brisbane with her husband and two sons.

GRACE'S

TABLE

Sally Piper

UQP

First published 2014 by University of Queensland Press
PO Box 6042, St Lucia, Queensland 4067 Australia

www.uqp.com.au
uqp@uqp.uq.edu.au
© 2014 Sally Piper

Cover design/illustration by Allison Colpoys
Author photograph by Christine Sharp
Typeset in 12/15pt Bembo by Post Pre-press Group, Brisbane
Printed in China by 1010 Printing International Limited

Cataloguing-in-Publication entry is available from the National Library of
Australia http://catalogue.nla.gov.au/

ISBN (pbk) 978 0 7022 5004 0
ISBN (pdf) 978 0 7022 5237 2
ISBN (epub) 978 0 7022 5238 9
ISBN (kindle) 978 0 7022 5239 6

University of Queensland Press uses papers that are natural, renewable and
recyclable products made from wood grown in sustainable forests. The
logging and manufacturing processes conform to the environmental
regulations of the country of origin.

For my mother, who always cooks with love,
and for my father, who benefits from it daily.

Grace hooked her nail under the sticky tape and pulled back the gift paper. Inside was a boxed polished-steel knife block holding six different knives.

'Knives,' Grace declared.

'Do you like them?' Susan sounded young again, eager for approval.

'They're very ... modern.' Grace looked kindly at her daughter, then gripped the handle of one and slid it from its slot. The new steel glinted from tip to haft and made Grace think of surgeons and torturers, and the cold impersonal touch of both. The knives' obvious sharpness also made her think of her father, but in a kinder way.

Grace's Pa had been a man with penchants for bitter mints, tool care and wheezing. Asthma had saved him from enlistment, though he cussed it for doing so long after the troops had returned home. Mother rolled her eyes at his cussing and muttered, *Ignorant fool* or

Tell that to Widow Parkes, like she knew something he didn't. He never challenged her. Instead, he'd take another bitter mint from the jar on the small round table beside his chair and suck on it in quiet contemplation of what he might have missed.

He was a tall, barrel-chested man. And despite his rickety breath, Grace remembered the firmness of his muscles when she'd swing, like a pendulum, from his strongman arms as a child. To her, they felt like rocks beneath his skin and she believed him to be as hardy as anybody's father. As a young girl she put his laboured breathing down to nothing more than difference, not ill health, though towards the end of his life she was less naïve and knew the two to be inseparable.

At the end of a day he'd come into the house in his dusty home-sewn shirt and trousers, at odds with the clean regime of their home. He'd position his boots compliantly side by side at the back door, tongues lolled to one side like a dog's, shoelaces undone and at the ready, as though a quick escape might be required at any moment. What he looked to escape from, or to, Grace could only guess, but she figured it related to territory. Where the house smelt of Sunlight soap and wax polish, the kitchen of vanilla essence, stewed fruit or simmering stews, Pa smelt of farm and sweat. The scent of one was always in conflict with the other.

'Go clean yourself up, Frank,' Mother would admonish.

Even after coming back in from the cement tub in the washhouse with his hair damped down and his skin smelling of soap, he'd stand around like a visitor who'd inconveniently dropped by at meal time. His lounge and kitchen chairs were his only sanctuaries. Mother eventually left them dusty and flat-cushioned, either despairing of keeping them clean and plump, or as an indictment of his failure to fit in with her meticulous hygiene.

The sheds and barn were where Pa felt at home. Grace, often seeking escape too from her demanding mother, would hunt him out at one building or another. She'd scrape mud from the deep tread of the Ferguson tractor tyres with a stick while he lubricated parts that moved with thick brown grease, or sharpened the blades of things that cut — cut grass, cut cows' horns, cut wood. He was a man who took great care with his tools and machinery, showing them a loving touch Mother lacked.

'Look after your things well, Gracie, and they'll last you forever,' he said once, as he ran a chisel across a whetstone in careful circular motions, periodically spitting onto the stone's surface.

'But the wooden handle's already broken so it hasn't lasted forever.' Grace felt smug in catching out the usually uncatchable.

'It's not the handle that does the cutting,' Pa said. 'And besides, that's easy fixed.'

'But the cutting part will wear away one day too and you can't fix that.'

'Won't happen in my lifetime, so it will have lasted me forever.'

'That's not a real forever.'

'Real enough to my thinking.' Pa spat with perfect aim onto the grey stone and worked the chisel blade through the white froth.

Grace had never used a whetstone on her own knives. She preferred the sharpening steel Des had brought home from the shop. She'd swipe her knives along the cylinder, switching the blade from one side to the other in a criss-cross fashion. It was a satisfying motion, efficient and controlled. Her favourite knife, a butcher's knife, which had also come from Des's work, wasn't unlike her father's old chisel. It too had a wooden handle and blackened steel blade. She'd recall Pa's story about things lasting forever whenever she sharpened it. Pa would be proud of this knife of hers. The blade, once wide, had worn down to be narrow and concave in the middle from years of being run up and down the sharpening steel. It fitted nicely over the curve of a tomato or the hard skin of a Queensland Blue and could still cut through either as if they were butter. She expected the blade to see her out, just as Pa's chisel had indeed seen him out. Grace often wondered where those tools were now. Joe took care of them after Pa died but with Joe gone as well, Grace supposed they'd reached the end of anybody's measure of forever.

'And here, this goes with them.' Now Susan passed Grace a second, smaller gift.

Grace opened it, revealing a flat object with two wheels sitting side by side. The modern knife sharpener.

'I hope you like them. They were expensive.'

Grace ran a knife through the sharpener. It dragged loudly across the coarse wheels, grinding metal on stone in a way that made her teeth hurt. She was inclined to spit on the thing just as Pa had spat on his whetstone. She tested the knife's edge with her finger.

'Very nice,' she said inadequately.

'They're all the go. Watch any of the cooking channels and you'll see this brand of knife on the bench in the background.'

'Is that right? Looks like I'm set to be quite the celebrity chef.'

'You'll be able to get rid of that other old thing now. It looks about ready to snap in half as it is.'

Pa would be disappointed with the measure of forever these days.

Grace slid the knife back into its slot. 'At least we'll be well-fixed for slicing and dicing today,' she said. 'We'll have to be careful when the little ones arrive though. Don't want any mishaps.'

Where Pa kept all things sharp at a safe height from inquisitive hands, her husband Des had considered small nicks here and there to be all part of a learned life.

One long ago Saturday, Grace had come in from the clothes line to find Des giving each of their three children a lesson in handling the largest of his butchering knives. It was a weighty thing with a long blade and timber haft worn smooth through use. He'd brought it home from the shop to sharpen. Peter was having first go – as the eldest, he usually did. Grace watched as he worked the knife backward and forward through the thick fatty layer of a large piece of beef rump. Susan, standing on the opposite side of Des to Peter, looked on. Claire, little more than three at the time, stood beside Susan on a chair that had been pushed up to the bench.

'That's it, son,' Des said, 'sure and steady. Show her who's boss.'

'My turn,' Susan said to Peter, as his slice fell away flat onto the chopping board. She held out her palm like a surgeon to Des, to receive the knife.

Claire jiggled up and down on her chubby legs and said, 'My turn, Daddy.'

'You can have a go after Susie, Claire.'

'Claire,' Grace said, 'you come with Mummy. You can learn to use the knife when you're a bit bigger.'

'Stop molly-coddling the kid,' Des said. 'How's she supposed to learn?'

Claire looked at Grace, triumphant, before turning back on excited, jiggling legs, to watch Susan make her incision.

The knife looked enormous in Susan's hands so Grace couldn't imagine how Claire would handle it.

'That's it. Keep it the same thickness as best you can. That's lookin' good, love.'

As Susan got close to completing her slice, Claire, sensing her turn was near, jiggled about more and more.

'Stop bumping,' Susan snapped at her.

What had been a small bump quickly became a large one as Claire's foot slipped off the side of the chair with her jiggling and she toppled onto Susan's shoulder. The movement pushed the knife off at an angle and into the hand Susan was using to hold the meat steady. The cut wasn't serious, Grace could see at once, but Susan howled, 'Stupid girl!' at Claire and gripped her hand to her chest as though the finger had been severed.

'You're a careless one,' Des said, lifting Claire roughly from the chair and plonking her on the ground. 'No turn for you.'

Claire burst into tears and ran to Grace, putting both arms around her legs.

Susan took a hanky from her pocket and wrapped it around her finger.

Des picked up the knife and handed it to Susan again. 'C'mon, love, back on your bike. Your sister's out of the way now. She needs to grow up a bit before she can have a go.'

'And you've only just realised that?' Grace asked him, feeling two small arms tighten around her legs.

Des, knife still in hand, reeled round to face Grace. He pointed it at her, said, 'Not another word outta you, d'you hear?'

'Hate you, Daddy,' Claire cried, then buried her face in Grace's thigh.

Now Grace looked at Susan's grown-up finger where the knife had made its mark all those years before but she knew there was no defining line left there. The cut had healed without trace. In fact, she doubted her daughter would even recall the incident.

But Grace did, and other incidents, equally careless, equally threatening.

Abruptly, Grace slid the new knife block to the back of the bench.

Just as brusquely, Susan opened a drawer and took an apron from inside, keeping her back turned while she neatly tied the strings in a bow behind her. When she faced her mother again, businesslike, she was ready for work.

Grace said, 'Why don't you start with the sauces.'

The ground between Grace and her daughter could be uneven. Grace supposed it was no different from the terrain she'd traversed with her own mother, sometimes steep and treacherous, at others flat, easy plains. Bev had tried to make sense of it for her once; old friends often brought logic to otherwise illogical situations. At the time she hadn't succeeded.

'Maybe it's not so much the difficulty of the climb you should be thinking about,' Bev said, 'as how you catch your breath along the way.'

Grace had just made some reference to how scaling Everest would be easier than understanding the workings of an adolescent mind, Susan's mind.

She must have looked confused, because Bev added, 'Do you pause now and then till you can breathe easy again? Or do you push on refusing to admit you're not as fit or able for the climb as you'd hoped, or asking yourself, even, if it's a climb you should be making in the first place?'

Grace, in no mood for wise counsel at the time – Bev's or anybody's – said, 'But that doesn't answer why she cut it up like that.'

Susan had taken a photograph of Claire from her album – one that captured her sister drawing, her brow typically folded in concentration – and got to it with a pair of scissors. She left the circle of Claire's face intact and a thin halo of her long hair. Reduced in this way it was an unflattering image. With all context cut away – the hand holding a pencil, the pencil pressed to paper – Claire looked defiant and sullen, not earnest. Grace had been livid, as much by Susan's destruction of the photograph as its inaccurate portrayal of her youngest child.

'It's mine. I'll do what I want with it,' Susan snapped, when Grace challenged her about it.

Some time later, Grace had found the circle of Claire's face stuck to a page in an exercise book. The book fell out from under Susan's pillow when Grace was changing her linen. Beneath it in thick, black print, were the words, NOT MY FAULT! written five or six times like a chant. Claire's look of defiance seemed enhanced by those words.

Grace didn't tell Bev she'd found the photograph of Claire in Susan's book. But seeing it helped her understand what Bev had meant. And she decided her friend was right: there were some climbs she had been neither fit nor able to make.

'Where's the flour?' Susan asked, rummaging through the shelves of Grace's pantry cupboard.

'Second shelf down. The container on the left.' Grace looked over her shoulder. 'Not that one. The one with the blue lid. The red's self-raising flour.'

'You've always had this colour system for anything in a packet – which is most of it!'

Susan came over to where Grace was preparing the lamb, looked over her shoulder.

'Should be big enough,' she said. 'Are you going to do anything special with it?'

'Yes. I thought I'd flavour it with some herbs.'

In small doses her daughter was good company, but for longer stretches Grace felt she was like a bird of prey, a secretary bird perhaps, all long legs and imperious plumage.

Susan watched Grace cook in a way that unnerved her. It wasn't just the presentation of Grace's food she eyed – beans cut on the diagonal when Susan preferred them left whole – but there were her low-fat long-life quips too. A raised eyebrow from her daughter had the power to make Grace shake fewer grains of sugar into the cream she might be whipping. Perched on a kitchen stool observing, Susan reminded Grace of how Matron had watched her do some nursing task years before. Sometimes her hands had trembled from the close scrutiny and she'd struggle to guide a needle into an ampoule to draw up a drug or to grip the tail of a suture. But where Matron's scrutiny had been to prevent mistakes, Susan's was to let Grace know that she was being observed.

'Isn't he meant to have one of the little pink pills in the morning as well?' Susan had asked, only fifteen or sixteen years old at the time.

By then Grace had taken to administering Des's medications for him – and there were many. She'd put them into an old ceramic pin dish and leave them and a glass of water on the table beside his cutlery, ready for him to have with his meals. He'd often lift the small bowl to his mouth and take them, unchecked, all in one.

Des poked through the coloured tablets with his index finger, looked from Susan to Grace.

Grace stopped filling the milk jug and studied her daughter's face. Those miss-nothing eyes looked back at her.

'The pink one can be varied,' she said finally, and returned her attention to filling the jug.

'You reckon she's tryin' to diddle me, Susie?'

'Just checking,' Susan said, 'in case she'd forgotten it.'

'I think I should know what I'm doing,' Grace said, putting the milk jug on the table.

Susan took it up, started pouring milk over her cereal. 'I suppose you should.'

But what did Susan, or any observer, see really, when they studied the actions of another? Grace wondered. Did she think she was witnessing the truth of her mother's life when she watched her, or was it her own version of it?

Grace inspected the leg of lamb she'd bought two days earlier. It was paler than the ones Mother had prepared. And though she hoped this one would be tender, she doubted the flavour would stack up as well. Mother had a deft hand for making the ordinary sublime.

It was through food that Mother's love was given voice, and just as well because in other ways it was mute. Grace marvelled at how something warm or sweet could speak like this. How a mouth stuffed with soft, freshly-baked scone, sweet jam and cream could take hurt into the stomach and lose it there. It proved to her that food, so taken for granted by some, was a powerful thing.

But Grace had learnt a trick or two over the years to bring out the best flavours. Susan might raise an eyebrow at the salt she used to achieve it, although it was a lot less now Des wasn't around.

Grace cut slits in the roasting joint until the knife's tip hit against bone; miniature pockets she planned to fill with garlic and fresh rosemary. Mother wouldn't have made such a fuss. She'd have grabbed it by the knuckle without ceremony, dropped it in her old blackened baking dish and slid it into the oven of the wood stove on the way out the door to church. It was the pinch of nutmeg and pat of butter she added to the julienned carrots later, the tiny thyme leaves she scattered across the roasted potatoes before serving, that showed Grace her mother cared.

Nowadays, Grace catered for a crowd who liked modern twists. She sealed each rosemary-filled slit in the lamb with a clove of garlic. Grace thought whether anybody would notice the pockets had been filled once the meat was cooked. Would her guests believe what they tasted when they ate the meat or would they need their eyes to see something of the garlic and rosemary, for them to trust their tongues? She doubted it. Such was the truth of cooking.

She poked the last of the garlic into the slits, grabbed it by the knuckle, just as Mother would have, and placed it in the baking dish. With her back to Susan, Grace sprinkled the leg generously with salt and rubbed it into the meat with her hands.

Grace studied her hands as they moved across the meat. They looked much like any others the same age – veined, lined, the backs stained with tea-coloured spots. But they'd felt their way through the past seventy years in unique ways. Much of their work had been to the benefit of others, some not. She'd known them as still, listening hands, but also as hands that moved with urgency and madness. For a while they'd been careful nurse's hands. Then hands that cradled three babies and clapped, tickled and taught in turn. She'd bruised, burnt and cut them; some scars suggested badly. They'd dismissed, beckoned, pleaded over the years, and not always successfully. Their goodbyes were too many to recall.

She held out her arms and studied the flat platter of her palms, red now from salt and friction. She turned them over, looked at the backs again. Her fingers were long and slender as her legs still were; the nails neater at seventy than they had been in her fifties – back when she'd had to scrub beds and bodies in the nursing home. She was fond of them, she decided, attached, beyond the obvious. She'd rather lose an eye or a foot than either of these two old friends. She'd miss the feel of one against the other as they rested in her lap, cupped comfortably like a successful marriage. Not that Grace could give anybody tips on that.

Her relationships, even now, were as problematic as they were when she was younger. She hadn't thought it unreasonable to expect she'd have them down pat by now. And she probably would have if it wasn't for her children. Unfortunately, they were determined to stand like a nagging conscience between her and Jack, forcing them to conduct their romance like sly adolescents.

'They'll all be coming?' Jack had asked her last week of the day's celebration.

'Yes. Along with Ada and Kath.'

He nodded, face impassive, typically hiding what he really felt.

'One day,' Grace said, and rested her hand on his arm.

He'd laughed then, a rich, generous sound despite his exclusion. 'Let's hope it happens sooner than later. It'd be nice if one of us could put in an appearance at the funeral of whoever goes first.'

'I'd show up anyway if I were you,' Grace said. 'You've earnt a seat on a pew.'

She put her hands back to work on the lamb, cold after the warm thought of resting them on Jack's arm.

The lamb was slow-cooking in the oven, the timer set for two hours.

'I'll make a start on the mint sauce,' Grace said and moved to the sink, half-filled it with water.

Earlier, she'd picked a large bunch of mint from the old cement tub by the tap at the back of the house. She dropped the mint into the water now and swept it about, separating the sprigs. A money spider made its way to the surface from the submerged greenery and tried to scramble up the sink. Grace gave it a helping hand and it scuttled off across the bench. Behind her, she could hear Susan moving a pebble of fresh nutmeg across the grater.

'I've never put nutmeg in a béchamel sauce.' Grace worked the mint leaves up and down in the water, picking off webs and browned leaves as she spotted them.

'I've never made mint sauce,' Susan said.

Grace had never bought it. Just as Mother had never bought tinned peaches.

Peaches had been one of Mother's favourite bottling fruits. The seasons at Harvest could be measured each year by the number of Fowlers Vacola preserving bottles that filled Mother's pantry shelves. If they were lined up three and four deep, then it had been a good year. The years there were few were the years Grace recalled wearing shoes too tight and jumpers too thin.

She'd looked upon those tall glass jars with their metal lids clamped down tightly on red rubber seals, and marvelled at the colourful patterns her mother had the patience to create. Deep maroon plum orbs pressed against the glass like eager faces and golden peaches, layered in symmetrical convex halves, forming hilly landscapes all the way to the top. There were sauces, chutneys and pickles too, made during times of plenty, plus pears, quinces, cumquats and stubby pieces of fibrous rhubarb. The change of seasons could be mapped in that pantry from summer blackberry jam through to winter pickled onions.

There had been a peach tree in Grace's city back-yard once, but it was a tree she came to despise. The people who sold them the house had praised the tree's fruitfulness. Grace was thrilled. Back then she still believed a well-stocked pantry said much about a woman. Each August the tree teased her with its weighty display of pink flowers. But by late October, when all the blossoms were gone and the fruit should have been plump with promise, they were still hard and ill-formed little nuts of bitterness. No amount of fertiliser or mulch helped; the tree continued to mock her optimism.

One year, in a state of frustration, or madness perhaps, she harvested the pathetic crop anyway, determined they'd be eaten. She spent some time rubbing the fuzz from each, tossed out the ones with grubs and blemishes, and kidded herself that what was left looked better than usual. She pricked each fruit to its stone with a skewer then stewed them whole in sugar and water.

The failure of the exercise was revealed early when they refused even to give up their skins. And the one she cut to try was tasteless. Feeling she'd be doubly damned by the tree if she wasted the two pounds of sugar in the syrup as well, she went to the greengrocer and bought peaches. She stewed those sunny fruits in the syrup but the pleasure in eating them was spoilt by the ones she'd thrown out. When the tree toppled over one windy January night, she was glad.

Grace reflected later that the real reason she'd hated that peach tree in her backyard was because in producing inedible fruit year in, year out, it had reneged on its purpose. But then Grace had not always done what was expected of her either, so who was she to question?

Grace pulled the plug from the sink, scooped up the mint and shook the excess water from it. She set the mint on the draining board and wondered, as she started to pinch the leaves from the branches between thumb and index finger, if Susan's years of watching her had taught her much that was useful.

Grace had learnt a good deal at her mother's elbow, especially about the art of cooking. Even as a small child she'd watched enthralled by the mystery and cleverness of it, as her mother scooped and poured and shook ingredients into pots and bowls and moulds. A slab of butter could be rubbed into a generous shake of flour and the two mixed into pliable dough by a good splash of milk and beaten egg before it was cut into scones. Some days they'd have mixed peel or sultanas added, on others, grated cheese and parsley.

As a child Grace believed the act of making some-thing sweet or savoury, spicy or sour, was down to nothing more than whimsy. Later, she came to realise that her mother had put much thought and effort into concocting variety, as much to prevent her own boredom, Grace suspected, as theirs. Unintentionally, Grace was being taught to live inventively.

There was rarely a cookbook open on Mother's kitchen table, only an assortment of bags and packets and tins. When there was a recipe, it was in a tattered and torn exercise book she had filled with handwritten slips of paper gathered from friends and neighbours. There was little in the way of explanation on those pages, just a list of the main ingredients, their quantity described in words like *generous* or *dash* or *sprinkle*. Flours weren't identified, techniques not explained; it was assumed the cook would know when to fold or cream or beat. The heading to the dish might read *Mavis's Chocolate Dessert* or *Freda's Pork Dish*. The ingredients to these recipes could metamorphose into something new like a Chinese whisper. But a little of the original person was always left behind in the recipe's name despite Mother's small, neat notations altering many of the pages, *try cinnamon*, *better with four eggs* or *cook longer*.

Grace's experimentation started with those butter-stained pages. As a girl, she set up her own mixing bowl and wooden spoon beside her mother's on baking days and she scrutinised the recipes encoded in that exercise book. She soon realised there was no code to break: 'Is this enough sugar?' she would ask.

Her mother would look across, thoughtful. 'A little more.'

Simply those extra granules, Grace learnt, made a pavlova's peaks more pert and creamed butter whiter.

Mother shook flour or cocoa or arrowroot into a sifter and Grace cranked the handle until a soft peak formed in a bowl. The height of those peaks started to make sense once knocked down to form a well, filled with beaten eggs and mixed to a smooth batter.

'How much salt?' she asked.

'A pinch.' These measurements were a secret language just for girls. 'Here, I'll show you.' Mother dipped her thumb and index finger into the salt pig and brought out a triangle of white grains.

A pinch seemed a funny measure. Grace held up her own fingers, caught the thumb and index finger together and looked at them. They made her think of shadow puppets and birds' beaks. She dipped that beak into the salt pig as her mother had done, and pinched. 'My pinch looks smaller than your pinch,' she said, looking at her own collection of salt grains, paltry compared to her mother's.

Mother looked up. 'Add another pinch, then.'

As Grace's young hands grew, so did the size of her salt pinches.

'What have you learnt from me about cooking over the years?' Grace dared to ask Susan.

'To use less salt.'

Grace knew that one was coming. 'But ... you've learnt nothing good?' Grace asked.

'Of course I have.'

'What?'

Susan stopped stirring the béchamel sauce. 'Let's see. You've taught me how to cook old-fashioned stuff, I guess, like Anzac biscuits, scones, Christmas puddings. That sort of thing. Most of my recipes come off the internet now though. You type in the key ingredient and it brings up dozens of suggestions.'

Sometimes Grace still pulled her mother's old recipe book from the back of a drawer and scanned the torn and spattered pages. She'd try to make the steamed puddings or pastries written there, not weighing or measuring a single ingredient but sticking instead to the dashes and sprinkles her mother suggested. Sometimes they failed. Other times they turned out perfectly. Grace wondered what would become of such a book. She imagined it at the back of a cupboard in Susan's meticulous home and paraded around friends from time to time as a quaint but ridiculous relic from the past, like sanitary belts.

'How long have these been on?' Susan stuck the tine of a fork into the hole where the saucepan lid's knob was once attached and lifted it to look at the potatoes inside. 'They've nearly boiled dry.'

'Long enough, then.'

Grace took one of the new knives from the block – a broad-bladed one that tapered to a severe point – and started chopping the mint leaves. The fragrance released from the herb made her salivate. She knew when she steeped it in vinegar that the acerbic taste of it would catch at the back of her throat, but in a tantalising way.

'Makes my toes open and shut,' she recalled telling Mother of her homemade mint sauce as a child.

There was a clatter behind Grace – she knew the sound. The saucepan lid had slipped from the fork and hit the floor. She'd done it often enough herself.

'I don't know how you put up with these old pots.' Susan had bent down to pick it up but it kept moving across the tiles as she struggled to catch it on the fork again.

'Here, use this one – it's easier.' Grace passed her a carving fork from the drawer.

'I should have bought you pots, not knives!'

Upright once more, Susan stuck the fork in the potatoes. 'These are too soft to roast now. I'll have to bin them. And the pot may as well follow.'

'I'm fond of both pot and lid, so don't throw either out.' Grace took the pot from the stove and tipped the overcooked potatoes into a colander to drain. She'd mash them later and use them to top a cottage pie.

She opened the cupboard under the sink and took a bag of potatoes from the basket inside. 'I'll do more.'

Guilt obviously had some advantages, as Susan took the knife that Grace was about to use and said in a softer voice, 'I'll do them. You go and get dressed or you'll be caught in your gardening clothes when everybody arrives,' and kissed Grace on the cheek.

In her bedroom, Grace swung back the doors to her wardrobe and sat on the edge of the bed. She cast her eyes across the clothes from left to right. Then back again. Nothing appealed.

Des had always liked to see her in fitted blouses with tightly belted skirts or trousers. Sometimes she'd felt he wore her on his arm like some people wear a Rolex watch. Mother had never allowed Grace bare shoulders or too much knee. And now Susan, Grace knew, would like to see her in the lavender floral frock with dainty pearl buttons she'd given her last Mother's Day. She'd expect it trimmed with pearls at throat and ears, the jewellery a gift too. Grace never felt her real self when she wore such an outfit. Jack wouldn't care what she wore; he praised her in a slip and bra as much as he did when she was dressed up for the theatre.

Grace stood again at the wardrobe. She ran a finger along the fabrics, stopping at a pair of lightweight cotton cropped trousers, relaxed at the waist. She took them from their hanger and laid them on the bed. Next she trailed through the tops; passed over cream, floral, pastel, bold fabrics, then lingered over a cotton blouse. Short-sleeved, button-through, loose. It was white like the cropped trousers. She took this from the hanger and laid it on the bed as well. She wouldn't look brazen, decorous, dressed up or striking. Instead, she'd look cool, clinical, efficient – just what the day needed.

With the pot back in service, the second round of potatoes simmering on the stove and an apron on, Grace turned her attention to the half-dozen mangoes lined up along the windowsill. She could smell them even above the chopped mint and the lamb roasting in the oven. She took a clean tea towel from a drawer and used it to polish a crystal bowl she'd brought in earlier from the china cabinet. She held the bowl up to the light that came in through the window. Satisfied that it was clean, she set it back on the bench, took each mango from the windowsill in turn, tested its weight. The last one she kept cupped in her hand. It was warm in her palm.

'It's a sensual fruit, don't you think?' Grace rolled the fruit gently between her hands as she spoke, allowed her fingers to caress its smooth skin.

'I've never really thought about it,' Susan said.

'Firm like a breast,' Grace said. 'A young breast, anyway.'

'Come on, let's get them cut up. We'll see how good these knives are.'

Grace ignored this. 'But inside, they're as soft and sweet as a puss—'

'Mum!'

Grace looked at her daughter and smiled. 'Yes, dear?'

Filip had once said Grace was *exotic* like a mango.

He'd brought one back to her at Harvest, after a visit to his family in the city. He often brought her unusual treats from these visits: syrupy sweet Macedonian specialities mostly – halva, baklava, ravanija. Grace imagined his mother – small, dark – pressing waxed-paper bundles or dented biscuit tins into her son's hands, as much a gift of culture as love.

Grace had neither seen nor tasted a mango before this gift, and was struck immediately by its sun-coloured skin.

'Smell it.' Filip held the fruit out to her.

She sat up on the picnic blanket, wrapped her hands around the warm fruit, embraced his fingers too, and breathed deeply of its scent. The sweetness she inhaled was like nothing she'd smelt before. It spoke to her of elsewhere.

'It is all the way from Queensland,' Filip said in his precise English. 'It is a tropical fruit.'

'Is that why it smells like the sun?' Grace asked.

'It smells exotic, like you.' He pressed the fruit to his nose then rolled it in his palm, just as Grace was doing these many years later. 'Firm like a breast,' he said, mock squeezing the fruit. Then, gentling his grip, added, 'But inside, so soft, so sweet.'

'Like me?' Grace teased.

'Yes, like you.'

He took out a pocketknife and Grace watched as he carefully sliced the side off the mango. Juice from it ran through the gaps of his fingers and onto the blanket. He passed Grace the cut portion, curved like the hull of a boat. She licked the flesh tentatively, unsure what to expect.

Filip laughed at her. 'You taste it like a kitten tastes milk from a bowl.'

Some firsts are not forgotten, her first taste of mango one of them. The flavour burst onto her tongue, declared itself as a fruit that needed to be eaten greedily, messily. Juice dripped from her chin and down to her elbows as she ate the flesh. She turned the curved-hull skin inside out to be sure not to miss any.

'Delicious,' she said, and held the thin golden skin up to cover the sun when she'd finished.

Laughing, Filip passed her the other half, which she ate as quickly, then the seed, which she chewed until its stringy fibres stood out like a brush.

After she'd licked the juice from each of her fingers, she then took her time to lick it from each of his.

Susan took a glinting new knife from the block, tipped a mango up, and made a decisive slice down the side of the golden fruit.

Grace gave her fruit one last roll in the hand before cutting it, gently, with her old knife, which fitted its shape so well.

She wished she could say the same of Filip and the other men she'd loved, that the lives of each had fitted hers like worn knife to mango. Not even Des had achieved it, and he'd had more than thirty years to work on the fit.

Now, she found, love worked in less explosive ways. It had neither the highs nor lows of her youth, nor the disappointments of middle age. It had become, instead, a gentle constant, unstartled by intensity. It was no longer waited on or waited for but taken, as needed, like sips from a cup. That's what Jack provided now, those small sips.

His birthday gift to her sat now at one end of the kitchen bench in a pretty ceramic pot. It was an orchid, a beautiful one. Its small white flowers were so intricate that Grace had held a magnifying glass to a number of them to fully appreciate their detail. Their tiny throats were frilled with cream, which gave way to a lower petal that curled up like a friendly dog's tongue.

It was an unusual gift to receive from a man who rarely gave any. It had stirred that memory of Filip and his long-ago gift of a mango. Today Grace was thrilled to discover that she could still be courted with the exotic.

Susan, however, had ignored the orchid since she'd arrived, knowing where it had come from. What a shame even beautiful things were perceived by some to have an ugly underbelly. Grace tried to think lightly of it. Thirteen at the table would have been considered unlucky.

Mother and daughter stood side by side at the bench, crystal bowl between them. In silence they sliced cheeks from the mangoes, Grace with her old knife, Susan with the new. Susan was brisk and efficient in the way she worked. She peeled the skin from each then sliced the flesh into long even strips on a chopping board. Grace's actions were slow and less measured. The skin of hers fell away in irregular pieces and the slices varied in thickness and shape. Each took it in turns to scrape the sliced fruit from their boards into the crystal bowl.

'You're dreamy today,' Susan said, after a while.

Grace selected another mango from the bench. 'Lost in the past ... I'm quite enjoying it.'

'I've not known you to spend so much time there.'

Grace shrugged. 'Turning seventy must have made me sentimental. Lamb. Mangoes. They're all bringing back old memories.'

'You? Sentimental?'

'Yes, today it's the emotion du jour.' Grace smiled.

'Sounds like a soup menu.'

'Ah, you see, just the word soup makes me nostalgic today.'

'Why?'

'Because it takes me back to Mother relaxing her rules.'

'How?'

'If it was cold and Mother had made soup, I was given a treat.' Grace dropped her voice to a whisper and leaned in towards Susan. 'I was allowed to sit on the floor to eat it.'

Susan laughed. 'Sitting on the floor was a treat?'

'Uh-huh. With Mother it was. She'd let me sit on an old cushion with my back pressed up against the warm bricks around the wood stove and a big mug of soup wrapped in a tea towel on my lap. I was even allowed to blow across the top of it to cool it.'

'Wow – that's really living it up.'

Grace laughed with Susan. 'As they say, sometimes it's the small things.'

Susan cleared another mango from her board into the bowl.

'Pa would come home and say, *Look, Grace's a hearth rug. Let's bring the dog in too and they can both lie in front of the stove.*'

'I bet Nan drew the line at that.'

'Definitely.'

Grace couldn't remember a more flagrant disregard of manners allowed by Mother at meal times than sitting cross-legged on the floor to eat – no bowl, no napkin.

There had come a morning long ago when Grace had wanted to show her own children the same freedom soup had sometimes brought her as a child. She'd woken with the coldest feet she could remember having since moving to the hot north from Harvest. As she got up from her bed, she said the word soup without any prior thought or reckoning.

The cold snap would be short-lived – they always were – but Grace was determined to celebrate its arrival all the same. Just as Mother had, when the first frosts came in hard and they lingered in the shade, even at midday. Out would come the heavy cast-iron pot. Mother would chop and dice anything to hand, then leave the brew to simmer and thicken on the old wood stove for the best part of the day. Grace's cold snap hadn't brought any frost but if she cooked soup she could pretend it was there. She saw it as a way of restoring a gentleness to the often hard memories of her mother.

A mean south-westerly pummelled Grace's windows as she boiled the soup bones that day. She cooked them until the meat fell away as tender morsels and the marrow had all but disappeared, the surface of the liquid glossy with it. The hard little pellets of barley became soft and plump at the bottom of the pot and the small squares of vegetables obligingly kept their shape.

But that evening, as the soup simmered gently on the stove, Des came in the back door in front of a cold draught: 'What's for dinner?' he asked, before his jacket had even reached the coat hook on the back of the kitchen door.

'Soup.'

'What else?'

'Well, there's bread and dessert, of course. But the soup's a meal on its own.'

'You know I don't like soup. I like chewin' me food. I can take it from a spoon when I'm old and lost all me teeth.'

'But it's so cold.'

'And why are those kids eatin' on the sofa?'

'Mum said we could play hearth rugs,' Claire called from the adjoining room. The music to *Gilligan's Island* jangled in the background.

Grace suddenly felt foolish, for imagining Des would be as easygoing as Pa.

He went to the fridge looking for leftovers, but there were none.

Then he slammed the fridge door shut and wrenched open the freezer door. He crashed frozen bundles about inside, eventually pulling out a plastic bag that held a slab of beef fillet. There for a special occasion, Grace remembered he had said when he brought it home from work.

Frozen meat in hand, Des went out the back door. Grace saw the light from his shed flicker on through the kitchen window. Fleetingly she thought how cold it must be outside, no jacket and a two-pound slab of frozen beef in your hands. Above the wind she heard the bandsaw start up.

A few minutes later Des came back in, a slightly less than two-pound piece of beef in one hand and a frozen slice of steak in the other.

He dropped the larger piece back in the freezer and threw the steak on the bench in front of Grace.

'I'll have it with mash and fried onion,' he said, and headed towards the bathroom. 'And there'll be hell to pay if you kids make a mess in there!'

Grace stopped peeling the mango and looked at a spot on the kitchen wall, as though the memory was projected onto it. 'There were so many rules.'

Susan shrugged. 'She was an old-fashioned woman, I suppose.'

'And your father's excuse?'

Susan stopped cutting the mango she was working on and looked at Grace. 'He was old-fashioned too. It's not fair to blame the person. Blame the era.' She went back to her slicing but with more force than was necessary for the delicate fruit.

It disappointed Grace to think Susan could justify Des's shortcomings in this way. With this thin excuse for bad choices. And Des had often chosen badly.

'All things considered,' Susan added, clearing the last of her mango, 'he was a good man.'

Grace took her board to the sink and turned on the tap, pretended not to hear. She rinsed board and knife under running water then made a show of seeing every orange fibre washed down the plughole.

4

The temperature in the kitchen rose incrementally with the level of activity needed to prepare a meal for twelve. Grace opened the window to move some of the hot air.

A soft Sunday hum drifted in. It was her favourite day of the week; the closest she got to her childhood quiet. She could hear insects going about their business among the star jasmine flowers on her back patio; birds making friendly conversation from the jacaranda's branches. Somewhere, a few backyards away, she picked up the rhythmic pop of someone hitting what might be a ball in a game of totem tennis. On the second-floor balcony of the unit next door, a woman was hanging washing over a clotheshorse. Grace watched as she snapped creases from a pillow case, shorts, a towel. Each action cut the air like a pistol crack.

On weekdays these sounds were lost. The city swallowed them up in its wakefulness, its business:

wheels turning, braking; car engines accelerating, decelerating; clip-clopping shoes and conversations on the move. There were the sounds of progress too: drills, hammers, angle grinders. And those of harm or danger: sirens, alarms, unknown crashes and bangs.

The smaller fibres of sound – those Grace could hear today – were the ones she liked best because they were the ones that revealed the true fabric of people's lives. It was odd to think that on weekdays they were mute. At Harvest, she remembered such noises – wind-cracked sheets drying on the line, the distant thunk, thunk of a fence-post driver – as the defining sounds of any given day of the week.

The eleven o'clock news broadcast came on the radio. Grace already knew what the headline would be – the same as it had been for close to three weeks now. But habit forced her hand to reach across the kitchen bench and turn up the volume anyway.

'Still no change to the state of residents' footpaths overnight,' the reporter began. One look out the window that morning had told her that. 'With waste reported to be chest-high in some areas ...'

Chest-high? Grace tried to imagine it. It could be fairly called thigh-high in parts of her street, and that seemed bad enough. Still, leave ten or a hundred bags stacked long enough in the February heat and the smell was terrible.

'Union officials and local government members have been in crisis meetings overnight but there's still no sign of a resolution to the dispute.'

'Nothing new there then,' Susan said, and turned the volume back down.

Grace went to the fridge, took a cauliflower and bag of parsnips from inside and sat each on the bench.

'Kath will hate having to come here today.' Grace thought of her old friend on the outskirts of the city, as she started cutting the cauliflower into florets.

'It'll do her good to get off her mountain. See what's happening in the real world.' Susan took the second pot of potatoes from the stove. 'Not too small,' she said to Grace on her way past to the sink.

Grace ignored her. 'The world's as real as she likes it where she is.'

'Each to her own, I suppose. But I couldn't stand it.' Susan started opening cupboards under the sink.

Mother had always said something similar about Harvest – that it was as close to the real world as she liked and that the far-away city could stay just that, far away. At the time Grace too had thought each to her own, desperate to be shot of Harvest, desperate to be nothing like her mother, as Susan probably felt now.

'She was always so outgoing,' Susan said to the inside of a cupboard. 'I never understood why she took herself so far off the social map in the first place ... Where's the colander?'

'The other potatoes are in it. I'll get something to put them in.' Grace took a plastic bowl from inside a cupboard and emptied the first batch of cooled potatoes into it. She then took the other pot from the sink and upended it into the colander, tilting her head back from the steam. 'Maybe after living a busy life she decided simplicity was the ticket.'

'Taken a ticket to sit and wait beside her grave more like. She's given in to it.' Susan moved in on the cauliflower, took over from Grace.

Grace knew the *it* Susan referred to was age.

'She never struck me as the type,' Susan said.

'There's no type. Ageing happens to everybody.'

'But she was always so out there. As a girl I wanted to be just like her when I was her age. Remember the zany-hat stage I went through? That was Kath. Just as my failed attempts at smoking were. Remember that tin Dad used for his rollies, the one you always kept full for him? Certainly came in handy during that particular phase.'

Grace remembered the tin because she had given it to Des. She still held the image in her mind of the male peacock that was pressed into its gold metal lid, tail feathers on full display. Bev had found her filling it with fresh rollies once. Grace was sitting alone at the kitchen table the day her friend came by, unannounced, to the back door. Not that an announcement was necessary, but if Grace had known Bev was calling in, then she might have found her doing something different.

'Are you doing it to keep busy?' Bev had asked, hand resting gently on Grace's shoulder.

Her friend's voice was anxious but Grace was in no state to soothe. She didn't look up from the cigarette she was crafting. Instead, she ran the tip of her tongue carefully along the gummed edge of the Tally-Ho paper and sealed it. She picked up a match and poked the hairy tobacco ends inside, then put the completed cigarette in the tin. She pulled another paper from the packet and started over again. 'Yes,' she said. 'Keeping busy.'

'Oh, Grace,' Bev said softly.

As Grace remembered it her friend had remained at her side, arm round her thinning shoulders, until she'd fitted the last one she could into the tin.

She got the rolling of Des's cigarettes down to a fine art – the tobacco tight, but not so tight that you couldn't move the air easily through it, and not so loose either that it burnt down too quickly. He never thanked her for keeping the tin full, but neither did she stop doing it.

'Kath was my idol,' Susan said, 'and now I have trouble remembering why.'

Who could deny Susan her feelings of betrayal: to have imagined a future for yourself, only to discover it wasn't the right one.

Grace looked up from the potatoes, quite drained in the sink now, and watched Susan as she worked the knife through the cauliflower. She remained a tall woman, and attractive in an unadorned way. Peter's Jane had always needed trimmings to create such a look; Susan could still pull it off with the assets she'd been given from birth.

Yes, she's carried herself well, Grace thought, admiring her straight back and long neck. Des had taught her not to round her shoulders on her height. Pull yourself up tall, Susie. Let the world see what my girl's made of, he'd say. And Susan would press her shoulders back and lift her chin in a way that made her look more proud than confident. Either way, Des was always pleased with the result.

But changes were at play with Susan, Grace had noticed, and age was the umpire. Her daughter's upper arms were going the way of an older woman's, a little saggy, and the V of her neck showed the tell-tale lines of the child who'd always enjoyed the sun. Her dark hair, a feature Des had admired from the moment he'd laid eyes on the tiny damp mop at birth, remained thick and shiny but Grace knew she'd been colouring it for a while to hold back the grey.

Grace felt a pang for her daughter's lost youth. And a greater pang for Susan's fear. No matter how hard people tried to run, age would always take hostages.

For Grace, the regrets had long passed. She'd come to accept that when she stood naked in front of a mirror now, features of her elderly mother looked back at her. There was the same short white hair and cartography of lines to her face. Her breasts hung lower than they once had and her abdomen was no longer flat. The once thick, springy pubic hair was sparse and wiry; a diminished crown above withered rose petal folds. Her legs were more bone than meat.

The image was an irony. Just as Susan had strived to be like Kath when she was younger, Grace had reached out, eagerly, for her future too – years ticked off by quarters; declared almost five, nearly ten, finally sixteen. Now, she wished she'd preoccupied herself more with remaining a child.

'Maybe you'll want to be like her again one day,' Grace suggested. 'Live a simple life on a quiet mountain.'

'Not likely.' Susan brought the knife down to cleave the last floret, a large one. 'There'll be no quiet mountains for me when I'm old.'

Susan started on the parsnips, left them long and quartered, just as she liked them.

Grace enjoyed making bus journeys within and to the edges of the city. She liked the way the cumbersome vehicle settled gracefully with a whoosh of air at each stop and floated off again like a hovercraft. The rhythm of the movement soothed her.

The previous week Grace had taken the bus to visit Kath and her mountain.

'I need some fresh air,' she'd said to her friend on the phone.

Kath had laughed her raspy smoker's laugh and said, 'And you're calling me?'

Ada made the trip with her – round, reliable Ada – a friend who'd been ticking the years off with Grace longer even than Kath had. They were a quartet once, with Bev, but she was gone now. As one of a long line of lopsided, breast-less women in her family, Bev had received her cancer as though it was a long-awaited visitor finally come knocking. It had escorted her out the door a dozen years ago now. Grace missed her as though it was only yesterday. Her friend's gentle hand had rarely been far from Grace when she needed it.

She and Ada sat in the middle of the bus where experience had shown them a smooth ride. Grace imagined how they looked to others: both white-haired and each dressed similarly for comfort, not high fashion, with permanent press and cautious hemlines. Short-legged Ada sat at the window, knees apart due to anatomy not choice, tips of her sensible shoes struggling to touch the floor, and the hem of her skirt pulled down decorously. She clutched her handbag to her lap with both hands, rarely relaxing her grip – but neither would she hesitate to lift it and use it as a weapon if required – and leant in to Grace a little to listen each time she spoke. Grace was a head and neck taller than her friend, with her long legs either stretched out in front or pulled back under her seat, ankles crossed one behind the other. Like Ada she had both hands on her handbag, but more for comfort than protection, and the top hand lifted from time to time to add emphasis to what she said.

The two friends talked for most of their journey to the city's north-western fringe. Much of their conversation was about the garbage strike – it consumed most conversations – but to a younger person's ear, Grace supposed they covered it in ways that were predictable.

Wouldn't have seen the city like this twenty years ago.

Never had so much to throw out, I suppose.

Not half as much.

Ah yes, times that weren't so good were lauded, proudly, as obstacles unique to a different generation, for building character, as if it were a construction project finally completed.

But Grace had grown from a family, and a community, where flaws and failings and wrong choices were worn like a hair shirt, suffered privately in fear of *pull yourself together* or *you've made your bed* gibes from people for whom stoicism was a way of life. But there had been Arnott's biscuits, strong tea and the indirect counsel of friends.

'What's the old maid doing here?' Des had asked Grace, more than half a lifetime ago, on finding Kath sitting in his lounge room one Saturday afternoon.

Des wouldn't have believed Grace if she'd told him of the lovers Kath had had, was still having. Depending on his mood, he could only see her friend as either a barren crone or a cigarette-rolling dyke.

'Shh – she'll hear you. The girls are coming in for afternoon tea, that's all.'

'Bloody hell. Don't any of you have jobs to do?'

'Des, please, keep your voice down,' Grace hissed. 'Besides, do you work every minute of the day?'

'No, and I shouldn't have to. Don't forget who puts the meat on the table.'

Bev's head bobbed past the kitchen window and along to the back door. 'It's only me,' she called, and opened the screen door to let herself in. 'You still here, Des. Thought you'd be long gone by now, knowing we were coming round.'

'No one informed me you were, otherwise I would've.'

'Consider yourself informed now.' Bev gave Grace a peck on the cheek and a wink.

Bev got away with more than most women around Des because of the shape of her arse. Des slapped it now and took himself outside. His jaunty whistle suggested he thought he'd got the last word – or hand – on the matter.

'He's no quality bottle of red, that one,' Bev said, rubbing her rump. 'Not likely to improve with age at all.'

Embarrassed, Grace changed the subject. 'Come through to the lounge. Kath's already here. Ada shouldn't be far away.'

'Don't you reckon thirty-eight's a bit young to be classed an old maid?' Kath asked, as Grace and Bev entered the room.

'You heard.'

Kath gave Grace a how-could-I-not look.

'Is that what he called you?' Bev looked at Kath, amused.

Grace distracted herself by clearing a place on the coffee table to make way for the tea tray they would share later.

Kath, dressed smartly in a fashionable scoop-necked frock, her curvy calves shiny in nylons, got up and did a hunched old-woman-walk across the lounge, stooped over an imaginary cane, one hand pressed to her back. Grace wished she could relax into the laugh along with her friends.

'What am I missing?' Ada came through from the kitchen.

'The wisdom of Des,' offered Kath, still chortling.

'Looked as though he was setting the shed alight when I came in.' Ada took a seat beside Bev on the sofa.

'That's where Des and I do understand one another.' Kath removed a slim and colourful tin from her handbag. Inside was a neat row of cigarettes she'd rolled earlier. She took one out, lit it up and blew a perfect smoke ring into the air with her first breath out.

'Those things are no good for you.' Grace passed her friend an ashtray. 'I wish you'd listen to me where Des won't.'

Kath scrutinised the smouldering tip. 'Maybe they aren't. But if I give them up, what will I have in common with him then?'

'You could start slapping my arse.' Bev's comment set off another round of laughter.

Grace envied much about Kath's life. In many ways her friend was living before her time, something Grace thought might be both frightening and liberating. With both parents dead early, Kath, an only child, had been left the family home, which had given her more than familiar surroundings and fond memories. It had allowed her to flout convention too, as only women of independent means could. Grace had often tried to put herself in Kath's shoes, to try on singleness, childlessness, not having to answer to anyone – but the fit usually pinched. On the days her children came home from school excited, not knee-scraped and grumpy, and Des walked in the door with the teasing smile and playful eye he'd worn when they first met, Grace felt her family around her like a warm blanket. At these times she didn't envy Kath her dinner for one or her big, lonesome house. But on the bad days, Grace would fantasise about those shoes of Kath's and imagined them feeling as comfortable as Cinderella's slippers.

Just then Kath slipped off her high heels and tucked her feet beneath her on the lounge chair. 'Bloody shoes are killing me,' she said.

Grace laughed suddenly and the others laughed

reflexively with her. Then she started to cry, and all fell silent.

'Time for tea.' Grace got up quickly and left her friends slack-jawed. In the kitchen she leant against a bench and focused hard on the bold patterning of the linoleum. The flooring was a good distraction – she'd always hated the brown and green design but it had been cheap, half-price in the sales. It reminded her of the rows of onions her mother had strung up in the shed, brown bulb riding on top of brown bulb. But now, through damp eyes, the design blurred into something more pleasing, the colours softer, the pattern less ordered.

Grace wiped her eyes on a tea towel, wrangled the cupboard door that always stuck, and took out the good china teacups. She felt the greater wrestle within, though, for allowing herself to act such a fool. But misery had a way of bubbling up like a gassy drink when least expected.

Bev came out, as Grace knew she would, but only after a decent amount of time had passed. Time enough for Grace to pull herself together.

'Need a hand in here?'

'I think I've got it under control.' Grace clattered the lid back onto the tea caddy then started laying the cups and saucers on a tray. Bev sat down at the kitchen table. She rested her generous hands on the grey and white Formica surface and waited. Grace knew Bev could wait any amount of time if she had to.

'There's nothing I want to talk about so you may as well fill your time putting these out.' Grace passed Bev a packet of Monte Carlo biscuits and a scalloped-edged plate.

Bev shrugged and took each. 'Nothing like keeping busy during times of despair.'

Grace gave her friend a sidelong glance, but Bev was concentrating on opening the packet of biscuits.

'I love Monte Carlos,' Bev said. 'Such a flashy name, don't you think?'

Grace didn't answer. The kettle whistled. She took it from the stove and poured the boiling water into the teapot. She slipped a knitted cosy over the top.

'But when all's said and done,' Bev went on, 'the biscuits themselves are really quite plain.'

Grace, her back to Bev, could hear the biscuit packet rustle as Bev removed each one to put on the plate. She knew she'd be doing it with care.

'It's what joins them that makes them special,' Bev continued, 'that seam of jam running through the white icing. That's the Monte Carlo's secret.'

Grace rested her hands on either side of the teapot. It was July and cool in the kitchen. She enjoyed the warmth of the teapot through the tea cosy and sleeves of her cardigan while she listened to Bev's talk of biscuits.

'I bought a packet once and they were missing the jam. Can you believe it? All icing, no jam.'

'Did you take them back?' Grace asked.

'No. We got through them, but I felt cheated.'

'You should have taken them back.'

'Ah, but you see, I think I got those jamless Monte Carlos for a reason.'

'Yeah, machine failure.'

'No, to remind me of what they tasted like without the jam.'

Grace brought the tray over and placed it on the kitchen table beside Bev's plate of neatly laid out Monte Carlos. 'I've gone off jam lately. I find it sickly,' she said.

'Well, that's a problem if you happen to have a packet of Monte Carlos in the cupboard.'

'Are you suggesting I buy a different biscuit?'

'Only if you can't stomach the ones you've got.'

The bus continued its stop-start journey towards Kath's.

'Arnott's have been good to us over the years,' Grace said to Ada.

They'd each had a few Arnott's moments in their day, and Ada nodded her head in quiet understanding.

'It's the shared biscuits I miss most about Bev,' Grace went on.

Ada nodded.

'She loved her Monte Carlos,' said Grace, still remembering.

Grace and Ada sat in comfortable silence as they travelled further up the mountain. Fewer people got on and off the bus, but when the doors opened for those who did, the air that came in was fresher each time. By the time they pulled into Kath's stop they were the last two passengers on board.

At Kath's they sat on the back deck and took in the view across eucalyptus trees. Grace breathed deeply of the musty smell of the forest floor, with the occasional waft of cigarette smoke (Kath had moved on to tailored cigarettes when she turned fifty, worried she'd outlived her role as swinging sixties icon and looked more like an old hooker with her tin of rollies). They shared a bottle of wine and ate sandwiches with the crusts cut off, like children. Then there were biscuits, of course – Scotch Fingers and Ginger Nuts. Ada dunked hers in her tea, as she always had.

To Grace's ear their conversations moved seamlessly, but to a stranger's she supposed they would sound disjointed and cryptic.

'Another birthday,' Kath said. 'One remembered and celebrated.'

'Yes, reach seventy and I finally hit the jackpot. Maybe I should deduct the others from the tally, pretend I'm younger.'

'Not so fast,' Ada laughed, 'we've kept count.'

And they had. But not so much kept count of the years as marked the day firmly in their diaries from one year to the next as Grace had theirs, even Bev's, still.

'You managed to talk Susan out of a restaurant then?' Ada asked.

'Only just. She had the thumb screws on me there for a while. Pulled the mother-guilt thing a few times. It'll make it so much easier for all of us,' Grace mimicked. 'But I played the daughter-guilt one right back at her.'

'It could be the last time I have the whole family round my table,' Kath chanted in her best old-lady-hard-done-by voice.

Grace laughed. 'Something like that.'

'Can't let them bully you,' Ada said. 'God knows it's a full-time job keeping my lot off my back. I've started teaching the grandchildren how to make papier-mâché masks out of the retirement home brochures I keep finding on the kitchen table.'

'Do you make sure the snowy-haired couples in the matching tracksuits are stuck on the outside?' Grace had yet to find the same kind of reading material left on her kitchen table, but she knew the pamphlets Ada meant. They were marketed like holiday brochures, except the faces at the destinations had more wrinkles and less cleavage on show and the highly whitened teeth weren't necessarily their own.

'Smack bang on the forehead,' Ada laughed, 'more noticeable there.'

'At least I don't have to put up with any of that crap.' Kath lit up another cigarette.

'Well, they can keep hinting and I'll keep pretending I'm good with glue and paper.' Ada dunked the last of her biscuit in her tea.

The three sat quietly for a while, listening to the hush of the bush. The loudest sound was of Kath's breath. Each exhalation rattled softly with damp. Grace kept quiet about her friend's habit nowadays, even though she'd seen the consequences of it often enough. Dusky-lipped men and women, whose stomachs were caved in and chests barrelled out, laboured to pull breath as though the air was being sucked through a pinhole in plastic wrap. Grace could still picture them, each sitting on the edge of a hospital bed, spindly legs dangling, shoulders hitching with effort. Some days she'd unintentionally set her respiratory rate to match theirs, compelled to breathe for them, compelled to ease their burden.

But Kath liked her vices, so who was Grace to deny her friend? Besides, at seventy-six, it was too late for Kath to go back; too late for Grace to make a difference. But she imagined trying to breathe for her friend when the time came, sucking the air in sync, wanting to ease her burden; pretending she could.

A distant grunting noise sounded from somewhere in the bush, eerie like the devil's laugh. They all strained to listen.

'Koala?' Ada asked.

Kath turned her good ear towards the stand of eucalypts at the back of her house. 'Wrong time of year.'

51

Then there was a new noise, almost like a child giggling. To Grace it sounded as though the bush was haunted.

'Lyre bird,' Kath announced. 'You hear them occasionally.'

They sat very quietly, hoping to hear more. It was a privilege to eavesdrop on such a secretive bird. But after the distant sound of what might have been a car alarm, which could have been the lyrebird or just a reminder that the city wasn't so far away after all, the bush fell silent again.

'I swear I heard one mimic a steam train once,' Kath said. 'God knows how old that bird must have been.'

The friends' laughter echoed across the trees.

Ada turned to Grace. 'Do you remember that time when the children were small and we took them to the zoo? Claire spent the day mimicking animals and you called her a lyrebird?'

Grace smiled, remembering, easily.

'She got so indignant,' Ada continued. 'I am not a liar. That is the sound it makes. She didn't half stamp her foot.' Ada shook her head, laughing with the memory.

'So very young, but so very righteous,' Grace said.

'A noble trait.' Ada took another Scotch Finger, broke it in two on her plate.

Noble seemed a word better suited to the aged than to a little girl. But Grace knew what her friend meant.

★

The bus journey back off the mountain that afternoon had been a rewind of the morning, only faster. It wasn't because the heavy vehicle was going downhill, Grace decided, but because the undesirable had a way of presenting itself with sudden force. The bush gave way to streets and kerbs and rubbish and cars all too quickly. Each time the bus doors opened, the buzz seemed cacophonous after the quiet of Kath's deck and the whispering eucalypts.

When they reached their stop the sun was almost through its arc across the sky. Despite her short legs, Ada managed an uneventful step down from the bus after it had settled itself like a fat yet graceful lady at the kerb. But then she slipped a little as her heel found a clump of litter, so Grace linked arms with her till they reached the nearby T-junction. There Grace unlinked her friend's arm and each stood on the edge of the footpath, Grace in the dip, Ada on the higher ground, reducing the height difference between them. They waited to cross the road.

Neither could have predicted the white delivery van would cut the corner in order to get its bulk round the narrow intersection, any more than they could have predicted which one of them would stand on the left to take the blow from its wide side mirror. That day it was Ada's turn to be on the wrong side of luck. The van's mirror struck the side of her head as she poked it out to check for traffic and she was reeled backwards by the force of it. Too shocked even to cry out, she lowered herself to the ground strangely, gracefully. Grace followed, coming to her knees, to comfort Ada, remembering fleetingly, shockingly, another time like this.

A crowd soon gathered around them, two aged women on the ground, one bleeding down the side of her face, the drops spilling onto her ecru blouse. Grace heard snatched words – *ambulance* and *elderly* and *mustn't have looked*. A hand came into view to press a wad of tissues to Ada's wound, another offered up a bottle of water. Ada stared up at Grace, abruptly searching for recognition in a face she'd known for decades. It unnerved Grace to see how the memories and the strong connection could be severed so easily. She was reminded of the mind's capacity to withdraw during times of deep shock.

Finally, the reality of pain, perhaps, told Ada she was alive and that she could come back to the here and now and she clung to Grace then like a terrified child.

They must have looked a strange pair, Grace thought later. She refused to take her arms from around Ada. She pressed her against her chest, protecting her, protecting herself, from their fear. And Ada, bag still clutched to her lap, didn't indicate she wanted to be released. It would be that first look on Ada's face that Grace would relive that evening and several after it, more than the kindness shown by strangers.

They waited like that, together, until an ambulance could make its way to them.

★

'Is Ada going to make it today?' Susan asked.

'She said she would. Her son is going to drop her over.'

'It was lucky she wasn't hurt more seriously by the sounds of things.'

'The bruising's bad enough. Looks like she's been in a boxing ring.'

'Still, it could have been broken bones, or worse.'

The measure of worse could be interpreted in odd ways, Grace had come to realise since the accident.

'I'm worried about her,' she said to Susan, tipping the drained potatoes back into the pot and covering them. 'Today'll be the first time she's left the house.'

This past week had taught Grace much about the fragility of confidence. She'd seen Ada every day and each time she'd listened to a once-robust voice cowed and quavering. To have trust in your body one day, know it would take you where you wanted it to, only to have its reliability cheat on you like a whoring husband the next, was enough to bring confidence to its knees. So how was worse to be measured? Could being in a coma for a week be worse than having your vulnerability exposed? Once she'd have said an emphatic *Yes*, but now she wasn't so sure. Ada had been forced to face her future, and what her friend saw was how short and unpredictable it could be.

'Maybe her family should find her somewhere for a stint of respite care,' Susan suggested.

Grace looked up at Susan, one hand poised on top of the pot's lid, the other gripping its handle. 'Isn't that just another quiet mountain but with a different view?'

Susan shrugged. 'If it helps.'

'I'll see her well again,' Grace said, and she used all her strength to shake the potatoes about in the pot, to the point where she doubted any would need further scoring with a fork before roasting.

5

Enough food cluttered the tops of Grace's benches and kitchen table to make a refugee weep and she didn't feel proud. But her family was a hungry one, for all manner of things – food, attention, victory – so there was a level of expectation they'd be fed well.

There were several kinds of vegetables to be steamed, roasted or baked in béchamel sauce. A rich master stock simmered for gravy. The shredded mint leaves and vinegar and sugar had come together to make an unattractive swampy green-coloured sauce, the look of which belied its pleasingly sharp taste. The lamb continued its slow spit and sizzle in the oven, and every time the oven door was opened, the smell of caramelising fat filled the room. Soft and hard drinks chilled down in the ice-filled laundry tub. And the kitchen sink was crowding with the dirty dishes needed to make it all happen.

Grace thought of those documentaries where images were sped up to show the life of a plant from seed to shrub or the decomposition of a gazelle, accelerated to seconds. Imagine doing that across a kitchen's lifetime. What quantities of food! What industry! What consumption! Other rooms would look like forgotten domains in comparison.

The kitchen gave a family structure, shape – a space in which to exist. And Grace imagined her cooking as its beating heart. She was tireless in the task, but despite the heart's unwavering commitment, the work was largely ignored. Yes, Grace thought, cooking was much like the hidden work of the heart, unseen inside the cage of the chest.

Mother's chest had been made of glass. Her skills and work in the kitchen were never overlooked, and certainly not by Pa.

Her preserved peaches and plums and chutneys weren't allowed to remain unnoticed in the dark cool of the pantry, gradually diminished by greedy appetites along with custard, cream or cold meat. Each year the better ones were moved to the produce competition sheds of the local Agricultural Show for a few days. There, housewife pitted herself against housewife in draughty, corrugated-iron sheds where their wares did their best to impress the judges. She entered fruit cakes and plum puddings as well. Pa's shoulders hitched with amusement at the frenetic lead-up and increased heat in the kitchen as Mother, red-faced and short-tempered, poured, chopped and stirred. Mother responded to his humour with tight lips or a snapped, *Well, I'm cooking them for Christmas anyway.* Pa, not so easily fooled, declared, *We're going to eat well after this weekend, kids*, when the Swiss rolls and jelly cakes and date loaves arranged on pretty plates appeared on the kitchen benches too, items that had nothing to do with Christmas.

But while Pa might have teased and chuckled at Mother's cooking madness before the Show, he was the first into the shed to see what she'd won when the judges finally opened the doors. He would lead the family round the long trestle tables, ebullient over the blue ribbons she'd received – and there were many – and disparaging of the lesser or absent ones. *Look, she's done it again, kids*, he'd say or *Judge must have forgotten to taste this one.* Mother, in her publicly pious way, would say little, but Grace noticed her town accent – the normally dropped 'g's suddenly finding their way back onto the ends of her words – even more noticeable when she spoke to those women who'd been less successful than her.

The Show weekend was an important one in a countrywoman's calendar, Grace came to realise. Those produce sheds gave her mother the chance to be recognised, known as the one who made the best lamingtons or Madeira cake in the district. Her recipes would be requested for inclusion in the church fund-raising cookery book and her plates of gem scones or ginger nuts were the first bought at school fêtes, usually by the women working behind the stall before the public had a chance to even see them. But success was also the feeding ground for jealousy, so sought-after were these small accolades. Grace would eavesdrop on the not-so-quiet mutterings from women as they studiously walked the aisles of the shed. *Looks a bit dry if you ask me*, they'd say at halved chocolate cakes, or *Couldn't call that one a blowaway* at the sponges. Grace would prickle with rare defence if she heard such utterings around any of her mother's winning entries. She'd scowl at these women until they shuffled off, pretending not to have noticed, but afterwards they'd speak in whispers.

When it came time to reload the boot of the car with the cakes and rolls and slices, her mother had a sad, faraway look despite the bundle of ribbons in her handbag. It was only as an adult Grace recognised the look as the same one people got when a much-enjoyed party was over. As the trestle tables were packed away and the produce shed locked up for another year, so too was Mother's moment in the spotlight. But Pa was right – they certainly ate well once the Show was over.

It felt a bit like Mother's pre-Show cooking frenzy in Grace's kitchen today. Susan stirred cheese into the béchamel sauce on the stove, with efficient clockwise then counter-clockwise motions. Grace ran hot water into the sink and started the dishes before the tap disappeared behind a wall of dirty pots and pans.

'I bet you're wishing now we'd gone to a restaurant.' Susan removed the wooden spoon from the pot, wiped her finger across the back of it, and tasted the sauce. She added a further pinch of nutmeg, three grinds from the pepper mill.

'Not at all,' Grace said. 'I'm happy to be having it at home.' She ran the pot scrubber over two knives, their blades fanned out in a victory sign, then set them on the draining board.

'On my seventieth I'm going somewhere nice like Fiddlers or The Croft.' Susan tasted the sauce again then poured it over the cauliflower she'd arranged across a baking dish. She scraped the sides of the pot with the spoon to get all of the tenaciously cheesy sauce from inside, craned her neck to look inside. 'Air conditioned. Someone else doing the cooking – and clearing away.' She banged the wooden spoon on the edge of the baking dish then brought it and the pot to the sink, dropped each in the sudsy water.

Grace retrieved the two glasses already in there before the water went milky.

'Where's the pride in that meal?' she asked Susan.

'In somebody else paying for it.'

Grace saw Susan's restaurant meal as one consumed out of duty: a family brought together on the condition of convenience and ease; the time-frame predetermined by the restaurant's hours or next bookings; the menu at someone else's discretion, their tastes, their preferences. Not a beating heart anywhere, Grace thought. And no blue ribbon moments, except in the opening of a wallet.

Sadly, many of the meals Grace had prepared in the past hadn't shown a beating heart either. Today she hoped to make amends. She wanted this food to mean something more than mere sustenance to her family and friends; she wanted it to be seasoned with goodness, to show them she cared, to make this lunch one to be remembered, just as Mother's Show cooking and preserves had defined her.

In the past it had been difficult to show love in the preparation of certain foods. Meat was one such food, or meat the way Des liked to eat it anyway. He took his roast beef rare, sinewy, the fat inside still pale and soft, which meant they all had to take it that way. It looked like the haunch of a recent kill when he carved it at the table. Grace would struggle to eat hers, push her vegetables to high ground on her plate to keep them from the blood pooled there. The children learnt to like theirs the same way as Des, having known no different, but Grace never did. Some days she felt as though she was feeding a lion when she placed the bloodied joint in front of him, feared he'd reach across and devour her arm along with it. *Delicious*, she imagined him saying as her blood filled the gaps between his strong white teeth, *Rare* – just how I like it.

Susan jiggled the baking dish back and forth on the bench. The thick sauce settled into gaps and gullies. She sprinkled the top with a mixture of grated

Parmesan and cheddar cheese then opened the oven and slid the dish inside.

'Next job?' she asked, slamming it shut.

'Peas.' Grace dried her hands on her apron and took a large bag of fresh peas from the crisper.

'Not frozen?'

'This is no ordinary restaurant,' Grace said, and up-ended the contents of the bag onto the kitchen table.

They each pulled out a chair and sat facing one another, shelling the peas into a metal pot. The empty pods started to build on sheets of newspaper beside them.

'Do you remember how I used to cook your favourite meal for your birthday dinners when you were young?' Grace asked.

'Yes, I do.'

'You always wanted curried chicken with rice followed by steamed chocolate pudding for dessert. You'd drown the pudding in cream – twice.'

'You remember that?'

'Of course. Peter always had steak and chips, no vegies, followed by trifle. Claire's—' Grace had to think a moment. She opened a pod with a satisfying pop and ran her thumb along the row of peas inside. Each hit the metal pot like rain on an iron roof. Then she remembered. 'Claire's was cocktail sausages and green jelly with Neapolitan ice cream. She'd ask for more chocolate than strawberry.'

'You've got a good memory.'

'For some things.'

Her memory for other things, the minute details of a day or season long past, were usually lost to her. Like the sun streaming in the kitchen window and onto the table now, warming her left arm. It was one of the everyday things from her past she no longer felt sure she knew. What had childhood summer sunshine been like? She presumed it had been hot and dry and often burnt her skin. She guessed it had made her sweat and caused the long walk home from school to be a listless, fly-flicking meander instead of her usual purposeful journey from ink-welled desk to door. She remembered swimming in the creek near her home in the summers but she couldn't recall the sensation of the cold, brown water as it hit her body. She even had a faded glimpse of a child shielding her eyes from the glare as she looked through a heat shimmer from house to horizon. But were these memories trust-worthy, ones she could claim as her own? Couldn't they just be visions loaned to her from a movie or a magazine? She never could be sure. Not anymore.

'Remember how you used to do a ring of rice round the plate first then fill in the centre with the curry?'

'Presentation's everything,' Grace laughed.

'And the curry was always bright yellow.'

'Straight from the Keen's curry powder tin. Never could tell what was in it but it was the only one your father would eat. Same flavour and colour regardless of whether I was currying egg for sandwiches or meat. Now there's so many different ones on the supermarket shelves I don't know how people choose which one to buy.'

'You try them all. Eventually the field narrows to a few favourites.'

Grace preferred to make hers from scratch. All she needed was a well-stocked spice rack. She'd juggle combinations of coriander, cumin, cardamom and turmeric. At times she'd add fennel seeds or fenugreek. And to fire it up she'd grind a paste of chilli, garlic and ginger and add to the mix. Some were tomato based, others of coconut milk. She'd rarely produced the same flavour twice.

'Do you make a favourite meal for Jorja and Jaxon?'

Susan shook her head. 'No, they choose a restaurant they'd like to go to.'

How times had changed.

'Jorja always picks Thai. Jaxon, Mexican.'

Grace had been an adult before she went to her first restaurant. At the time Des was trying his hardest to win her over, to give a country girl a taste of life with a city boy. What she'd really got was a false taste of the man he'd never be. Later, when they were married, she'd ask him to take her out for a meal and he'd rarely agree. He'd won his trophy and preferred to enjoy the culinary accoutrements that went with it, in his own home.

'Why d'you wanna eat out?' he'd ask.

She couldn't tell him she needed to break the pattern of the same sounds from the same people at the same table every night. He wouldn't understand or care how the monotony of such a routine crushed a woman's courage to be able to live a different meal-time performance.

'Besides, who'd look after the kids?'

'Bev says she'll mind them any time. Come on, it'll be good to get out.'

Once he'd agreed to take her to their local hotel for dinner. To recall the day now was like viewing an old silent movie.

She could still see herself – the memory not borrowed, but real – spending an hour shaping her eyebrows and pressing her best dress in between feeding and bathing crying children who were sensitive to a predictable pattern being suddenly hurried. Des came in from work and got ready like a man preparing for a hat-in-hand appointment with the bank manager. Later, she wondered if he'd spent his journey home from work thinking about ways he could get out of it.

At the hotel, he hesitated at the junction in the hotel's long hallway that brought the choice between turning right into the Ladies Lounge or left into the Public Bar. Grace gently steered him through his hesitation to the door on the right with an arm she'd linked through his.

Her silent movie showed her scanning the menu for some of her favourites – grilled flounder, baked snapper – but not finding them. She couldn't remember what she ate now, only that Des cleared his plate quickly; her own meal was still only half-eaten by the time his was finished. He sat back in his chair then; licked food from his teeth; fidgeted with a corner of the tablecloth; wound his watch.

The hotel's dining room was a characterless backdrop to the picture ticking over in Grace's head. The walls weren't adorned beyond their flocked wallpaper and the backs of curtains were yellowed by the sun and cigarette smoke. When people spoke she saw their lips move but heard nothing. She could see their knives and forks working at their food but there was no audible scrape or clatter. She and the other diners looked like extras in some staged drama with the real actors, the important people, yet to arrive to bring on the action. She remembered how part of her missed the chaos of home, where food fell or was thrown to the floor and a spoon or cup was slammed up and down on a highchair table. The other part of her, the one eager to play the role, ate her meal slowly and with care, savouring tastes she could no longer recall the flavour of.

Des declined dessert; Grace ordered one. When it arrived, Des spoke to her, said something about nicking in next door for a minute, left Grace to finish on her own.

Grace's dessert bowl had long been cleared but Des still hadn't returned. She watched the odd assortment of couples around her – some chatted intimately, held hands across the table; others didn't say a word to each other, but stared off, instead, at some undefined spot in the room. With calm resolve, Grace gave one final dab to her lips with her napkin, gathered her handbag and got up from the table to take herself home. On the way out she saw Des in the public bar. He was with a group of men who each had their hands round a glass of beer. Grace remembered how his white teeth flashed as he laughed, sharing a joke even the barmaid enjoyed. She never knew if he went back to check on her. She never asked to be taken out again. Grace clicked off the reel to the memory.

'Your father never liked eating out much.' Grace rained another row of peas into the pot.

'That's because you fed him too well at home. Keep them a bit hungry. That's my motto.'

'Is that why Richard's skinny as a pin – you starve him?' Grace joked.

Susan laughed. 'His mother says he's been scrawny since birth. Just before we married she told me if she'd never been able to fatten him up then I didn't stand a chance either. I didn't hesitate to tell her he put on a kilogram in the first month after our wedding. She put it down to inactivity beyond the bedroom, not my cooking.'

It was Grace's turn to laugh. 'Did he lose it again – the kilogram?'

'Yes, by the next month. Like I said, you have to keep them a bit hungry. Not that I ever told his mother he'd lost it. For years she always thought he weighed a kilogram more than when he left home. Richard said she'd squeeze his sides whenever she saw him. I think she was trying to work out just where that extra kilo was. Middle age takes care of it for me now.'

Richard's mother's inability to relinquish her role as feeder – reduced as it was to an advisory level, and even then the advice taken begrudgingly, knowing Susan – didn't surprise Grace. She supposed it was the only means by which his mother could continue some sense of control over her son's life. To hand over the secrets and idiosyncrasies of his eating since birth, packaged like precious memories and entrusted to the care of another to be remembered. For some, Grace thought, this must feel like a blood-letting, but for others the task of feeding could carry a more malevolent power. It provided an avenue through which perceived wrongs could be redeemed – the worst, fatty cut to the belligerent; the yolk with a blood spot to the cruel; a disliked dish to the ungrateful.

Grace had sometimes taken pleasure from these acts, having few other ways of demonstrating her hurt. She supposed it was a childish victory, nothing more than school-ground retribution. And often the punished failed to notice they had been anyway.

Unless, of course, she'd served up something Des disliked. Then she was sure to get his attention, especially after that time she took over buying the meat.

Some of Grace's friends had envied her a husband who took the responsibility of meat purchase off the weekly shopping list. Grace had resented it. Des would bring home the week's supply of meat on payday, already wrapped and labelled for her to put straight into the freezer. Some days he'd even take a bundle out to thaw, leave it in the sink on his way to work, without so much as a *Thought we could have pork chops for tea* or *What are the chances of beef casserole tonight?* Just icy chunks left to seep blood down the drain and attract flies. And if the label had come off, sometimes she had to wait till it thawed before she could work out what it was she had to cook for that evening's meal.

But there was a day when Grace had opened that freezer and been faced with the usual two-pound bags of mince for rissoles, steak or chops for grilling, joint for roasting – and she'd slammed the door shut on the predictable lot, making the old Kelvinator rattle on its feet.

It was a determined woman who got in the car that morning and drove to the shop where Des worked. She went there wanting skirt steak to make beef olives, or a boned leg of lamb that she could keep the tin of Keens from, season it instead with a mixture of spices from India or Africa or fill it with a farce flavoured with lemon peel and garlic then wrap it tightly in foil and slow-cook it. She wanted meat that could be served with pasta or rice – no mash, no fried onions, no pumpkin, no frozen peas. She wanted to make complicated dishes, dishes fragrantly exotic. Dishes Des wouldn't like.

Sitting in the car she watched him work his lady customers like a craftsman. She didn't know if he saw her there, though he easily could have. All he had to do was look up when he was taking sausages or liver or bacon from the window display and he'd see her sitting behind the wheel of the Belmont, watching him. He didn't wave if he did notice her, not that she would expect him to. The footpath had always marked a fine divide between his place and hers and he rarely acknowledged her across it when she'd walk past the shop on her errands.

Inside, she could see it was busy – two, three deep at the counter – but this didn't dampen Des's enthusiasm to give each of his customers time for a laugh and a longer chat than was necessary. Grace could see the way he held a woman's eye as he handed over packages of meat. He'd rest his hand on the bundle for a moment when he placed it on the countertop, not releasing it until he was ready, once he'd got one more smile, one more blush. Young or old, he'd flirt with them. The only difference was he'd pass the older customer's packages over more quickly, then scan left or right again to see who was next, showing whoever it was his perfect teeth.

Did her butcher husband recognise the intimacy he shared with these women as he guided them on what might be good to feed their husbands, those wives who were always looking for new ways to please? He could hint at what would get them the greatest praise, a kiss even or more, if the cut was particularly flavoursome, especially tender. She imagined him saying, *The lamb's at its springtime best, it'll melt in his mouth* or *Leave the front door open when you roast this pork and he'll smell how much you love him even before he's unlatched the gate.* They'd leave his service with a wink and a tightly wrapped package containing the promise of a good night, not just a meal of meat.

The Casanova of quality cuts, that's what Grace thought as she watched him work.

Once numbers had dwindled inside, Grace got out of the car, locked the driver's door and crossed the footpath divide. She'd come for choice, not false affection. She entered the shop and stood behind a slim woman in hugging tweed trousers and a knitted sweater that made a prize of her breasts. Grace looked down at her own fitted skirt and button-through blouse and thought: *You'll do.* If Des looked at her, thigh-level first then up to her face, as he had previous customers, then, yes, she'd definitely do.

It had been so long since Grace had stepped inside a butcher's shop that she'd forgotten the smell. Quarters and halves of carcasses hung along the back wall. There were trotters and honeycombed tripe and hindquarters, small and large, held up by hooks through knee joints. What animal they once were, or part thereof, was awfully clear. One of the butchers was using a bandsaw to dismember those larger sections into smaller portions. Grace watched the marrow and fat gum up the blade as he sectioned a lamb's back into loin chops. The sawdust on the floor caught the bloody drips and made his footsteps soft.

Des worked over a forequarter of beef at a deeply worn and stained wooden block. The open chest cavity glistened at Grace and the white rib bones that showed through reminded her of the toothy, laughing entrance she'd seen at Luna Park. She'd always considered that mouth to be a macabre welcome to a place of fun, like being swallowed by a greedy giant. This rib cage had a similar effect.

Des held a large cleaver in his right hand. He raised it above his head and brought it down hard on the ragged and bloodied neck end. The action was done with such authority and strength that she imagined if the animal's head had been still attached then he could just as easily have hacked it off in one blow as well. A quick and efficient beheading. For a moment she faltered in her cause, even considered turning around and leaving the shop before he noticed her there. This wasn't a place for the unsure, not when things were being done around her with such certainty. But it was too late for that.

'What can I get for you, love?'

Grace's gaze was taken away from Des's back and she looked into the playful eyes of one of the other butchers.

'I'd like a pound of thinly sliced veal, please.'

'Grace, what are you doin' here?'

Grace tried to appear brave. She looked around her as if Des might have lost his senses. 'Buying meat,' she said.

'We can't have run out at home.'

'No, we haven't,' she said, 'but I wanted something other than what was at home.'

Des looked at her incredulously, like she might be the one who'd lost her mind. 'How could you want somethin' other than what's at home? There's a pile of meat in the freezer.'

'I want veal,' she said. 'There's no veal in the freezer.'

Des looked flummoxed. 'Veal?'

'Yes, veal.'

'I don't like veal. It's got no flavour.' Des embedded the cleaver into the timber block then picked up the severed neck end and flung it into a bucket on the floor.

Grace shrugged. She noticed the man who was serving her had paused, knife edge resting on the pink slab in front of him, torn between slicing it thinly and putting it back in the refrigerated cabinet.

'A pound, please,' she said.

'So what're ya gonna do with it?' Des sounded sulky, like Peter when he'd been told off.

Grace wouldn't be put off, she decided. She smiled sweetly at the man as he carved off the slices.

'Make veal parmigiana,' she said, 'with garlic bread, I think, and a nice green salad.'

'Bloody wog food.'

The butcher serving Grace secured her paper-wrapped package with twine, looped the long end of it round his index finger then snapped it free from the roll with a jerk of his hand. He placed the parcel on the counter in front of her, held his hand on it as though she might consider returning it. She didn't wait to see if Des would offer to put the cost of the meat on his tab. She opened her purse and handed the man a note.

Thanking him, she left the shop with her neatly wrapped package, but not without hearing, 'You've got yourself a feisty one there, Des.'

The cleaver came down hard again as the shop's door closed behind her. She imagined the animal's spine severed in two.

For a while after that Grace had made her own weekly meat list. She'd stand and wait her turn like all the other women, flirt even with some of the butchers on occasions, and order her meat for osso buco and stroganoff and moussaka. Her inventiveness proved short-lived though, because before long she went back to giving Des exactly what he liked.

'There were plenty of times your father thought he'd been starved.' Grace took another pea from the diminishing pile.

Susan snorted. 'Not the way I saw it. You always gave him a mountain of food – much more than he needed.'

'That's because he'd complain if he saw too much of his plate at the start of a meal.'

'Do you think those comments about being expected to live off china flowers were a complaint? They were jokes, Mum. He wasn't really asking for more but you always gave it to him. And given the state of his heart – his diabetes – it would've done him good to see a bit more of his plate, not less. It was a dangerous habit you got him into.'

'Dangerous habit I got him into? Don't blame me. Your father was responsible for his own eating habits.'

Between them, in the sudden quiet, peas popped into the bowl.

Des had always been a dangerous eater. The closeness to animal fat all his working life – fat that kept his hands soft, clothes stained and hair slick – never deterred him from liking his food cooked in it. If asked about his favourite meal, Grace knew, he'd say it was a breakfast fry-up: *The working man's heart-starter*, he called it. But Grace thought his eating habits marked him as a weak man. It was a weakness that would eventually strangle him by the coronary arteries at the age of fifty-four.

'You're a damn fine cook when you put your mind to it,' Des said to Grace, long after her triumph at the butcher's had served its purpose.

Des appraised his plate. Two thick sausages, their ends turned up like old boots; two long rashers of streaky bacon, the fat brown and crispy as he liked it; two fried eggs, sitting like perfect breasts, bathed in oil and out sunning themselves; and potato cubes fried with onion.

'Tomato?' Grace asked.

'No. That'd spoil it.' Des pinched a generous amount of salt between thumb and forefinger from a small bowl beside his plate, a bowl Grace made sure was always full, and sprinkled it over his food. 'You not eating?'

Grace shook her head. 'I'll have something later.'

'You should be having something like this.' Des pointed to his plate with his knife. 'You're looking scrawny.'

Grace sat down and sipped her tea. She watched as he trawled a square of toast through a ruptured yolk and lifted it to his greasy-cornered mouth. The sound of cutting and scraping across a china plate filled the otherwise quiet kitchen. In the distance Grace could hear the rhythmic squeak of a child's swing toing and froing and the busy attempts of a fly trying to find its way out of the flyscreen at the kitchen window.

'Get us another bit of toast, would you.'

Grace got up, cut a slice from the loaf and put it in the toaster. She waited at the bench while it cooked.

'Another hot one,' Des said, looking out the kitchen window.

Though it was still early, Grace could feel the weight of that heat pressing against the stillness in the room. 'I miss the cold,' she said, almost to herself, as she watched the heat shimmer above the toaster.

'Miss the what?'

'The cold. From Harvest. When I was a girl.'

'You can have your cold. Give me the heat any day.'

'But it's all the same. If we're lucky it gets cool at best. But usually it's just one day as warm or warmer than another. When you feel really cold – hard frosts, a bit of snow on the hills, that sort of thing – you have to make adjustments and it's those adjustments that let you know you're still alive. Otherwise how can you tell the difference from one day to the next?'

'By the six o'clock news. That toast ready yet?'

Grace hooked a nail under the metal edge of the drop-sided toaster. The Bakelite handle had broken off long ago. She passed the hot toast from hand to hand and onto a small plate she'd taken from the cupboard. She embedded a butter knife into the dripping tin beside the stove and dragged it across the bench toward her. From inside she dug out a generous measure of the fat and spread it right to the edges of the toast.

She handed Des the plate. He slid the toast onto his and set about cutting it into symmetrical squares, which he used to mop up the leftover juices and fat on his plate. She always marvelled at this attention to detail and the neatness with which he ate, which never went beyond his meals and the dissection of slabs of meat.

Des rested back in his chair, flicked crumbs from his shirt to the floor. His front was much flatter than it should have been. But nursing had shown Grace that disease didn't always present itself as expected. Sometimes it worked covertly, mostly under the surface, like an iceberg. Des rolled his tongue around his teeth, licked and smacked bits free from the gaps. He washed down whatever he'd collected with a swill of tea.

Peter strolled into the kitchen, eyes half-closed with sleep and hair sitting every-which-way but flat. The smell of stale alcohol secreted from his skin as much as it came from his breath and dominated the musty smell of sleep.

'Big night out with the lads, mate?' Des asked.

'Ugh.'

Des chuckled in between taking slurps from his tea.

Peter opened the fridge, propped himself up against the door, scanned the shelves before closing it again, empty-handed.

'There's nothin' to eat.'

'There's plenty. You just need to be here when it's served,' Grace said.

'Give the kid a break. Can't you see he's had a big night?'

'So?'

'C'mon, help the young fella out and cook him a good recovery breakfast. Sit down, champ. Mum'll rustle you up something.' Des pulled a chair out from the kitchen table, slapped the seat of it.

'You can wait until I finish my tea.' Grace sipped at her tea slowly, tried to savour it, but the flavour was lost. Disgruntled, she got up, tipped the last of it down the sink. 'I'll make you poached eggs,' she said, clanging a saucepan onto a burner.

'Give the kid a fry-up like you gave me. It's the best cure for a hangover.'

'I've used up all the bacon and sausages,' she lied.

Des slid his cup across the table. 'Any more tea in the pot?'

Grace took the empty cup back to the bench. She added a dash of milk then filled it with tea from the pot. It was dark and strong now. Stand a spoon up in it, Pa would have said.

'Don't forget to sugar it,' Des called. 'Just the one.'

Grace added two, and stirred.

'I don't think he knew how to take responsibility for what he ate,' Susan said, after a silence, wrapping her empty pods into a bundle with the newspaper. She got up and took the package to the bin.

'Compost,' Grace called.

Susan changed tack from bin to compost bucket. 'After all, he left school when he was barely fourteen. Wasn't one to read much. How was he to know better?'

'The doctors told him, so he knew well enough,' Grace said.

'I suppose you both did.'

Grace picked up the last pod, a malnourished looking thing whose failure to thrive made it not worth the effort.

'Which is the odd thing really.' Susan rested both hands on the edge of the sink and stared out the kitchen window.

Grace watched her daughter's back, stiff, straight, and wondered if she was taking in the view or considering the paradox. Given the view wasn't much she could only assume it was the latter.

Grace wrapped her pods up neat and tight like a butcher's bundle for the compost bucket, and forced it down on top of Susan's.

6

'They look like op-shop specials.'

'Eclectic, I'd call them.' Grace defended her twelve assorted dinner plates, from finest bone china to heavy earthenware. 'That one I painted myself, when I was going through a crafty stage. Thought I was the next Clarice Cliff.' This was a plate lurid with simple but bright purple and yellow crocuses. 'And this one ...' she held a white porcelain plate up to the dining room window, where the sunlight made it appear translucent, and thereby revealed its quality, 'was one of a pair given to me by Bev. That's what makes it special. More than the Wedgwood mark on the back.'

'Aren't you worried it'll be broken?'

'Better to have it out to enjoy but at risk, than tucked away in the back of a cupboard where there's no pleasure in owning it.'

Susan shrugged. 'I suppose so, but once it's gone, it's gone.'

'Aren't we all.'

'What about this thing?' Susan lifted a large and weighty nut-brown stoneware plate from the table. 'Scratching around to find a twelfth?'

Grace laughed. 'That's the one I keep to remind me of church.'

'Church?'

'The church plate. It was ugly as sin too.'

Just as the plate Susan held was the ugliest on the table, the Catholic Church in Harvest had been the ugliest building in town. It dominated a large bare block on the outskirts, across the road from the equally austere Catholic primary school. The grass along its concrete paths was trimmed with precision and there was never a trace of the last wedding's confetti to be found on the ground. Not even its wide, stepped entrance or fancy tiled floor in the vestibule made it softer on the eye. Whenever Grace walked into the building she felt as though she was entering a large, red-bricked coffin. Each Sunday, as Mother drove towards it, Grace's spirits dropped.

'Why doesn't Joe have to come with us?' Grace knew the answer but was in the mood for goading her mother.

'You know why – he has to help your father.'

'What – read the paper?'

'Don't start, Grace. This is just what we do. Accept it.'

Did she only have to accept it for another two years, until she was sixteen like Joe, when she too could fabricate some plausible excuse not to go? Somehow Grace didn't think it would be that simple.

Sitting on the hard pew listening to Father Donnelly was enough to make a girl, even a good girl, consider passing the time by scratching her name into the blond timber seat. Most Sundays she would just sit there, flicking a nail across the inside seam of her glove or looking around at the different pudding-topped hats on the women's heads, wishing it would end, and soon. But the minutes still ticked away too slowly to the sound of Father Donnelly's voice. The worst Masses were at Lent when the portly priest made his slow pilgrimage round the Stations of the Cross. Grace was guaranteed to nod off then, usually brought round by her mother's sharp elbow.

Father Donnelly was a man who tried to instil faith through fear. The slap he'd delivered Grace's face during her Confirmation ceremony felt more like a punishment from Mother than a welcome to receive the sacrament. Whether he'd got some pleasure out of it or if he really believed his was the hand to pass on God's message, firmly, Grace couldn't be sure. What she did know was that he spoke with a city boy's private school voice – all big words and confident delivery – so she never understood why he needed his lofty altar to speak down to his farming congregation.

'Hard times befall us all,' he said, 'but that does not mean – cannot mean – the giving must stop until those hard times are behind us.'

Grace fidgeted in her seat, shifted from one buttock to the other to relieve the pressure on her tailbone. She felt a firm nudge from her mother's arm, warning her again to keep still.

'Did Jesus abandon you during the hard times? Care less? Give less?' He paused here for effect, Grace guessed, more than to give the congregation time to mull over the question. 'No. No, He did not.' Father Donnelly looked down and shook his head reverently. Then, looking up again, he startled those who'd not had the benefit of Mother's elbow with the fervour in his voice. 'No! He became more resolute. He made more sacrifices. Gave more. Suffered more for His people.'

Grace thought about how Father Donnelly's cheeks often went dusky during his sermons. The purple spider veins on his nose stood out all the more too, as did the red lines tracking across the whites of his rheumy eyes.

'And that, my children, is the thought I'd like you to hold as our bearers pass the plates round today. Of those sacrifices Our Lord made for us. Of the suffering He endured in our name. And then ask yourself – can I give a little more? Can I suffer a little too, just as He did for me?'

There was a general rustling in the congregation as people reached for wallets and purses. Mother passed Grace some coins as she did each week, but this time Grace refused them. She made fists of her gloved hands on the tops of her thighs so that her mother couldn't force them upon her. She watched the plate pass along her pew from hand to hand, cupped palms passing low across its top to hide what they dropped.

She couldn't think about the generosity of Jesus as the plate moved towards her. Not while the clouds remained scarce in the sky and the holes in the soles of the men's shoes showed cardboard through them when they kneeled to have the wafer put on their tongues.

'I call it my greedy plate,' Grace said to Susan.

'A good one for Tom, then,' Susan joked.

The previous day Grace had cleared much of the clutter in the dining room in preparation for her family coming to lunch. Until then, the room's prevailing smell had been of dusty doilies and aged timber. And the moss-green velvet drapes had always depressed the sunny look of a day so were now folded up and in the back of a hall cupboard, where they would likely stay. Now a new kind of light entered the room through net curtains.

Jack had helped Grace with the makeover. She'd felt guilty that he wasn't going to benefit from his efforts, but then again, they rarely ate in this room, so he would only be missing out on her company, which on this occasion was probably just as well.

When at Grace's home, they took their meals together at the kitchen table. They would sit facing one another, chairs placed on the long sides of the rectangular table. Close enough that the small, often subconscious, acts of intimacy could be shared: a hand to a sleeve, fingers laid over fingers.

Des and Grace had sat facing each other too, but their chairs had always been positioned at the distant narrow ends.

Jack, a man who couldn't abide idleness, would cook for Grace in her home. He was a brave cook – adventurous and experimental. He'd often arrive armed with special ingredients, ones that had rarely seen the inside of Grace's kitchen before – robust-flavoured olives, large as a man's thumb; delicate orange-bearded scallops with cushions of white meat in a half-shell; once, a whole, pale duck. Some of his adventures and experiments tasted better than others, but it was fun to watch the alchemy of his cooking.

His specialities – pasta sauces and marinades for meat, poultry and fish – always started with a base of ground garlic and onion – *scaffolding*, he'd call this pungent paste – and he'd build from there. He'd season generously, and taste regularly with a long-handled teaspoon. Sometimes he'd hold the spoon out to Grace, his other hand cupped under it to prevent drips getting on her shirt.

But generally he was a messy cook, a dish for every element or stage of the process. Grace would clear the clutter away for him, wash and dry his dishes, either during the cooking chaos or after they'd eaten, and initially with some vexation. But gradually she recognised that accommodating the long-term habits and idiosyncrasies of another requires respectful patience and some concessions. Eventually she simply saw it as her job, while Jack took on the one that she'd laboured at for years, and not always so joyfully.

It was a novelty to sit down at her kitchen table to a meal that had been prepared by someone else. Jack would look at her, expectantly, as she took her first taste of his rustic puttanesca sauces (no two the same) or the marinade used for the duck (a second never attempted), and she would give him an honest appraisal, as Jack demanded.

'Don't gloss it up for me, Grace,' he'd say. 'You either like it or you don't. Only rule is you've gotta tell me why, so I can work on it.'

In this way food was often the focal point of their meal-time conversations, their voices vibrating with satisfaction as they ate.

Kath said, *That's because food replaces sex the older you get.*

To which Grace had replied, *Speak for yourself!*

So Grace would tell Jack – respectfully, mindfully – what she thought of the food he served her. And in so doing, it awakened her palate to new and interesting flavours again. Often, all she need say was *Delicious!*

At other times, Grace raised her judgements as questions: *Maybe duck breast would have been less fatty?* or *If the sauce was simmered for a little longer, then the flavour of the tomato might be more intense?*

In this way she hoped Jack would know that in tasting his food she noticed all of the stages that went into its creation, and wasn't just delivering him a blunt response to the final product.

She'd been served enough *yuk*s and *disgusting*s in her life to know that it often forced those tasked with providing family meals to cater to the lowest common denominator of taste, a state that not only threatened the cook with culinary boredom, but was also a sure-fire way to take those all-important ingredients, *love* and *care*, out of the process.

Through Jack, Grace learnt to show food kindness again.

She also rediscovered the rich and complex pleasure that food provides. Once again, she stopped to marvel at how the rough, crazed husk of a lychee could give up such a tender, sweet fruit. For the first time in years she shared the same food from the same plate as another: crispy-skinned whole fish, the unwounded white flesh of a nectarine. And as for the duck, Grace learnt that the best cut was its tender, succulent breast.

And sometimes after Jack's meals, she would leave clearing away till the next day.

Back in the dining room, Susan liked the makeover.

'Oh, that's much brighter,' she said when she first entered the room. 'And smells less grandmotherly.'

A framed photograph of Grace's five grandchildren sat on top of an old china display cabinet. It was given to Grace as a gift for Christmas just passed. The shiny chrome frame and colourful clothing the children were wearing brightened the dark mahogany of the cabinet.

Susan picked up the picture, studied the faces in it, then set it back down on the doily Grace used to protect the timber.

'It's a great shot,' Susan said. 'Look even better without the old doily under it.'

'Then you'll be pleased to hear I threw a number of them away yesterday.'

The factory-made ones anyway. Those she'd stitched as a younger woman, and those worked by her mother, she'd put to one side. Grace hadn't been able to bring herself to throw them out. She knew each stitch had been made with care, an act that was owed respect. Besides, Susan might want them one day, though the clutter-free lines of her daughter's home didn't indicate it would be any time soon.

Susan hadn't been one to squirrel items away to fill a glory box as a young woman. In fact, Grace didn't think her daughter had kept much from her past at all. There were no favoured items of child-hood clothing or books tucked away in a dusty box. No special teddy bears, toys or dolls to pass on to her own children. Grace had envied those mothers who complained their spare rooms were made unusable by the boxes of treasured items their children kept stored in them. Her spare room had always been disappointingly uncluttered.

Grace recalled how her daughter would burn her class notes in the incinerator at the end of each school year; did the same with those she'd accumulated from teacher's college.

'Why don't you keep some of them?' Grace had asked. She knew many were marked with *A*s.

'What for?'

Grace shrugged, not really certain why herself, but knew in burning them Susan lost any opportunity to know why in the future.

'Burning them is so final,' she said.

'Exactly why I'm doing it. That stage of my life is over. Time to move on and make room for the next one.'

Grace had flinched each time she saw the plumes of smoke generated by Susan's need to *move on*. It reminded her of Des. Too much had been burnt over the years. There were too few boxes.

After inspecting the dining room, Susan slipped her hands into oven mitts, opened the oven door and removed the baking tray from inside. The lamb erupted in a firework of fat as she lifted it onto the stove top. Once the spitting settled, she started basting the meat. The smell of roasting lamb, garlic and rosemary filled the room.

'Smells good,' Grace said. 'Brings my appetite back. It's been off lately.' Grace, with mitts of her own, took the tray of roasting vegetables from the oven. She shut the door to keep the heat in before starting to turn them.

'Why's your appetite off?'

'Maybe because of the strike. It used to get a good workout when I went for my walk.' Grace hadn't allowed the garbage strike to break this daily practice. 'The smell of backyard barbecues, Stern's bakery at the top of the road. Some days I felt half-starved by the time I got home. Go straight to the biscuit tin when I walked in the door. I'm hardly tempted now.'

'I'm surprised you still bother with the walk.'

'Idle bones make for greater moans.' Grace had always feared stasis and the new routine it could unwittingly bring.

Susan returned the lamb to the oven and closed the heavy door with a thud. Grace gripped a potato with the tongs, turned it over, moved on to a piece of parsnip. She leant over the baking tray and inhaled. She was pleased they smelt like vegetables. Des would have complained that today's roasted potatoes and parsnips were being cooked in vegetable oil and not in with the meat. *Where's the bloody flavour in doing them that way?* he'd have asked. She'd always given him the ones that had sat in the deepest puddle of the meat's juices. They were probably equal parts fat as vegetable by the end of their cooking time, but that was how he liked them.

'Ah, taste,' Grace said, turning the last potato. 'That's the best sense of all to put to the test.' She slid the tray back in the oven.

'I bought these as a special treat.' Grace picked up a cellophane bag to show Susan.

'What are they?'

'Syrian Nuts.'

'Syrian? What's in them – apart from nuts?'

'I don't know. That's why I bought them.'

She had spotted the cellophane bag at her local deli. It was tied with twine, just as school fête rumballs or coconut ice might be. They had been expensive, but what made them worth the price was the absence of an ingredient list on the packet. There was no use-by date either, no allergy warnings for gluten or lactose, and only a fool would fail to notice they contained more than a trace of nuts. She'd bought them to see if she could guess the flavours of the spices by taste alone.

Grace cut the twine with a pair of scissors and took a cashew from inside. She ate it while reading the label: *Syrian Nuts, 400gms* then the name of the deli. Nothing more.

Syrian, Grace thought. As a child she'd never have known a country called Syria even existed, let alone where it was. *Syria* was never written on the blackboard of the one-roomed timber building that served as Grace's first school. And neither was *space travel*, *sperm* nor *spamming*. A girl called Betty or Barb or Bonnie had sat beside Grace; she couldn't remember her name now, only that it started with a B because of the emphasis the teacher placed on the first letter of the girl's name. What Grace remembered most about this girl was that she had her knuckles rapped with a ruler by a teacher determined to cure her left-handedness. And the boys, the ones who never saw futures much beyond their father's farm, had to bend over the teacher's desk for the cane. Now she supposed most schoolchildren of a certain age knew where Syria was and none of them went off each day fearful of their teacher's contempt for genetic difference or scholarly disinterest.

Grace put her glasses on and looked closely at the contents of the packet. She could see in the mix – other than the nuts – rosemary leaves, sesame seeds and something she at first thought were caraway seeds, but soon discovered was the licorice-flavoured anise seed. There were other tiny black seeds that could have been cardamom. She tried a pecan next, covered in a sticky brown coating. She ate it slowly, still unsure of all the flavours. After an almond she decided with some certainty the mix contained cumin and coriander. The macadamia told her there might also be nutmeg, cinnamon and cloves. But the sweet aftertaste made her think all these had been combined with icing sugar. She didn't know if Syria had all these herbs, spices and nuts, but that didn't seem important. Because in eating them she could imagine she was sharing something of the Middle East.

'What are they like?' Susan placed a serving bowl she'd been wiping over with a tea towel onto the bench. She picked up the lid, wiped dust from it that Grace knew wasn't there. She'd cleaned both earlier.

'They're an unusual combination of spicy curry, savoury herb and sweet spice. Here, try one. Tell me what you think.' Grace held the packet out to Susan.

Susan put the lid down and took a macadamia from the bag. She put it into her mouth and chewed, eyes lifted in expectation. Then, shrugging, she said, 'Tastes like a honey-coated macadamia gone wrong, if you ask me. I prefer them dipped in chocolate.'

'Chocolate's old hat. This flavour's more …' Grace searched for the best word to describe what she'd tasted, 'unexpected.'

'It's a nut,' Susan said. 'Not an event.'

'Eating it can be made an event. Here, have another one and let's celebrate its difference.'

Susan reached into the bag and took out an almond. With raised eyebrows she held it up in salute to Grace. 'To the nut!' she said.

If Grace could be sure which nut Susan saluted – her or the almond – then she might have knocked her cashew against Susan's almond playfully. But there was no telling, so she just slipped the cashew into her mouth and munched.

Susan's own search for difference had led her to call her children Jorja and Jaxon; they'd be spelling their names out to others for the rest of their lives. So was novelty a preserve only for the young? Grace wondered. Were parents to maintain a predictable sameness, not testing, or tasting, new things, so that their children might better see their own development? Grace thought with some bitterness that finding your aged mother sharing toast with a strange man one morning, both parties still in their night attire, was obviously not a welcome development.

But Grace said nothing of this.

'Could you pass me the donkey dish, please? It's on the bench behind you,' Grace asked. 'It's for the nuts.'

She knew Susan thought the dish ugly but it was one Grace had always loved. It was a painted figure of a grey donkey with a sway back, drooping ears and a solemn face. The high-sided timber-look cart at the donkey's back was where the dish served its purpose. It had been a wedding gift from a girl she'd worked with at the hospital, given from girlfriend to girl-friend, not left alongside other gifts on a long wooden trestle table at the wedding. She could still recall the words the girl had written in the card: *Don't become the burro.* They'd stopped seeing one another not long after she'd married Des. Grace hadn't been sure at the time if it was because her friend recognised that Des had never liked her or if she believed that Grace had failed the words in her card. Later she suspected it was a bit of both.

As Susan turned to Grace with the dish in her hand, the donkey's legs clipped the edge of the bench. Grace saw a colourful flash – and the dish dropped from hand to floor and smashed on the hard tiles.

'Oops,' Susan said. 'Looks like the donkey's carried its last load.'

'Oops? Is that all you can say?' Grace bent down to the shattered pieces and started gathering the larger ones in her cupped hand. She longed fleetingly for the cheap old lino back; it might have saved the breakage.

'Who was it saying having special crockery out was worth the risk?'

'But you don't even sound sorry!'

'I am sorry. But it was an accident. I'll get the dustpan and brush and help clean it up.'

Grace gathered up the donkey's sad ears. Remarkably they were still attached to the top of its head, like Goofy's ears on a Disneyland baseball cap. Its solemn face and handy cart – save one wheel – were in smithereens. She recognised one of its little pink nostrils, now cleaved in two. Its sway back was a mosaic of jagged pieces. She could only find one eye.

'Fifty years I've been looking at your sad little face.'

'At least you acknowledge it was a miserable-looking thing,' Susan said, coming back from the laundry with the dustpan.

'I loved it,' Grace snapped.

'It's only a dish, Mum.'

'Which once carried an important message.' Grace scouted around the floor looking for far-flung pieces. It was important to her that all its broken parts should be disposed of as a whole. To do otherwise seemed like a betrayal. 'You wouldn't understand.'

Susan said nothing. Instead, she held the dustpan out for the pieces Grace held.

Grace watched as Susan swept the smaller fragments up from the floor then dumped the lot in the bin.

'My poor little burro,' she said. 'The rest of your time spent as landfill.'

Susan slammed the bin lid down. 'Oh, for Pete's sake, Mum, you didn't go on half as much when Claire broke your favourite serving platter of Nan's that time.'

Grace looked at Susan, stunned. She tried to recall the incident. She remembered the platter and remembered its absence but not so much its breaking.

'She was a child,' Grace said, not knowing what else to say.

'A spoilt one,' Susan mumbled, then blushed and turned away.

Grace wished she'd misheard the words.

She'd always thought Claire too hard to pin down to spoil. Even her conception had proved elusive. She was born four years after Susan – who'd come along back-to-back with Peter – and only then when Des's clever hand had mixed more sherry than lemonade in Grace's drinks one night.

From the day Claire crawled, she revealed herself as a child whose inquisitiveness would allow trouble to find her. It sought her in stair tumbles and bee stings, stuck high up in trees and lost down lanes. It found her in sibling squabbles and daredevil cycling, in errant cricket balls and wayward pogo sticks. It never caught her around dolls or tea parties or dress-up, because she did none of those things. She was the bright full stop to Grace's three children and the one who made Grace laugh and cry in equal measure at her antics and escapades.

In comparison, Peter and Susan had been serious for their tender years, and each had a preoccupation with themselves.

Daddy, Daddy, look at me! they'd call from their safe positions on low branches. *Do you think I'm clever, Daddy? Do you?* they'd demand from their stable bikes. But where her two older children worked their father for favours and praise, Claire showed no desire to have either. She was happy to find her accolades within herself, by achieving clever deeds and brave acts.

Come and give your old man a hug, Des would say to her, arms outstretched.

In a minute, Claire would say, but that minute never came. She'd forget or he'd tire of waiting.

Sometimes I wonder whose kid she is, he'd say to Grace, despairing of this third child, the one who didn't seek out his lap or come running at the first call. He'd shake his head at her aloofness but there was always one of the other two at his elbow to take his mind off the one who chose to be elsewhere. And when she proved shrewd enough to spot his mean streak, and comment on it, he was less interested in encouraging her around him much at all.

So for Susan to say Claire was spoilt ... did she not *see* the reckless free spirit and energy of her younger sister, the difference.

'How can you say such a thing?' Grace was more hurt now than by seeing her treasured burro in pieces.

Crimson crept to the neckline of Susan's pale silk blouse. 'Forget I said anything!' Hurriedly she left the room to take the dustpan back to the laundry.

But there were some things Grace didn't think age would allow her to forget.

The air remained tense after this exchange.

Grace tried hard to hide her disappointment and Susan fussed over broccoli florets, leaving the stems long the way her mother liked them.

Right or wrong, Grace took this small gesture to mean more: it was Susan's penance. The day could yet be salvaged by long broccoli stalks.

7

Susan was the wearer of masks. She had a number she could draw on, depending on the occasion. The one she'd worn with Grace most of the morning was that of efficient helper. This mask was almost flawless: no frown, lips passive and her chin kept in a kind line in relation to her neck, not jutting forward in angular defiance. This mask had slipped momentarily when she slammed the lid on the remains of the donkey, and Grace had seen the viper-face that sometimes emerged from the surface of her daughter's skin.

Now, as the doorbell rang for the second time that day, Susan applied a new mask. This one was Mother, all teeth and big, interested eyes directed towards her children, saying, *Look, I've noticed you, now notice me.* Except, why would they? Most children, Grace had learnt, failed to notice much beyond their own shadow, especially when adolescence was forcing them to apply so many masks of their own.

Just as a big-busted girl rounded her shoulders or a tall one stooped, Grace's fourteen-year-old grand-daughter hid her insecurities and faltering confidence behind a long fringe that swept across half her face. The Western girl's veil. Among close family the fringe might be swept to one side and Jorja would look out with her sharp green eyes, surveying the people she was forced to live with. At other times – hormonal highs and lows or enforced gatherings – the veil of hair would be dropped across her face again, letting everyone know there would be no engaging today.

Grace would read her granddaughter's moods like an astronomer read the stars: join the dots and a complete constellation could be drawn. Starting with Jorja's fringe, the trail led from lips to jaw, shoulders to arms either folded across her developing chest or dangling free and open at her slim hips. Today the veil was drawn, the lips were thin, shoulders rolled in on themselves, and those growing buds were compressed by the weight of her arms. Enforced family gathering, Grace decided, and gathered her granddaughter into an embrace.

'Thanks for coming, Jorja. It's lovely to see you.' Grace felt her girl soften a little and was grateful.

'Grace,' Richard said, holding his arms out wide in a look-at-you way.

'Richard,' Grace replied, drawing out his name as he had hers.

'Well, what can I say? Congratulations.'

Not *Happy Birthday* or *You don't look a day over sixty-nine*, just *Congratulations* as though she'd achieved some unexpected milestone, like graduating with distinction or getting a mention in the Australia Day honours list. Grace couldn't help but laugh, 'Yes, Richard, looks as though I've made it. And everything pretty much still in working order,' she said, slapping her sides.

'Come in off the porch,' Susan, the hostess, ushered. 'It smells good inside. Jaxon, turn that off, sweetie, and wish your grandma happy birthday.'

'Happy birthday, Grandma,' Jaxon said to his electronic game.

Jorja sniffed the air like a lioness. 'Roast meat,' she said, top lip curled.

'Yes, lovely lamb but there's plenty of vegetables to go with it. Jaxon, she needs a hug too. Come on, love. Turn it off.'

'I can't. I'll die. And I've just got to the next level.'

'It's all right, Susan. I'll get my hug later.'

'That's not the point. Come on, Jaxon, you know you'll get to whatever level you're at again.'

'But I've never got this far before.'

'Are the vegetables cooked *with* the meat?'

'No, they're not. Richard, will you please get him off that thing.'

'Sure.' Richard reached over his son's shoulder and took the gadget from his hand, mid-game.

'Da-ad! Why'd you do that?'

'I didn't mean like that,' Susan said, exasperated. 'I'd hoped you'd reason with him.'

'That's how we reason at work – give the boss any grief and you lose privileges.'

Susan looked to the ceiling and placated the now tearful Jaxon with an arm round his shoulder. 'He's not on a board yet, for God's sake.'

'I just know the potatoes will be cooked with the meat and I love roasted potatoes.'

'Jorja, we're roasting them separately. Okay?'

Grace watched as Susan transformed her face to suit one person then the other. She remembered the tediousness of diplomacy, of being the mediator, the negotiator, the fall guy. The funny thing was Susan – or any child – would never recall just how easily she'd been able to unhinge a moment in the family's life by a simple act or statement, sometimes with devastating consequences.

It takes a lot to raise kids these days. You can't imagine, Susan would say to her. Grace thought her imagination had only improved with age. That aside, *Do you think I bought you fully grown off a supermarket shelf?* she'd say, and Susan would splutter some reply like, *Things were easier in your day*. Grace never could see the ease in a mangle over a spin cycle.

Grace often thought of her mother's masks. There were three, each perfectly crafted from the roles she served.

One was simply called Mother: thin-lipped, lecturing and stern. Then came The Boss: lofty, dominating and forceful. And finally there was the mask called Cook. This was the one Grace remembered most fondly, as it made Mother gentle.

It was this face that toiled over delicate and airy sponge squares, holding each carefully between two forks and dipping them in chocolate sauce before rolling each in coconut to become lamingtons.

'They're the devil to make!' Mother would cuss, but her cook's face would look on pleased as they devoured them.

Over time, her Christian name became lost, to Mother, The Boss and Cook. Even Pa would say, *Better ask The Boss* or *What's in the pot, Cook?* Sometimes Grace had to stop and think what her mother's real name had been. Then she'd remember – Mary – and feel relieved that not all of her mother had been lost to a role.

Not only could Mother change her face three different ways, she could split her personality too. She had a personality for home and another for town. The damns, bloodys and belches that Joe got away with in the house provoked a twisted ear or a pinch if he let slip in the street. Her perpetually red and chaffed hands – from the old laundry copper, the kitchen sink, the sponge bucket used to wash the shit and mud from a cow's udder – didn't cause shame at home. But in town, she'd hide these working-class hands beneath pristine white gloves and wouldn't take them off until the brown paper bags of groceries were sitting on the kitchen table. Then Mother whistled while she put those groceries in the pantry – though her town lips had been pressed together, except when she exchanged pleasantries with other women using her town accent.

Grace never saw her parents kiss or embrace but with her own coming of age assumed they once had, and possibly still did long after she was an adult and had left home. The slim-spined romance novels Mother bought on mail order and kept hidden in a box at the back of her wardrobe were testimony to that. Grace would sneak into her parents' bedroom and take one at a time, reading it on the sly in the bush or with her back against a sun-warmed barn wall. It seemed a brash thing for a girl to do, to read of snatched kisses and startled gasps by women who always got their man.

In middle age Grace read them purely for the happy endings they offered and assumed her ageing mother did the same. Why else would one have been on Mother's bedside table the night she forgot to wake up, a page marked somewhere near the end with an old shopping docket? At least her last thoughts that night she died would have been of the happy ending only pages away.

So Grace grew into two different people as well. One who longed to coax some feminine camaraderie from her distant mother, and another who was more irreverent than a follower of the family party line. She could switch either on or off depending on what she hoped for. And Filip eventually provided her with the perfect arena in which to practise.

'You're too young for a boyfriend,' Mother said.

'But I'm seventeen.'

'Exactly. Too young. And he's too old. And your teacher. It isn't proper.'

'*Was* my teacher. School's finished now. Remember?'

'Don't get smart with me, young lady. Besides I don't care if you've finished school or not. It's still not proper.' Meaning tongues would wag, the country woman's dread. 'There are plenty of nice local boys for you to see. That man isn't like us.'

On that point her mother was right. He wasn't bigoted.

Grace didn't want any of her mother's nice local boys. She was attracted to Filip because he was different. He didn't have farm stuck to the soles of his shoes or have a vision limited to his father's boundary fence. He was dark, but not outdoors–swarthy like the boys who hung around the front of the picture theatre or dance halls on Saturday nights. His darkness ran ancestrally deep. He kept his hair cut short because that's what suited his European legacy. He didn't bother with the James Dean sideburns or the teddy boys' ducktails the way the others did. It was as though in accepting his difference he decided he might as well live it.

And neither did Filip seem too old at twenty-six nor Grace too young at seventeen. Initially he was the teacher, she the student, but eventually they taught each other. In class he taught science, guided her through the workings of a plant or chemical reactions and the way a magnet could attract metal. Once classes were over, the science was more experimental and grounded in life.

Their extra-curricula learning started over mating ladybirds. Grace was sitting out of the sun under the eaves of a school building. She had one of her mother's novels open in front of her. From the centre of the rickety wooden table, a plaque naming the donor had long been prised, but a rectangular dent remained in the timber. Grace was absentmindedly running her finger around this depression as she read – the ladybirds only catching her attention when one of them travelled across her hand.

She put the book face down then carefully removed the orange-and-black speckled insect with her finger, placed it back alongside the other. She watched as the two small domed bodies bumped against one another like fairground dodgem cars. Eventually the male, its legs grappling for a stronghold on the female's shiny back, mounted its mate. Grace had seen farm dogs locked together in an awkward sexual frenzy often enough, and Pa's bull mounting the backs of cows, leaving Grace to wonder how the cow's legs didn't buckle under the bull's weight. But with these dainty ladybirds, it seemed a quaint affair; small, discreet, tidy, the way Mother would like it, Grace imagined.

She was in the shade and didn't notice it deepen with his approach.

'Nature in action,' he said, sitting on the seat beside Grace and watching the tiny spectacle before them.

More than fifty years on Grace would still feel the heat in her cheeks.

'Their spots are like fingerprints,' he said, 'no two are the same.'

Grace tried to appear indifferent to what the ladybirds were actually doing, to be worldly, confident, mature, like the heroine in her novel, despite the heroine's likely swoon and knee-crumpling submission by the story's end.

'They'd never get away with a crime then,' she said.

He laughed – something he rarely did, she thought, but this proved to be true only in the classroom.

'Unless you consider passion to be a crime,' he said, 'in which case we have caught them red-handed.'

Grace must have felt brave that day, buoyed by the novel's anticipated happy ending, perhaps.

'I don't think passion's a crime,' she said. 'It's just another kind of science.'

He nodded his approval. 'Life science?' he offered.

'Hmm, I guess so.' Her books had never showed how to look deeply into the controls and reasons behind passion, only that it was something every girl should seek.

The 1960s were still around the corner, so they couldn't blame the freedom of that decade for the ease with which they sat together and observed ladybirds mating. She was tall like her father, and slim, stretching out of her school dress; and he'd seen that Grace, unlike most people in their small town, didn't look sideways at his differences.

Soon after, Grace stopped reading her mother's romance novels.

Girls, Grace suspected now, learnt the foolishness of expecting too much from love earlier these days. Where it had taken Grace twelve months with a lover and years with a husband, Jorja, at the age of fourteen, was probably well on the way to knowing it already. *Cosmopolitan* magazine or *Cleo* might tell her the truth, where Grace's romance novels had only told lies and given girls a false sense of reality. But what was worse, she wondered, going into love believing it would be perfect or going into it a young cynic?

Unlike Jorja, Jaxon kept his face so open that every sorrow, delight or victory could be read as easily as if the emotion was tattooed on his forehead. He was uncomplicated, honest and consistent – just like Claire – so Grace always knew what to expect from him. Grace had known where the scene over the electronic game would lead even before the tears started, just as she knew the tears would stop soon after his mother put her arm round his shoulders. Grace knew her birthday hug would come, voluntarily, once things were right for him. And she knew, also, that he wouldn't hold a grudge for any of it. Her eleven-year-old grandson never dwelt on the past, not while the future was unfurling so rapidly before him. He came over to her now, reached up his thin arms and wrapped them round her.

'Happy birthday, Grandma. Did you know you're the oldest person I know?'

And with a child's innocence the events in the hallway were forgotten and faces relaxed again.

Grace had worn masks to hide difficult truths from her friends, back in a time when marriages were only allowed to be sound. Her children had witnessed her happy mask often enough, snapped on as they came into the house when the air was heavy with unspoken accusations. Others she'd worn to appease Des. There'd been those that disguised her anger – the jaunty smile to stop the spit and crackle of thoughts from bursting to the surface – and those that disguised her deceit. Some concealed hurt, others worry or regret. And another had helped her manufacture grief: a special one required just to get her through Des's funeral.

Grace's eyes that day had proved as dry as Father Donnelly's consecrated bread. She was grateful for the dark glasses she wore, slipped on even before she'd left the house. Her mother would have stared Grace down with pursed lips until she'd removed them, if she had been alive to share the day. Solitary grief, Mother always said, was a selfish act. Grace didn't dare think what she might have said about her daughter's inability to show any grief at all.

Peter had sat on Grace's left, watching his hands and blinking fast; Susan to her right, tears running freely down her cheeks and onto her collar. Grace wished, with a kind of crazed desperation, that she could squeeze out tears of her own.

She wore dark clothes, as was expected. Navy though, not black. Black had never suited her so there was little in her wardrobe appropriate for the day. And Des would have thought it a folly to buy something new, just for a funeral – his or anyone's. Grace buried him in the suit they'd married in, which would have pleased him. He always maintained he'd barely changed from when he was a young man, and to his thinking this would have proved it. For all his fry-ups and sugar and beer, he carried most of his extra weight on the inside, around his heart. But not all. She'd had to out-stare the undertaker when he pointed out that the trousers' waist button failed to meet the button hole.

'Would Mrs Baker have a better suited pair of trousers?' he asked.

Grace looked round for this third person before deciding to claim her. 'No, Mrs Baker does not.'

She'd felt a kind of thrill at the time at not being cowed by the man. Remembering the feeling in the church later, she'd smiled. So there was some aspect of their marriage that both she and Des would have still agreed upon, even laughed over: practical frugality.

The coffin was one of the few unmoving things in the church. Those seated behind her fidgeted with quiet respect. Grace could hear the soft rustle of pages as hymn books and readings were flicked through and the squeaking of pews as people adjusted skirts and jackets. Occasionally there was a stifled cough or a delicate blowing of a lady's nose. The men, she noticed, tended to go for short, sharp sniffs.

The minister, a fresh-faced young man who made Father Donnelly of Grace's Catholic youth look like a decaying scholar, steadied his papers and spent a moment scanning those present. Des, the lucky bastard, reclined and oblivious to the waiting discomfort of those gathered to see him off, would have been pleased to know that time had stood still, just for him, for a moment. Finally, the minister's eyes rested on Grace, where he inclined his head ever so slightly as if the one had shared a pact with the other in acknowledging when the show would begin. Grace felt tempted to nod back but was conscious she had a role to play. Dropping the starting flag wasn't part of it.

'We come together today …'

Grace stared straight ahead through her dark glasses, neither listening nor caring to. She just wished the show would end so that she could go home and get on with her life.

For years afterwards she believed she'd got away with her charade that day. But Susan, it seemed, had noticed.

'Why didn't you cry at Dad's funeral?' her daughter asked out of the blue one day while they were preparing another meal, another time.

'I cried!'

'No, you didn't. Ada said it was because you were shell-shocked, him dying relatively young. I believed it at the time, but I'm not so sure now. I remember looking at you at one stage during his funeral and you were smiling.'

Not trusting herself to turn to Susan, Grace had focused instead on the circular motion of the electric beaters as they wove their way round the bowl, whipping cream.

'I cried later,' she finally said to Susan, when the cream was thicker than she liked and the weight of the question still lay uncomfortably between them.

'I never heard or saw you cry.'

'Jesus, Susan. What did you want, a flood?'

'I don't know what I wanted. Some display of grief, I suppose.'

'I'd been grieving for years. Did you notice that?' Grace left the kitchen forcefully, with the bowl of whipped cream. She was angry, not so much with Susan and her close-to-the-bone questioning, but at the realisation she'd been impaled on her own deceit, after having thought she'd got away with it.

Luckily she'd been able to disguise her anger from her other guests by the thickness of the cream: she'd had to bang the sides of each of their bowls to get it to leave the serving spoon. Wearing this mask, she spoke in a falsely cheery voice to everyone – jollying along, her mother would have called it – while Susan looked on bewildered.

And the question was never raised again.

Susan's husband, to his credit, didn't do jollying along or any other false emotional state. What Richard displayed on the surface come from his core. If he was angry or bored, he showed it; tired or happy, the same. Grace liked this about her son-in-law, and his boy Jaxon: you knew what to expect just by looking at them. Today Richard looked ebullient. He liked Grace's cooking – reminded him of his own mother's, he'd said more than once. Susan would say, *And what's wrong with mine?* to which he'd reply, *Generally nothing.*

If there was one fault to be found in Richard's chemistry it was that he was a perfectionist. His polo shirts were always buttoned to the top, shoes polished to a glassy finish. No hair was permitted to grow awry, from anywhere that it should choose to sprout, and his nails were always clipped to a millimetre-neat, white line across the tips of his fingers. Susan had been sacked from ironing his shirts a few years back, for the misdemeanour of leaving dual iron lines down the sleeves. Grace thought her daughter should have felt thankful, not demoted; Des had demanded Grace try harder.

But people who insisted on perfection were hard work, Grace knew. They only ever commented on shortcomings; things done well were considered mandatory anyway, so didn't warrant a mention. Consequently, Grace had observed, Susan spent much of her time aiming to please and looked for compliments, much as a dog watched a table for scraps. What riled Grace most about this type of man who believed he had a right to demand perfection from others was that he rarely recognised his own lack of it. In Richard's case, this usually presented itself through bluntness.

'Is it a good leg of lamb, Grace?' Richard asked, following his nose to the kitchen.

This translated to butcher-bought, not supermarket – a joint recommended over another, not randomly selected – and its cooking timed just so, not left to luck or chance.

'The best, Richard,' Grace said.

And her son-in-law, who reminded her of Des in this one particular way, opened the oven door to be sure.

Pa would often come home from the dump with more in the trailer than he'd taken away. He'd bring back busted sets of drawers, old machinery parts – cogs, wheels, brackets – and lengths of rusty wire, with comments like *Never know when you might need 'em* or *Should be able to fix this up a treat*. Once an old meat safe, despite the fridge they'd had for a couple of years. The girl Grace assumed fandangled appliances, as Pa called new technology, were still something to be mistrusted, so best to have a back-up.

At those country dumps, people backed their trailer to the edge of what was once a great hole and tossed the contents over the edge. There was no benefit of sorting or separation. Broken chairs tumbled on top of old letters or long-ago Christmas cards. Garden waste mixed with car batteries, broken toys with *Playboy* magazines. There was the odd dead animal too – a calf or cat – which riled Pa; he was a man who took careful responsibility for his dead. Papers were lifted from the top by the wind and strung out in a wide radius, caught in branches, fences or skewered on tussock grass.

These dumps could be a scavenger's paradise or a child's treasure chest, opening windows into otherwise private lives. Grace had read of those other lives on the backs of postcards she'd found there, postmarked from places she'd never heard of; small cameos from unknown coastlines and mountain ranges that were no less exotic for the stains and pungent aroma that marked them.

Once he brought back three boxes of sewing patterns for Mother. Corners of the delicate tissue paper poked out from the openings of the Simplicity and Butterick envelopes like the handkerchief from a fancy man's jacket. Mother had looked through the various packets muttering, *Pattern's one thing, money for fabric's another*, but had kept them all anyway. Grace took them back to the dump years later when she returned to clear out the house after her mother's death. Finding them at the back of a hallway cupboard had caused Grace deep regret on her mother's behalf, as sorting through her clothes hadn't revealed any of the pretty frocks or skirts or blouses pictured on the patterns' envelopes. She had to assume her mother never did get to feel any of the recommended fabrics glide under the foot of her old Singer machine.

The chooks got Mother's vegetable scraps; the dogs cleaned up the meat ones, and the slow combustion stove was fed anything that burnt. It made Grace wonder now, what it was Pa actually took to the dump. Maybe very little – broken china, tin cans, farm equipment or furniture so clapped out even he couldn't repair it. Perhaps this explained why the dump from Grace's youth never grew much larger in the eighteen years she lived up the road from it. There was a balance.

Grace still tried to maintain something of this balance. She kept hens – a mixture of Isa Browns and Rhode Island reds – which she'd recently increased to four; tiny compared to Mother's large flock. She composted as well, and kept a good-sized vegetable garden. She'd come down now to pick baby carrots, but felt inclined to take her time. Susan was in the kitchen reassuring Jorja of the vegetarian elements of their meal. Grace imagined Richard standing over her, questioning again the sense in removing a whole protein group from a developing girl's diet. Jorja would be hiding behind her fringe while this debate went on, and Jaxon, Grace expected, would be trying to get back the life he'd lost. Grace dawdled, pulled a few weeds while she was there. She found a caterpillar on the basil, tossed it to Ruth who was fossicking in the grass nearby. The hen spotted it with her flinty eyes and snapped it up in her beak.

It was hot outside – but then again, so was the kitchen, so Grace didn't mind.

In the city, the bricks, tiles and concrete absorbed the day's warmth, holding it for days. In Harvest the heat had pressed against timber buildings but the timber was never as obliging as concrete: it didn't allow the heat to embed itself within the grain for long periods of time. Grace placed a hand on the timber sleepers that formed the garden's retaining wall, bent down and placed the other on the cracked concrete path that led down the back garden. One surface burned more. She removed her hand from the path and kept the other on the sleeper. She knew in winter the concrete would sting with trapped cold. She'd observed this simple difference soon after she arrived in the city to live. She took this as a good sign: it proved she was far from the static landscape she'd left. But some days – the bad ones – she'd longed for more timber.

The screen door slapped shut. The noise startled Ruth enough to stop her foraging. She swivelled her head in jerky movements assessing the danger, red cone joggling with the motion. Grace looked towards the house and saw Jorja picking her way down the path. Ruth relaxed, returned to scratching and pecking at the ground.

Grace watched the way her granddaughter avoided stepping on the cracks in the cement, putting one foot cautiously in front of the other like a funambulist. It reminded her that beneath all the posturing and deep sighs Jorja was still really just a child.

'Do you need a hand?' she asked, coming up to Grace.

'I'm not doing much. Just wasting time, really!'

Jorja sat on the wall of the vegetable garden. She picked up a broken bamboo stake and started to poke it into the mounded straw mulching the plants.

'Did you like the knives?' she asked.

Grace sat alongside Jorja, tomato bushes to their backs. 'Yes, they're very – sharp,' she said.

'Sharp.' Jorja laughed. 'I told Mum it was bad luck to give knives as a present.'

'Your mother's always been more practical than superstitious. Besides, I thought they were only unlucky if given as a wedding gift.'

Jorja shrugged. 'I read once that you should never give a present to someone that could hurt them. I reckon knives have to be near the top of the list.'

'I'll be extra careful when I use them. And if I cut myself on one I won't hold a grudge. How's that sound?'

'Forgiving, as always.'

Forgiving, Grace mused, as always. But was she – had she been – always? Was it possible for anybody to forgive all past grievances, and should they be filed away under headings like *Resolved* or *Atoned* or *Forgotten*?

Des had wanted her to forgive, and forget. 'Let it go, Grace,' he said. 'Move on.'

What had provoked him? Grace wondered now. One place too many set at the dinner table? Five bowls on the bench, not four?

121

What she did recall was that she'd been enraged by the way he'd reduced Claire to it.

'Let it go? Just like that?' she said.

Des nodded. 'Why not?'

Why not? she wanted to scream. Because it would let him off, spare his conscience, put things back as they were before. But nothing was as it used to be and neither would it ever be again.

She said nothing.

Instead, she turned her back on Des, started serving dessert – apple pie, the top golden and grainy with sugar. She shifted the knife to the left; cut him a large wedge, the sweetened apple oozing from its sides. She added lashings of cream and put the bowl in front of him without care.

Grace went back to pulling weeds, Jorja to poking at the mulch, Ruth to the far end of the yard. Jorja had news she wanted to share, Grace could tell. Her granddaughter wasn't one to seek out company then sit in silence. Grace waited with the patience of the aged.

'Guess what?' Jorja finally said, barely able to conceal her pride.

Grace looked up expectantly.

'I finally got my period.'

'Congratulations!' Grace was genuinely pleased. To date, her granddaughter's body seemed to have put so much energy into her intellectual development that her physical development had been overlooked.

'Mum only said *Sorry*.'

'Well, I suppose she's still living them. I stopped years ago now, so I forget that some days they can be a pain.' Deep down, the real question for Grace was why Susan hadn't mentioned it.

'There's a lot about them not to like,' Jorja conceded.

'Yes, there is.'

'And Mum won't let me use tampons.'

'Ah. Tampons.'

When Grace first started to bleed, Mother silently passed her a neatly folded pile of soft rags.

'Don't know how I'm s'posed to swim. All the other girls use tampons.'

'I'm sure she'll let you try them soon enough.'

'Could you talk to her? She'll listen to you.'

Jorja occasionally sought Grace for this go-between role; it wasn't one she enjoyed. To Jorja, her grandmother might appear the matriarch, but Grace knew there were careful lines drawn over what she could and couldn't say to Susan. And Grace felt duty bound to respect those boundaries.

'Your mum probably has very good reasons for not wanting you to use them just yet.'

'She reckons I'll die from some infection. You were a nurse. You could tell her that's not true.'

'But what if it is true? I haven't been a nurse for a while and they're learning new things all the time.'

Jorja poked her stick more forcefully. Grace felt sorry for her granddaughter's frustration; neither of the two generations ahead of her seemed prepared or able to give her what she wanted.

'You and your mum are still new to it all,' Grace soothed. 'Give it a bit more time and she'll change her mind. You'll see. She was a girl once too, wanting to do all the same sorts of things as you, swimming included.'

Jorja poked a little less aggressively.

Grace picked two ripe cherry tomatoes. 'Here, let's celebrate you officially becoming a woman.' She passed one of the small fruits to Jorja and put the other in her mouth. 'Not quite champagne,' Grace said, 'but I do love the way they go bang in your mouth.'

She picked two more.

'You haven't sprayed them with any bug killers have you?' Jorja eyed the red orb suspiciously.

Grace looked askance at her granddaughter. 'This is your composting, green granny you're talking to, not Mrs Yates.'

Jorja flicked her fringe back and put the fruit in her mouth. Grace enjoyed seeing both her granddaughter's questioning eyes for a change.

'Mum reckons you've never lost your country roots.'

Grace laughed. 'She's right. You can tell by my hands.'

She held her hands out for Jorja to see. They weren't as stained and worn as Mother's had been, but they still showed a line of soil under the nails and in some of the deeper seams of her palms as well.

'These are my roots.' She waggled her fingers at Jorja. 'But they wash up all right, just like carrots.'

Jorja laughed, held her smaller hands out and turned them up then down to compare.

Grace gripped each of the pale, slender hands in hers and ran her rough thumbs over the backs of each. 'Pah,' she joked, casting them free. 'City girl's hands. Pretty, but soft.'

Yet they were the exact hands Grace had wanted once. Soft, pretty hands that proved she'd taken a different path from her mother's. Harvest had offered few options to a 1950s girl that didn't lead to hands like Mother's.

Her most likely, and expected, occupation had been housewife, but at seventeen that had no appeal to Grace at all. She could have tried for work in the local shops. There was the haberdasher, whose proprietor was a woman with a nose long and thin like a pencil pleat. But she only took on girls whose mothers she was sweet with, and Grace's mother wasn't one of them – she couldn't afford pretty lace trims or expensive lengths of gabardine. And Grace believed she was owed something more, for having made it all the way through high school, than to end up like those girls who hadn't. They weighed beans or quartered cabbages at the greengrocer or made spiders for children yet to learn their pleases and thankyous at the milk bar. Or they cleared away the greasy counter-meal plates from tables at the pub. There was the occasional office job – at the accountant, council chambers, the doctor – but Grace was sure she didn't want to miss even what sleepy Harvest had to offer by being stuck in some stuffy back room as a typist, a fluorescent light as the only sun.

Grace had looked for alternatives, ways to escape, even as she feared she wouldn't find the courage to take the opportunity, should it present itself. Mother had never supported her in this, so Pa wouldn't either. At the time Grace thought her mother was reluctant to lose a useful worker from the farm. But later, after Grace had gone, and letters from her mother arrived asking her to describe the intricate details of her city life – the decorative stair inside a department store, whether a tram swayed like a train, the exotic plants found in the Botanical Gardens – she came to wonder if the real reason was that her moving away proved there were other, possibly better, options than Harvest.

Up until then, Grace supposed her mother's vision of the future had been built on lush good seasons, the drought-ridden ones hidden by the forgiving undulations of her mother's memory. But the young Grace couldn't help seeing her own future from decades down the track: and she saw a wizened Grace looking back on pastures bristling with lost opportunities.

So at seventeen, just three years older than Jorja, Grace had wanted a different vision, and certainly no more country dirt under her nails. And it was Filip, his differences, that became the catalyst to change her life.

'What will your hands eventually do, d'you think?' Grace asked Jorja, who was picking her own tomatoes now.

'Maybe nursing, like you.'

'Really?' Grace was surprised, and a little proud.

'Uh-huh.' Jorja put two cherry tomatoes in her mouth, filled each cheek. She smiled a swollen smile at Grace then pushed a finger into either side of her face. Grace heard them pop inside her mouth.

'Why nursing?'

Jorja shrugged. 'I don't reckon it'd be boring.'

Nursing had beckoned Grace from a photograph in a magazine. The picture of the nurse was a good one for catching a restless girl's eye – it conveyed seriousness and possibilities. The uniform was serious, with its creaseless fall, the collar demurely high, the starched cap like a crown on the girl's head. A fob watch rested above her right breast like a medal and her hands, one resting on top of the other in front of her tightly belted skirt, looked soft, and pretty. The girl's face captured the possibilities. She looked out at Grace not with the empathy that the job would demand, but with a *Come and join the fun* dare, and the corners of her mouth, turned ever so slightly up, implied the girl was happy. That photograph was all the job description Grace needed.

She'd gone to the city with the hope of becoming that girl, but she never did, not really. Adult life proved more complex than that one-dimensional snapshot. Sometimes the work was too serious; the possibilities too few.

She found other things though. Anonymity for a start, a freedom she'd only dreamt of in Harvest. She could walk the streets of the city late at night with friends, coming home from a dance or the pictures, and not have to worry about who might see her. There were no phone calls to Mother the next day by a neighbour or a relative, calling on the pretext of a chat, only to let slip that Grace had been spotted, out late, shoes swinging in her hand. She loves a good time, that Gracie, they might say with a small laugh, which had the power to fold Mother's brow and leave it folded for days. In the city the magnifying glass was removed.

But she never did achieve those soft, pretty hands. As a nurse she found a different kind of dirt. She found it in infected wounds and soiled beds or on the dead when she washed and laid out their bodies. Her palms and fingers discovered blood – thick, sticky – when she lifted half-limbs, bandaged broken heads. Vomit, piss, pus; they all left their mark. Some days she struggled to touch her own food. And her hands became chapped and reddened too, just like Mother's, abraded by scrubbing brushes, harsh soaps and disinfectants.

But they remained gentle, she was told.

★

'You've a gentle touch,' a woman, diminutive both in stature and confidence, said to Grace. 'He'd be grateful for that. I'm sure he'd tell you himself if he could.'

Her husband hadn't been able to say much at all for several days, though when he'd first been admitted to hospital the things he did say as he fought his delirium tremens didn't suggest to Grace that he cared too much for gentleness. But she smiled at the wife, complicit with her attempts to recall only the good.

Grace remembered the day as hot and humid with no breeze for the ward's open windows to catch. The woman fanned her husband with a folded newspaper, giving herself purpose, Grace suspected, rather than him relief, as he was oblivious to the heat. He was mostly unconscious, and when he did stir he muttered incoherently or plucked at some invisible lint or bug on his starched sheet. Grace supposed liver failure could be a kind death in this way, though she knew enough about its causes by then to suspect that his family had probably known lesser kindnesses. He could, of course, have been the type of drunk who simply went to sleep after two or six too many. But the confused looks of pity, contempt and disinterest on his sons' faces told a different truth. As did the way the mother jumped when her husband shouted some curse from his semi-comatose state.

Grace was still struggling to lose her country girl's gait, her country girl's drawl, her country girl's startled look at the helter-skelter of city life, despite living there more than a year. She was never sure if it was her long legs or her cow-eyed country innocence that attracted Des.

He was the youngest of the five siblings around that bed, all of them men. Grace supposed if a woman was to be widowed in mid-life, as Des's mother was soon to be, then five able sons were her ticket to some comfort in her old age. Years later, she realised the stupidity of the thought.

When Grace was attending to his father, she could feel Des's eyes following her, as she worked her way round his bed, straightening covers, checking a chart, taking a temperature, a pulse. With a country girl's trust – that took many more years to lose than the drawl – she'd look up, fingers still pressed to his father's thin wrist, having lost count of the thready beats, and stare right back at him. Sometimes he'd look away first. Mostly she was the coward.

When she was at another patient's bed, and out of Des's line of sight, she had the opportunity to watch him instead. She decided there were contradictions at play in this man, contradictions that only revealed themselves when he thought he was alone and unobserved. Grace would watch as he carefully adjusted the sleeves of his father's pyjamas, pulled them out straight where they'd been rumpled or twisted up to his elbow in a way that would be uncomfortable for the conscious. At other times, when his father was flushed and sweating, he'd gently lift his head and turn his pillow over to the cooler, dry side. Grace had seen wives and mothers perform these small caring acts without a second thought, but rarely men. And yet there were other times when he'd sit in a chair beside his father's bed and spin his hat round and round in his hands between his knees and not even raise an eye in his father's direction. Or he might only stay a short while, study the form guide, then leave without so much as laying a hand on his father or saying a single word to him.

As his father's stranglehold on life slipped further, Des would sometimes look across his gasping, jaundiced body and wink at Grace. The first time he did it she was confounded, and looked to check nobody had seen, especially his mother. But she stared blankly and didn't notice.

It became a game then. He might let a single finger caress her back or arm as she leaned in to his father to freshen up the stale acid smell of his breath with a mouth swab, or to reposition a limb.

Are you always so gentle? he'd whisper, genuine in his enquiry. At others, he'd be more playful: *You're enough to make a bloke wish he was dyin'.*

She couldn't deny she was flattered by his attention and figured it was the kind of thing that had lifted the corners of the girl's mouth in the recruiting photograph. But she also sensed confusedly that he was both a man who cared, and one who didn't.

'I kind of hope the ol' man lingers on as long as possible,' he said to her on one occasion when he was at his father's bedside alone.

'I can't see him lasting much longer,' Grace said, her voice gentle, like her hands. 'I'm sorry.'

Des laughed. Grace looked at him, mystified.

'We've pretty much accepted the ol' bugger isn't going to dodge this bullet,' he said. 'What I meant was when he goes I'll have run out of excuses to visit the hospital. I could always slip one of my brothers something, I suppose. That'd give me reason enough to come back to visit.'

Nineteen by then, Des's pluck appealed to Grace.

'Mind you, I wouldn't trust any of them getting tucked in at night by a pretty girl like you. So unless you wanted to make it easier for me ...'

Grace felt a fresh plume of warmth creep up from her neck.

His father did take more days to die, more than Grace would like to have seen anybody have to fight for each breath.

Des remained, caring, then not.

'So do I have to poison one of my brothers or not?' he whispered urgently on the last afternoon, behind the closed screen of his father's bed.

His father had taken on the type of breathing that left a family poised at every exhalation, waiting and wondering if there'd be another breath in. Grace could smell the defeated sweetness that fermented in the air above his bed. She knew it as the smell of death.

Des's persistence made her want to resist him, to show him she was choosy and not won over by such jokes and winks.

But city girls took risks, Grace reasoned. Only country girls accepted boy-next-door mediocrity. She'd felt taller, and prettier, since she'd left Harvest. And this taller, prettier Grace felt confident that day.

'Here.' She passed Des a folded slip of paper.

'It's fair to say you won't be bored nursing,' Grace said to Jorja. 'But your hands will get dirtier than you know.'

Grace started to work at a troublesome run of couch grass that had threaded its way between two beetroot plants. She dug deep with her fingers to loosen the weed's roots. 'Gardening – it's tough love,' she said, holding the extracted weed up triumphantly to Jorja.

'Like nursing?'

'Yes, I suppose like nursing.' She looked at her hands, the fresh dirt under her nails. 'Who'd have thought they'd happily dig in soil again.'

'I'm glad they do. These taste much better than any Mum buys.' Jorja held another cherry tomato out to Grace.

Grace put the fruit in her mouth, enjoyed the sweet acid burst as she crushed it between her teeth. 'I'll have to teach you how to grow your own.'

'Why, when I can come round here and eat as many as I like?'

Grace gave her granddaughter a wry smile. She'd been as ignorant as Jorja at her age, assumed the patterns in her life – people, places – were fixed and unchanging.

Now when Grace thought of her childhood home, she could see it more as her mother had. She saw the flat and fertile flood plains cupped in the hands of the surrounding mountains, scooping the land towards the southern coastline. She considered it a pretty landscape. Those mountains, she realised now, were more changeable than she'd given them credit for. They could be lost from sight to heavy rain, capped with white or shimmering purple behind a veil of heat. Sometimes they were grey with smoke; at others crisply green or frosty-footed under a clear blue sky. She could see the dams in the paddocks too, sparkling like diamonds on fingers. Except in the years when they were empty with drought and the landscape took on the appearance of an old sepia photograph. But now, even when she thought of those various shades of drought brown, she considered them as colourful as an artist's paint box.

How did she fail to see the beauty of those mountains when living at their fingertips?

Ada's son dropped her at the door the way a parent delivered a child to a party. He was already turning back down the stairs to leave, calling, 'Have fun,' as Grace answered the chime.

'Oh. Hi, Grace,' Max said, looking up. 'Happy birthday. Hey, I've got a bit of running round to do today so any idea what time things'll wrap up?'

'I don't know, Max,' Grace said, annoyed. 'It's not your regular two-and-a-quarter-hour party slot. It'd take me that long just to blow out the candles.'

Ada, with her poor bruised face, shuffled uncomfortably on the front doormat.

'How about you call later – when you get a chance,' Grace said. 'I can let you know how things are going then.' She gave Max a tinkling-fingered wave goodbye then put her arm round her friend's shoulders and coaxed her inside. 'Bloody kids,' Grace said, supporting Ada as she lifted her tender leg over the door stop. 'Setting curfews – at our age.'

Ada's purple cheek creased into a smile and closed her already swollen eye even more. 'Happy birthday.' She embraced Grace, tentatively. 'I'm sorry, but I haven't been able to get to the shops to buy you a gift.' Ada lifted her hands then dropped them in a helpless gesture.

Grace shooed the apology away. 'We both know there's nothing I need.'

'Still, your seventieth!'

Grace laughed. 'So now I've reached the same decade as you.'

With arms linked, Grace and Ada moved slowly through the house.

There was a time when the two women were on all fours together on the grass in one or the other's backyard, small children at their knees or riding on their backs. Ada's son had enjoyed a good tickling then, or tying himself in knots over a game of Twister. Max and Peter had all the time and imagination in the world to run amok with costumes and sticks and large cardboard boxes. Now their creativity stretched no further than what was required to complete their tax returns.

Some couples' closest friends had been decided by their children's friendships. Ada was exactly one of those child-forged friendships, created by Peter's schoolboy mateship with Max. The sons were only acquaintances now, but the bond between their mothers was made of stronger stuff.

And Grace had found other friends in a variety of places. Bev she'd met in her new-to-the-city nursing days over a cheap bottle of cider smuggled into the nurses' quarters. It was the first of many, and over them they'd laughed or moaned at all manner of things from Matron's unfortunate lazy eye, magnified behind her thick glasses, to night shifts – that scourge to their social life. Kath came later in Grace's life, on a long train journey back to Harvest. Even on that first day Kath, who'd never had to share her life with a man, could comment on Grace's need to do so objectively.

Grace remembered a day Ada and Bev had come to help her with a sixth birthday party. Ada knew the skills of getting order from a bunch of littlies. Bev was keen to learn whatever would be needed by the large bulge beneath her floral maternity dress. Bev had maturity on her side. She'd come to marriage later than Grace, and to a man who didn't think conception necessarily need take place on the honeymoon; he'd let her have her career first. Des reckoned Bev's husband was a man shy on pride. Grace reckoned Bev was lucky to be given a choice.

It was Claire's sixth birthday party. She was a popular girl at school and had refused to cut her list of ten guests by a single one. She greeted each six-year-old at the door like the lady of the house, gave them their allocated party hat, before marching them through to the backyard where all the games were set up.

Susan, who'd not long before hit double figures in age, had been put out over Claire's party. 'How come she gets to have ten people? She's s'posed to only have six.'

Grace's party rules were one guest for each year celebrated. Susan had been reminding her all week she'd broken her own rule.

'I wasn't to know they'd all be able to make it,' Grace had said again and again.

'It's not fair. You should've sent out only six invitations.'

'Come on, you'll get to play the games and eat the party food as well. You can be my big helper.'

'I won't play any of their stupid games – they're babies.'

And now the sulkiness continued into the party.

Susan didn't move from the day bed, where she lay in a knot of skinny arms and legs, as Grace went in and out from kitchen to backyard with snacks and drinks. She knew her eldest daughter was only pretending to read the comic book in front of her; mostly her eyes strayed over it to the backyard. But if the younger children were noisy when they came inside the house, she'd make a great show of lowering the magazine to her chest in order to scowl at them. Once, she even yelled *Get outta there* to one little girl, who mistook the closed door to the girls' bedroom for the one to the toilet. As if this wasn't enough, Des had bellowed from his shed more than once for them to *Keep that damn noise down*, because he couldn't hear the races being called on his radio. Grace imagined Claire's young party guests quivering with relief when their mothers finally came to collect them.

Claire, fortunately, was oblivious to her sulking sister and cantankerous father. She led her gaggle of friends confidently through one party game after another, making sure the parcel stopped fairly along with the music and that blindfolds were secure when each girl faced the donkey.

'Chocolate brownies, as requested.' Bev had placed a square Tupperware container on the kitchen bench when she arrived.

'You've put the recipe inside, of course?' Grace now removed the container's lid to reveal a perfect display of brown squares dusted with icing sugar.

'Can't a girl have her secrets?'

'Not one this tasty. I could eat them every day.' Grace took a square and bit it in half.

'Which is why I won't give you the recipe. If you could make them for yourself they wouldn't be special when I made them for you.'

Bev's brownies were gooey and rich; seamed with caramel and studded with walnuts. Grace had been trying to get the recipe from her friend since she'd first had one. The only clue she'd been able to extract from Bev was that she'd been sent the recipe from a

Canadian penfriend. They were dark as a cave and not so much crumbled in the mouth as dissolved. Some of the ingredients Grace could guess, but any attempt to copy the brownies had produced nothing but a poor second cousin. They were destined to be loved by all but made by no one but Bev.

'Chocolate brownie?' Bev called to the still supine Susan.

'Are they your brownies?' Susan asked.

'The one and only.'

Susan's eyes lit up.

'If you want one, though, you'll have to come and get it.'

With some eye-rolling and much huffing and puffing, the comic book was dropped to the floor and Susan levered herself up from the day bed. She came over to Bev and took a piece from the container offered.

Bev winked at Grace.

'Now, I'll put two more pieces aside just for you, but only if you take these out to the others.'

'Do I have to?'

'I'd like you to,' Bev said.

'I'm not playing their stupid games though.'

'No one's asking you to. But I know Aunty Ada would appreciate you helping her to organise them, you being the older girl.'

Grace kept cutting oranges into quarters, trying not to look at Susan. If her elder daughter thought the request came from anybody but Bev, then she'd be back on the day bed quick-smart.

'All right then.'

Bev took two brownies from the container and put them on a small plate. 'Yours for later.' She passed what was left to Susan.

Grace noticed Susan's slow journey outdoors was fortified by another brownie. Once among the hungry revellers, though, and she heard her snap at a child, 'Just one, you greedy girl.'

'She got out of the wrong side of the bed this morning,' Bev said.

'She does most mornings.'

Bev rested her hands on the kitchen bench and pushed her spine up like an angry cat's. 'Ah, that feels good.' She swung her sizeable belly from side to side. 'So what's triggered today's humph?'

'Ten guests when there should have been six.' Grace arranged the quartered oranges on a plate.

'So why are there ten? I thought you had some rule.'

Grace shrugged. 'I do. But it just didn't work out. All the girls here invited Claire to their parties earlier in the year but I didn't expect them all to accept in return. So Susan's feeling hard done by.'

'She's a sensitive girl.'

'Too sensitive some days.' Grace started to peel and quarter apples.

'So what will you do next year?'

'Hope Claire's got it down to seven friends.'

'And if she hasn't?'

Grace shrugged again.

Claire burst into the kitchen, breathless and with her conical hat tipped to one side like a dunce's cap on a drunk. 'We're one piece short,' she panted.

'How can you be short?' Grace asked. 'There were plenty there.'

'Well, all my friends had a piece, so that's ten. Then Ada had one, and Dad took two ... and so did Susan, because she said she had to carry them out so she deserved them. So that makes ... how many? And I haven't had any yet.'

'Here, have these.' Grace passed Claire the plate with the two pieces put aside.

Claire took one and ate it in two bites, then scuttled to the back door again.

'Do you want the other piece?' Grace called after her.

'You have it,' Claire said, and disappeared.

'Here.' Grace pushed the plate across the bench to Bev. 'You seem to be the only one who's missed out.'

'No, keep it for Susan.'

'It doesn't sound as though she's gone without.'

'Still, a deal's a deal.' Bev pushed the plate to one side.

'Look at you, having to help me along like I'm a frail old woman,' Ada said.

'You are, aren't you?'

'Feels like it.'

'Your confidence has taken a battering, that's all. It'll come back.'

'Do you think confidence is something that continues to grow at our age?' Ada stopped walking to look at Grace. 'It might do for children – they can only get stronger, more knowing. But with us, confidence eventually has to hit the ceiling and from there the only place left for it to go is down.'

Grace looked into her friend's troubled face and saw the plea coming from those sore eyes, begging her to help find that distance from the ceiling she needed.

'There is no ceiling, Ada. We'll always live with the stars above our heads.'

Ada looked up. 'I see a ceiling,' she said.

Grace refused to follow her friend's gaze. 'Then we need to spend more time outdoors.'

Ada patted the top of Grace's hand and the pair moved on.

Grace didn't know how long she could help and protect her friends. Those years she had on them, years that had made no difference in their middle age, did now that they were all in their seventies. For Ada to be struck by a truck's mirror regardless of whether Grace was there or not showed that the benefit of those few years was finite.

The two friends moved past the lounge and along to the dining room, where Ada stopped and looked in. 'Table looks nice,' she said. 'You've used the plate Jimmy and I gave you.'

The plate, at one end of the table, was busy with English cottage garden blooms. It had been a gift from Ada and her husband to Grace and Des for their twentieth wedding anniversary. It had come decorated with an assortment of dainty petit fours Ada had made. She'd wrapped the plate in clear cellophane and tied off the top with colourful curling ribbon. Grace had admired the plate and its contents, told Ada it looked like a piece of art, too good to eat. Des had said, *Might look pretty, but let's see how they taste*. He'd got to the bow with a pair of scissors and tossed the cellophane to one side. The petit fours obviously tasted as good as they looked because he consumed the lion's share, taking each in a single mouthful.

'Yes, some of the old favourites out.'

'The church plate. Bev's.' Ada knew many of the stories behind Grace's plates. 'And the commemorative one from Moreville. Sixty years, wasn't it?' Ada craned her neck to see.

'Yes. Sixty.'

By the time Grace retired, Moreville was celebrating more than sixty-five years of caring for the aged. She found she couldn't eat off that particular plate, though she valued it. It reminded her too much of the puréed food she'd fed to people, homogenised blobs of grey or green or brown that were rejected more often than swallowed. She'd set the plate at

Meg's place, the youngest member of her family, and therefore furthest from needing such a diet.

Ada looked round the table, nodded, almost imperceptibly, at each plate as she passed it. Grace knew she was counting the places. 'Only twelve, then?'

'Only twelve.'

'Shame.'

The word shame was one of those with disparate meanings. The first, as Ada used it now, expressed sympathy, the other, as Susan and Peter would have it, expressed disgrace.

'Just the thought gives me the creeps,' Peter had said, after learning of Jack. Grace remembered how he'd visibly shivered.

Susan must have phoned him that morning. She had called in early and unannounced to find Grace and Jack sharing breakfast in their pyjamas. Unfortunately Susan hadn't seen the quiet intimacy of the moment – the sectioned newspaper shared between them, teapot handle turned for the other's ease, the casual touch of one foot against the other's under the table. Instead, she'd looked at Grace as if to say, *How could you?* Grace had felt dirty under her gaze.

'I don't ever want the kids to know about this. It's not how they see you.' Susan left at once and Grace never did find out why she'd called in.

Jack left soon after Susan that morning – believing, Grace guessed, that he'd contributed to the filth.

But eventually he returned, and Grace received him keenly.

Ada limped slightly on her left leg as Grace moved them on to the kitchen.

'Ada,' Richard said, as the two women entered the room, 'tell me who it was and I'll get my best men onto him right away.'

'Whoa!' said Jaxon.

Jorja leant up against a kitchen bench, flicking through a magazine. She half-saw Ada's face from behind her fringe, and winced at the sight.

'Oh, Ada. I had no idea how bruised and swollen you were. You poor thing.' Susan fussed with a kitchen chair for Ada. 'Come. Sit. Sit.' She gestured towards the seat. 'Or maybe you'd rather lie on the sofa? We can take you in the lounge, if you like.' Susan looked torn between pushing the chair back in and steering Ada out the way she'd just come in. 'I could prop you up with some pillows. Bring you in a drink – a nice cup of tea, maybe.'

'Stop fussing. She's fine.' Grace manoeuvred Ada towards the chair. 'I've got a good bottle of Chardonnay in the fridge. How does that grab you?'

'Perfectly.' Ada accepted the chair.

Grace hoped no one else noticed the soft tremor in her friend's hand as she gripped the chair back and the cautious way she lowered herself into the seat.

Grace took the wine from the fridge and passed it to Richard. 'Would you mind doing the honours?'

Richard cracked the seal on the bottle. He poured three glasses and passed one each to Grace, Ada and Susan; Susan's was three-quarters full, Grace's and Ada's less than half.

Grace held hers up and inspected it. 'Tide's out a bit, isn't it?'

'Oh, sorry, do you want more? I thought you'd want to take it easy.'

'Why?'

'Well, you know – Ada already being a bit wobbly on her feet.'

'She's not on her feet now,' Grace said, 'and mine are rock solid.' She worked the hinges of her knee joints up and down. 'Do I look like a well-sprung grandma to you, kids?'

Jorja grinned.

'You look as springy as a slinky to me, Grandma,' Jaxon said.

With wine glasses topped up, Grace raised hers to Ada. 'To the stars,' she said.

'Yes, the stars.'

Susan and Richard looked at one another.

'Stars?' Grace said, encouraging Susan to raise her glass as well.

'Ye-es – stars.'

'Celebrity stars?' Jorja asked. 'Which one?' She held up her magazine to show Grace a page covered in women with scant parts of their skin covered by glittering sequins.

'No. The real ones. Above us.' Grace lifted her glass to the ceiling. 'More inspiring.'

Richard looked troubled as he went to the laundry to get a beer from the tub of ice. Was it the ambiguity of the toast that had unsettled him, suggesting the start of dementia, perhaps, or concern about their alcohol consumption? Either notion annoyed Grace.

The empty wine bottles at Grace's house now were insignificant compared to the number of beer bottles that once accumulated against the back wall of Des's shed. They were stacked almost a metre high. Get me half a dozen tallies, Des would say to Grace if he knew she was going to the shops. Once he started brewing his own, an obsession that kept him in his shed for hours at the weekends, a balance was struck between those he emptied and those he filled with home brew. Sometimes during the week, Grace would hear one of the bottles explode in his shed. It would remind her to check how many there were in the fridge. She always restocked it if there were less than four.

But perhaps she was being unfair on Richard, perhaps he didn't think they were going senile or drinking too much. What if he considered himself their protector, just as Grace saw herself as one to her friends? Her toast might have set off a small blip on his radar; nothing more than a note-to-self moment alerting him to keep up surveillance.

If Bev had been here today, she might have stirred Grace's conscience again: reminded her that careless comments or actions didn't necessarily mean there was a lack of care, so much as a lack of understanding. There were many such things Grace would like to talk to Bev about, to have her wisdom again.

The last thing Bev had given Grace had been the recipe for her chocolate brownies. In some ways, Grace would rather not have had it.

Bev wrote it for Grace in a shaky hand on a square of hospital paper towel. Bev's eldest daughter, the one who had been the large bump under her dress at Claire's sixth birthday party, had not long left the room. She had just changed the coloured scarf covering her bald head, taking the old one home to wash.

Bev wrote the title *Bev's Brownies* on the yellowed paper.

'No, keep it a secret,' Grace said.

But Bev ignored her, added a subheading, *Ingredients*.

Grace watched her friend's once neat hand – the neatest of any nurse she'd worked with – struggle to grip the pen.

Under *Ingredients* she wrote *½ cup dark chocolate, chopped*, then *¼ cup chopped walnuts*. At this point she rested a moment.

Grace watched without willing the tears to stop; they embarrassed neither of them.

Next, Bev wrote *½ cup chopped soft caramels*, followed

by *1 chocolate brownie packet mix*. Under a heading of *Method* she wrote *Follow packet, add chopped ingredients to mix*.

Grace laughed when she read it, filled the room with the first sound of humour in ages.

'No wonder you never told me. A packet – you cheat. You said it was a secret recipe from a Canadian penfriend!'

'It was – once. Then brownie packet mixes came in so I changed to those. None of you noticed.' Bev was weak but smiled still. 'A girl has to have her secrets.'

The brownies never tasted the same, though, not even when Grace bought the most expensive chocolate and caramels.

Bev had been right, without her hand beating the mix they were no longer special. And neither were they as sweet. Grace still protected that recipe, written on its original paper and tucked safely away in a plastic sleeve, as much to protect the memory of Bev as to safeguard those secret ingredients. She looked at it from time to time, had even memorised every letter of every word that had a quiver to it – the vertical line to the 'l' in caramels; the horizontal bar to the 't' in packet.

She used to make them from time to time, just to pretend Bev was there in her kitchen. She'd even ask her friend's advice as she chopped ingredients or beat the batter, questions posed out loud. But the silence was cruel, so she stopped doing it.

10

A deep voice called, 'Hey,' from the back door. Grace looked up to see Nick clattering through the kitchen screen, esky in one hand and a bunch of carnations in the other.

'I'm here,' he announced, as if there was any need.

Grace still struggled to associate her first-born grandchild with the young man who stood in front of her now, a full head taller than anybody else, pressing pink blooms towards her. But she struggled even more with the fact he was Peter's. Peter, the methodical accountant, the one who ruminated over his columns of numbers just as his father had ruminated over the careful weighing of meat, each taking great care to ensure the balance ended up just right. Nick, on the other hand, breezed into Grace's kitchen in all his scruffy, clumsy, loud recklessness, esky banging against doorframe and cupboards, and sporting a new piece of silverware to his eyebrow and a t-shirt with an Andy

Warhol nude on the front, the black and red claws of something tattooed on his skin showing just below the sleeve. His whole chaotic and colourful arrival seemed like a one-man carnival entering.

'Happy birthday, old girl,' he joked, and lowered the esky to gather Grace into a two-armed embrace.

'Thanks, Nick,' she said, and hugged him back.

'How are you, Nick?' Richard extended a hand to his nephew.

'Still breathin'.'

'That must be a relief.'

Jorja stared, starstruck, at her cousin. Jaxon gave him a high-five.

'Holy shit, Aunty Ada. What happened to you?' Nick's brow-piercing got lost in a fold of concern.

'Mike Tyson,' Ada said. 'This is nothing – you should see the state of him.'

'Respect.' Nick gave her a gentler high-five than he'd given Jaxon.

'Hey, Aunty Susan.'

Susan offered her cheek to Nick. 'You not with your mum and dad?' She looked to the back door.

'Nup. Mobile now. Anyone want to see my new car?'

'I do,' cried Jaxon.

'Me too,' said Jorja.

'I might have a look next time, if you don't mind, Nick,' Ada said.

Touching her friend's shoulder as she passed, Grace joined the conga line out the front door.

Parked in the driveway was what could have been a large item of rubbish, but was in fact Nick's red Suzuki hatchback. It showed signs of having been a workhorse: small dents and scratches to most panels, the hood and roof dulled and whitened in places by a long life in the sun, and the blistered paint at the bottom edge of the driver's door suggesting rust. It featured recently blackened tyres.

Nick placed his hand on its faded roof and beamed back at the family. 'What d'you reckon?'

'Awesome,' reckoned Jaxon.

'Looks like a death trap.' Richard bent to check the tread on a tyre.

'Is it roadworthy?' Susan asked, looking from one end of the car to the other, face crinkled.

Grace watched Nick's smile shrink a little.

'It's a beauty,' Grace said. 'Will you take me for a spin?'

'Sure.'

The passenger door rolled back soundlessly on its hinges as Nick opened it for Grace. 'Your chariot,' he said with a flourish and helped her into the car.

'Can I come?' Jorja called.

'Me too?'

Jorja and Jaxon clambered into the back, and their parents looked on as though the children were being abducted by aliens.

Grace wound down the window. 'Don't wait up,' she waved as they drove away.

Looking into the back of Nick's car, it was hard to imagine fitting three children there – the car wasn't as wide as Des's Belmont had been and her two grandchildren's tangle of bare arms and legs took up most of the seat. The nudging went on the same these days though, but with less meanness, and Grace couldn't imagine it would ever end in the same violent outbursts she remembered from Des.

'Enjoying the ride?' she asked them.

'Great,' Jorja said.

'Does it go any faster?' Jaxon asked.

'Not with you in it, mate. Your dad'd have a fit.'

'Where'd you get the money to buy it?' Jaxon ran his hand over the cloth seat, flipped the back ashtray lid open then snapped it closed again.

'Weekend jobs – saved nearly every cent. Took a while, but I got there. I know it looks a bit rough but it gets me to uni and back, all right.'

'I think you've done very well,' Grace said. 'Not many young men can boast buying their own car at nineteen.'

'I'm gonna do the same,' declared Jaxon. 'How old do you have to be to get a job?'

'You won't even pick your schoolbag up off the floor so how are you going to do a real job?' Jorja asked her brother.

'If I was paid to pick it up, I would.'

'You are. It's called pocket money.'

'Get real – ten dollars a week is nothin'.'

Grace smiled as she listened to this exchange. Yes, little had changed. She recalled similar conversations when the going rate was twenty cents a week.

Nick cruised the suburban streets; his greatest challenge was when he had to dodge a bag of rubbish that had rolled onto the edge of the road from the nature strip.

He was a careful but confident driver, unlike his grandfather who had been a slow and nervous one. Car journeys with Des that went beyond the local shops had frustrated Grace beyond any of his other tedious ways. She'd sit there willing him to press the accelerator further to the floor. He never did though, apart from the odd occasion when he had to overtake another, even slower, vehicle. And rarely did he take a hand from the steering wheel, unless it was to smack at legs along the back seat. Instead, he gripped it in two places as though it might try to steer itself off in another direction altogether. If the kids played up, he'd shout quickly, easily, so that everyone could feel his tension, palpable as a pulse inside the car.

Grace would offer to drive before they set off from home, but she'd always get the same response: *How would it look for a man to sit up front while his wife drove?* She supposed she should have thought him brave, for not taking the easy way out – she knew he feared the machine. But she couldn't get beyond his cowardice.

The slow pace meant family trips of more than an hour required a roadside stop – sometimes two – for Des to have a smoke. Grace would stay seated and gaze absent-mindedly at the countryside during these stops. Des leant against the bonnet of the car, one foot on the front bumper, casually taking his cigarette. She would listen to the tick of the cooling engine or the erratic buzz of insects. Sometimes, if a good song was playing on the radio – Johnny Nash or Neil Young – she'd turn up the volume and sing along, drumming her fingers to the beat on the door's armrest. The kids might get out of the car if Des allowed it, and they'd busy themselves taking potshots at trees with stones or foraging with sticks in roadside gullies, which was all the better fun if there'd been recent rain and they held pools of water.

After five minutes Des would bellow, 'In the car!' and they'd come scuttling back up embankments or from behind trees while Des carefully ground his butt into the dirt with the heel of his shoe, checking it was all out once, twice, sometimes three times, before getting back into the car himself.

As Peter got older, his conversation invariably turned to cars on these slow journeys. 'Hey, Dad, what d'you reckon about me getting a Charger when I'm old enough to drive? A yellow one with a black hood and side air-extractors and a spoiler on the back *and* the front.'

As Grace remembered it, he was still a long way off being able to reach the clutch at the time.

'Nah,' Des said. 'Bloody dago's car. Stick with a Holden.' He risked taking one hand from the steering wheel to slap the dash. 'You know what you're gettin' with a Holden.'

'What about a GTS Monaro then?'

'Too powerful. Kill yourself in one of them.'

'I'm going to get a Datsun,' Susan said. 'A lady's car.'

'Can't trust 'em,' Des said, 'more plastic than anything else, being made by the Nips.'

'Well, I'm getting a pony,' Claire declared. 'A white one.'

Grace turned to look at Claire, sandwiched between her two older siblings on the back seat, and tried not to laugh. Her youngest child had thinned her lips to a stern line and folded her arms across her small chest, daring anybody to tell her what she was or wasn't going to use to make her mobile in the future.

'Gonna take you a long time to get anywhere.' Des laughed.

'Maybe she reckons a white one will go faster.' Peter nudged his sister who wasted no time in nudging him back.

'How many horsepower you reckon it'll be, Claire?' Des asked. "Bout four legs and a tail?'

'Don't tease her,' Grace said, looking at Des.

Peter pushed Claire again, which sent her into Susan who pushed her back into Peter.

'Oi,' Peter shouted, and pushed her again.

'Clair-e,' Susan whined, as Claire was sent rocking back into her sister like the smallest of a matryoshka doll.

'It's not my fault,' Claire said. 'Peter keeps pushing me.'

'Do not.'

'Do so.'

'Do n—'

'Shut up, you two,' Des thundered.

Grace turned round to placate them. 'Come on,' she said. 'Be nice to each another.'

'It's Peter's fault, Mummy. He keeps pushing me.'

'Do not,' Peter said, and he pushed Claire again.

'Clair-e,' Susan whined, and it was about to start all over again, except Des stopped it.

He risked a hand off the steering wheel, reached behind him and brought it down hard half-a-dozen times at random on the bare legs along the back seat. Most of the blows landed on Claire, an easier target in the middle.

All rocking and shouting was shut down in the back. The only thing Grace could hear was the restrained sniffs of Claire. She knew she'd be fighting back the urge to cry.

Grace reached her hand over the seat back and caressed Claire's leg, hoping she'd fallen on the spot where Des's hand had landed the heaviest.

'Don't care. Still getting a pony,' Claire mumbled.

When Nick pulled back in front of Grace's house, she saw Peter's clean, white Statesman parked in her drive.

'Looks like the olds are here.' Nick pulled the handbrake on and turned off the engine.

'Thanks for the drive, Nick. And you're right, she runs like a dream.' Grace patted the dash.

Peter came down from the porch to meet them. 'You're back in one piece then?'

'I'd expect no less,' Grace said. 'Nick's a very good driver.'

'A driver's only as good as the vehicle he's in control of.'

'Have you been here long?' Grace asked, changing the subject, knowing where her son's conversation was headed.

But Peter was never easily circumvented. 'About ten minutes. I offered to take him to the government auctions, you know – help him buy a good solid Holden or Ford. But he took himself off and got this Asian rust-bucket from some dodgy backyard dealer instead.'

'At least there's no question of ownership,' Nick said.

Peter guffawed. 'Not now, maybe.'

'There wasn't when I bought it either.'

159

Father and son locked eyes. Nick's face looked the more dangerous, given his stubble and glinting metal. Peter's showed his age: he'd lost some of his menace with his receding hairline and puffiness under the eyes. His words could still pack a punch though.

'How could you tell? You didn't even know to look for a compliance plate.'

Grace reached out and squeezed Nick's arm, willing him to let it go. The muscles felt taut under her fingers.

'You should be proud of him,' Grace said to Peter. 'At least he had the gumption to go out and buy his own car and with his own money. If my memory serves me correctly, you were more than happy to accept your father's Belmont for nothing – regardless of how old it was or its history.'

Grace subtly propelled Nick forward. 'Let's go inside,' she said, carefully.

Why couldn't her children be more kind?

Susan looked flushed when they got back into the kitchen and her wine remained untouched on the bench. Ada, glass empty in front of her, was nodding politely at Richard, who was enlightening her about the efficacy of one pain reliever over another. Richard loved nothing more than an ear to bend on the wonders of pharmaceuticals.

Jane's wine glass was nearly empty. 'Happy birthday!' She clicked across the tiled floor on high heels to drape both arms and the glass round Grace's shoulders. The many gold bangles on her daughter-in-law's wrist clattered against Grace's back, and what she always suspected were breast implants pressed firmly into her front. 'Sorry we're late. Bit slow out of the starting blocks this morning, weren't we, Pete? Work function last night. A biggie, as it turned out.'

Susan scraped the last of a salsa dip from its jar into a serving bowl. She banged the spoon loudly on its edge. Grace hoped the bowl wouldn't break too.

'Well, you're here now.' Grace patted Jane's back – the biggie, she noticed, still laced her breath.

'Happy birthday, Grandma,' Meg said from the table where she was colouring in. 'If you come here I'll give you a special birthday kiss.'

Grace obeyed, bent down to her youngest grandchild.

Meg gripped Grace's face in her small hands, kissed one cheek, then the other. 'That's how the French do it. Mummy told me.'

Grace smelt Jane's fragrance on her granddaughter's neck.

Stroking Meg's hair, Jane said, 'She's a sponge, this one. Remembers everything I tell her.'

'Don't bump, Mummy. I'll go outside the lines.'

'You didn't tell me we had to be here by a certain time.' Peter looked at Jane. 'I thought it was a late lunch.'

Jane pulled a *Don't ask me* face and took another sip from her glass.

'At this rate it'll be three o'clock.' Susan tossed the empty jar into the bin.

Grace didn't think this the right time to mention recycling.

'Sorry, sis. If I'd known I'd have made sure we got here earlier.'

'Three's good,' Grace said. 'After seventy years of watching the clock, it'll be good not to have to for a day. Here, let me finish that off, Susan. Take the weight off your feet.'

'I'm fine. It's your party.'

'And yours to enjoy as well.' Grace took the bag of corn chips Susan was opening from her and filled her daughter's hand with her untouched glass of wine.

'What can I do?' Jane asked, looking around, brow furrowed and glass held up as though toasting the mess in Grace's kitchen.

'You could refill Ada's glass.' Grace knew her friend would need it, should Richard move on to beta-blockers or respiratory inhalers.

'I better do mine while I'm at it then.'

Susan sat down opposite Ada and sipped at her wine like a bird, looking every bit like she'd rather be elsewhere.

But Susan often looked like she had some place else she needed to be when at Grace's. Visits were regular but brief, though always pre-planned nowadays. And as a young woman, just as Grace had looked towards the day when she could leave Harvest, Susan had looked just as keenly to when she could leave her family home. It took no time at all for her to find a share house once she'd completed her teacher training and had secured her first job.

'I'm gonna miss you, Susie,' Des had said with genuine sadness. 'Who's gonna protect me from your mother now!' He'd laughed when he said it but Grace felt she'd gained a small victory from those words, because the laugh was thin and hollow.

Grace looked on with sadness too, the day Susan packed up the last of her clothes and loaded them into the boot of her Datsun. She remembered being shocked by this emotion, and not because she thought she'd be pleased to see her daughter leave home, but because for the first time Grace realised just how her own mother must have felt the day she'd left Harvest. Grace felt ashamed that it had taken her this long to realise it.

She'd tried to coax Susan to sit with her at the kitchen table for a short while before leaving, to have afternoon tea at the place where Grace hoped her daughter had felt her greatest sense of belonging.

Grace even remembered what cake she'd made – a moist carrot cake with plump, juicy raisins and the top frosted with snowy, cream-cheese peaks. One of Susan's favourites.

But Susan couldn't stay.

'Sorry, Mum. The others are expecting me. They're putting on a welcome dinner for me tonight. I'll take the cake with me, though, for dessert.'

Grace put the cake into an airtight container, one she valued.

'Bring the container back to me, won't you?' she'd said to Susan.

It surprised Grace that she'd give Susan this particular container – she'd never have considered giving it to anybody else. It was one she used regularly and would miss, even for a week. Later she recognised why: it would guarantee Susan return it and therefore Grace would get to see her.

Each time Susan visited, Grace would have another sweet treat ready to send off with her. But the containers weren't always returned as quickly as Grace would have liked.

Susan's packing had been easy – all done in two hours, having so few boxes.

Grace had tried to appear upbeat as her daughter put the last of her things in the car.

'All grown up, eh?' she said, but then felt silly for saying it. Of course she was ... a young woman now, able to live by independent means.

'It was always going to happen.' Susan laughed. 'That's what kids do ... they grow up.'

Grace remembered the fear she'd felt upon boarding the train to leave Harvest. So uncertain, so alien was this proposed new life in the city that she briefly questioned the logic of her decision to leave at all.

Apparently there was no such uncertainty for Susan. 'I can't believe it's finally happened!'

Grace supposed Susan wouldn't recognise the sadness in such departures till she herself was a mother.

She felt her daughter's absence acutely as she waved her off.

With Peter already left home a year earlier, Grace remembered thinking: *With Susan gone now, what's left?*

But children must leave home to return to it with more. One came into Grace's kitchen now.

'When's lunch? I'm starving,' chubby Tom asked.

'Here's my big, strong boy,' Peter said. 'Needing some fuel, mate?'

'Oh, sweetie, can't you wait?' Jane ran perfect nails through Tom's imperfect hair.

'Nah. But *these* look int-er-rest-ing.' Tom's fingers played together at being a miser's. He scooped up a fistful of Syrian nuts from the less valuable dish they'd ended up in and shoved the lot in his mouth. 'Yuk,' he mouthed after a moment, and with some difficulty, to his mother.

Jane obliged her son with a paper napkin held out flat in the palm of her hand. Tom let the macerated nuts fall into it.

'Curried nuts – disgusting,' he said, pulling a face.

'Here, have a bread roll.' Jane took one from the wicker basket on the bench and thrust it towards him.

Tom took it and ran to the back door, leaving his mother with the napkin to dispose of.

'Have you said Happ—' Peter called after him, but stopped with the slap of the screen door. He looked at Grace and shook his head. 'Kids, eh?'

Jane busied herself with finding the bin.

Meg piped up from her seat at the kitchen table, 'He's just being a boy, Daddy,' then went back to her colouring. 'Just a silly boy.' She shook her head wisely as she filled in the spiralled horn on a unicorn's forehead with an orange pencil.

'Well, we're lucky we've got you then, aren't we, princess?' Peter said, and he stroked her golden hair.

If she could, Meg would have purred like a kitten.

Jane considered herself an epicure. She would sample food believing her palate was capable of recognising greatness. But at the end of the day what she really tasted was brand – Lindt above Cadbury, Bonne Maman jam over Cottee's. Take the packaging away and Grace reckoned her daughter-in-law's taste buds were no better equipped to pick greatness than the next person's.

'Divine salmon, Grace. Atlantic, I bet.' Jane took a second blini from the plate. Grace had prepared the small pancakes earlier, topped each with cream cheese, smoked salmon and a sprig of dill. 'Good cream cheese too,' she said, lips rolling with pleasure. 'Hard to beat the old Kraft Philly, isn't it?'

'Actually, the salmon's from a bit further south, Jane – Tasmanian,' Grace said. 'And the cheese is a home brand, but you're right, it is good.'

Jane gave Grace a well-I-never look and failed to take a third.

Susan, on the other hand, considered herself a food hack yet Grace thought her daughter was more the food connoisseur than any of them, and packaging never took priority above taste. 'Tasmanian's good,' she said. 'The right balance of salt and smoke. Pick one with an even texture, no zigzag splits in the flesh, not too pale, and you'll get the best flavour.'

They were sitting on Grace's back patio. They'd all agreed it was worth trying the outdoors given the heat inside the house. This had proved a good choice as a gentle easterly breeze came in across Grace's large backyard. Although it was still a warm wind, the air moved and the star jasmine vine latticing one side of the patio added its fragrance.

'Jimmy reckoned smoked salmon was a food fit only for fish hooks.' Ada laughed. 'He was a man of his time though – simple tastes, but no less appreciative for it.'

Grace remembered her friend's late husband as appreciative of everything.

'I've got to agree with him, Ada,' Peter said, 'not that I'd say my tastes were simple. But when it comes to smoked salmon – horrible stuff. Too slimy and fishy for my liking, Atlantic or otherwise.' Peter took a corn chip instead, and dipped it in the salsa.

'You should learn to love it, Pete. It's full of omega-threes – nature's medicine.' Richard held up a blini to Peter and put it into his mouth whole, like a pill.

'I've got nature's medicine right here.' Peter lifted his stubby of beer to Richard. 'Which tastes a whole lot better than your omega-threes. And if it's chasing down a good piece of wagyu, then you won't see a happier man than me.'

From when Peter was young enough to understand there was a difference between vegetable and meat, Des had taught him that meat had priority above all other foods. It, and beer, had remained at the top of Peter's favoured foods ever since.

'You are your father all over again,' Grace said, with some regret.

Peter looked torn between pride and anxiety.

'You're killing me, woman,' Des had said to Grace once. He was eating a T-bone steak at the time, which covered three-quarters of his plate. He'd cut it into chunks, even the thick fatty edge, and dipped each into the salt bowl beside his plate before putting it into his mouth.

'You could cut the fat off,' Grace suggested.

'It's not the fat you're killing me with, it's the vegetables.' His laugh was deep, infectious. It was one of the things Grace had loved about him when they first met, this laugh that could trammel a bad mood.

'You're killing yourself if you choose not to eat them,' Grace said, good-naturedly, though she was disappointed by the bad example he was giving to the three small faces at the table, two of which hung off his every word. Peter, Grace noticed, had already pushed his beans aside, just as his father had, and Susan looked torn between passing up something she liked and wanting to be part of the show. Claire gnawed on a bean she held in her chubby fist and looked from one person to the next, lost to what all the talk was about.

'We don't need beans, do we, champ?'

'Nope,' Peter said.

'Nope!' Claire mimicked with a toothy grin. She held her bean up in the air like a charging horseman's sword.

'And we certainly don't need cauliflower.' Des budged the white floret with his fork so that it rested alongside the beans.

Peter giggled behind his hand.

'A man needs meat, though, doesn't he, mate? And spuds, of course. Those two'll keep a fella going forever.'

'Spuds!' Claire shouted with joy.

'That's my girl. Spuds!' Des reached over and ruffled Claire's hair.

'Don't listen to your father, he's being silly. You eat everything on your plate. It's all good for you.'

'Nup. Won't. Dad says I don't have to.' Peter crossed his arms over his chest.

Grace looked at Des, trying to implore reason with a stare. She mouthed please and he relented.

'Come on, kids, you heard your mother, eat up your dinner.'

'But you said—'

'That's not fair if—'

Claire threw her bean at Des, hitting him on the nose. 'Won't!'

'I said eat up. Now!' Des brought the flat of his hand down with a crash on the table, which set the tomato sauce bottle rocking. Claire burst into tears.

'I reckon I got his good looks.' Peter preened his hair now and beamed at his mother. 'But I'm in much better shape than Dad ever was.' He moved his hands from his head to the front of his shirt, which he smoothed to reveal a far from flat stomach.

'Yeah. Right,' Susan said. 'And I'm Twiggy and Jane's Kate Moss.'

Jane giggled behind her wine glass.

'How can you be in better shape?' Nick said. 'From what you've told me, Grandad could carry a side of beef and not even strain with the weight of it. You're flat out carrying a briefcase and laptop without getting breathless.'

Those at the table laughed.

'Very funny. Who are you to talk, anyway? What was the last thing you carried besides an esky holding a few poncy boutique beers or some arty-farty textbook round uni?'

'I'm not the one telling everybody how fit I am.'

Peter came in with a quick mock punch to his son's arm. Nick saw it coming, but was too late to move aside and miss it. He flinched.

With a wink and a pointed gun-finger aimed at Nick, Peter said, 'Still fit enough to beat you when it comes to reflexes, kiddo.'

Grace could remember a time when Peter wasn't so unkind. He had been given a tent for his eleventh birthday, as she remembered it. Des had promised to take him camping. Peter, still waiting, decided he'd camp in the backyard. He invited two mates round – Max, his best mate, plus another boy from school, whom Grace hadn't met.

The boys spent the afternoon erecting the canvas structure, muddling through the instructions, positioning tent poles at one corner then taking them down and repositioning them at another. She could hear a great deal of discussion, and not necessarily all of it in agreement, about what went where. Grace left them to it – and Des was at the races – figuring they'd sort their way through.

Eventually the tent stood proud, if not off-square, at the bottom of the garden. The boys came in then, *for rations*, they said, and made themselves sandwiches and jugs of lime and raspberry cordial. Grace remembered coming into the kitchen after them to find a trail of honey and jam across the bench tops and the little that remained of the high-tin loaf was off-square, just like the tent's corners. All that was left in the biscuit tin was crumbs, and a box of Roses chocolates she'd been keeping for a treat, and which Grace thought she'd concealed well behind a wall of Tupperware storage containers in the pantry, had gone. Camping was obviously hungry work.

It was getting dark and the boys announced they were going to sleep in the tent for the night. The other parents were notified, pyjamas and pillows were gathered together, and soon the tent glowed with the light of a kerosene lamp.

Des wasn't yet home – most likely at the hotel after the races – and Grace and the girls were happy enough to be inside for the evening, despite Claire's earlier attempts to be included that day, which were thwarted, repeatedly, by the boys with shouts of *Get lost!* or *No stupid girls allowed!*

The loudest of the boys had been the one Grace didn't know. He was a hardy lad for his age, stocky, with crooked, home-cut hair. Peter and Max seemed to be in awe of this boy, acquiescing to his authority in a way she'd not seen either of them do before. She could hear him tell the other two what war game they would play next, of which he seemed always to be General, and he'd scoff at any suggestions of an alternative as *boring* or *for sissies*. Later, he told them where they were to position their bed rolls in the tent. He, declaring himself *the bravest*, would have the place at the tent's opening, *to keep guard*. Peter and Max didn't argue, though Grace thought them gullible to the other boy's clever engineering in securing the best place to capture a breeze in the hot tent.

Grace didn't like to admit it at the time, but she felt no fondness for this boy at all. She considered him to show all the traits of a bully.

Not even Grace got the full story from Peter when he came into the house about ten o'clock that night in tears, and this from a boy who rarely cried. It was something to do with the bully boy and urine and Peter not understanding how Max could have played a part in whatever it was that was done, laughed even, which suggested it was more than just a childish prank gone too far. Humiliation and betrayal seemed the more hurtful act, with no foreseeable way back from either.

Grace had tried to console Peter, held him close against her chest on the sofa, stroked his hair and told him that friends sometimes acted in poor judgement. Eventually he'd stopped crying but refused to go back out to the tent. Looking back, she wondered if she'd done enough.

Thankfully, Des was still not home as he would have told Peter to *toughen up*, or to *go thump the culprit*, trivialising it or ignoring the emotional hurt of a friendship betrayed altogether.

The next morning Max and the other boy had gone by the time anyone in the house had got up, leaving Peter no opportunity to redeem the events of the night before.

The incident marked a time of shift in what had always been a close bond between Peter and Max – they grew further and further apart from then on. And thankfully, the other boy never came to their home again.

Grace supposed such experiences from childhood contributed to the moulding of character, not being called the formative years for nothing. As to how much of Peter's putdown comments today were attributable to this and similar incidents as a child or from having learnt a lack of kindness from Des was anyone's guess. But what Grace did know was that sometimes it was difficult for her to recall this tearful and vulnerable boy when faced with the man.

'Whatever makes you feel like a tough guy, Dad,' Nick said.

Grace offered the plate of blinis between the two men. 'You like smoked salmon, don't you, Nick?'

Nick took one. 'Thanks, Gran. And for the record, Dad, the esky's got poncy *soft* drinks in it. Zero blood alcohol for P-platers. Get with the times.'

'Found ya!' rang out from somewhere down the backyard.

The younger grandchildren had been running from one hiding spot to another since they'd all moved outdoors. Grace reckoned their excited squeals were as much about being released from their own small garden plots as being with cousins. She'd never seen them enjoying the same games at their own homes. In Grace's backyard there were enough sheds and secret spaces to keep up a steady supply of new places to hide. Jorja moved between joining in on the game and sitting with the adults, keen to relinquish her role as child but not yet getting enough from adult company to keep her away from her younger cousins altogether. Nick shifted more comfortably between the two groups, as he was called in to help unearth a particularly clever hider from time to time, and then returned to the patio.

'Don't know how they find anybody out there.' Peter looked down the long backyard.

His gaze travelled past Des's shed – used for gardening equipment now – the hen house, a trellis covered in a lush passionfruit vine. There were pawpaw trees, fruit hanging like old women's breasts, and three bamboo tripods still in place from last season's sweet pea. There was old corrugated iron – some sheets leant against fences, others formed a retaining wall to a mound of compost topped with recent lawn clippings. Empty plastic and ceramic pots were stacked along one fence; rolls of chicken wire and piles of timber stakes continued on from them. At the very end of the block was a large, blackened brick incinerator that hadn't seen a lick of flame in years.

It had all served a purpose at some time or another – and a lot of it still did – though Grace suspected to others it looked little better than years' worth of accumulated junk. It was a landscape she was familiar with; Pa's backyard had looked no different.

'We should dump a heap of it out the front while the garbage strike's on. You'd get a better feel for how much land you've actually got then – realise its potential. Might tempt you to do something else with it then.' Peter indicated somewhere off in the backyard. What was behind him, her home, was excluded from the sweeping gesture.

Ada snorted. 'Fortunately for Grace, and us, we're here to celebrate her birthday, not her relocation.'

'Thanks, Ada,' Grace said and looked sharply at Peter.

Out in the garden it was Tom's turn. He did a rapid count to seventy for the next game – the designated number chosen by Meg in recognition of her grandmother's age. Each loud number blurred rapidly into a long rush of breath out and breath in.

Grace had nursed many people much older than seventy, especially when she worked at Moreville, a gloomy place with its fragile sense of permanence. She remembered how eyebrows lifted with childish expectation when she entered a patient's room, as though she'd come to rescue them, take them home. Once they realised she'd only come to hand over a meal tray or make their bed they must have felt sharp disappointment. Not that all of them showed it. With some, the eyebrows simply dropped again and the passive mask of calm waiting returned to their faces. But there were those who never stopped railing against where they'd ended up. They'd slap and bite and scratch; throw things – trays, combs, accusations – or sob, sometimes for hours. In many ways, Grace respected them more. They refused to give up the energy that proved they were still alive.

Peter, imperturbable, went on, 'I don't think you appreciate how much these big inner city blocks are worth if you subdivide them. Besides, it's more land than you need. If I was you, I'd carve off one of the blocks and sell it to a developer. I bet six months from now you'd be asking yourself why you didn't do it sooner!'

'Not to mention the financial security it would offer you.' Susan nodded approval at her brother, looked to Richard for support.

'Oh, yes. Security,' he said. 'Very important at any age.'

Pa never saw the need to decrease the size of his farm by so much as an acre and neither did anyone suggest he should. He'd kept it all, right up until the day he collapsed down a back paddock where Mother eventually found him, virtually unconscious and plucking at the grass with one hand. Her mother always believed he was trying to keep a hold of the land he'd loved so much. It was a comforting idea.

'I'm quite attached to my backyard clutter,' Grace said. 'But by all means bin it, subdivide it and spend it when I'm dead.'

'You cheat!' chorused from somewhere behind Des's old shed. 'That wasn't seventy.'

'But until then I think it's doing a pretty good job as a playground for your children, so let's just enjoy the space for as long as we can.'

Susan blushed. Peter shrugged: 'Only thinking of you,' he said, 'and all the upkeep. It's fine while you can still look after it. But ...'

Each person was left to fill in the last line.

'But,' Ada said, voice quivering, not with the tremors of age or injury, Grace knew, 'when it comes time for you to be so concerned, you'll be here like a shot to cut the grass for your mum, won't you, Peter?'

'Well – yes. I could certainly do that.'

Turning seventy wasn't proving to be a simple transition from one decade to the next. Sitting here, Grace had begun to feel a sense of trepidation. Like it or not, the psychological baggage that came with the number seventy was presenting itself – in the minds of her children. She'd just been nudged over the line into old age, and new unspoken words pressed at their lips.

It looked like the only thing holding them back for now was courage. A courage that was growing in strength with each beer or glass of wine.

'I'm going to check the lamb and bring out some more dip.' Grace was eager for the solitary comfort of her kitchen, away from what her children might want to say next.

'Can I help?' Ada turned with difficulty to face Grace.

'Thanks, Ada, but I can manage.'

Back in the one room of her house that had seen more of her life than any other, Grace felt calmer. This was her space, her haven, her bolthole. The kitchen was the vault that stored her memories, witnessed her everyday actions, kept her secrets.

Grace remembered how she used to embrace herself in this room. She'd stand in the centre of it, between the fridge and the table, and wrap her arms tightly round her body. She did this late at night when the house was most still and sleep had come to everybody else but wouldn't come to her. There, she'd turn slow circles, always anti-clockwise, and with each turn she'd take in the four walls, over and over again. Throughout this circling she'd will the colour of the walls to go back through beige to lemon to soft, soft blue. Her turning, she knew later, was nothing more than a crazy attempt to shift time backwards. A foolish unscrewing of the mind.

When she finally accepted that the walls would remain beige, she took up sitting at the kitchen table for long periods of time. Sometimes her fingers worked in the dark at the scratches and dents on the Formica surface, trying to read them like Braille. At other times she'd simply sit and watch the moon move across the sky through the kitchen window. Some nights it was so bright she could see the veins and tiny hairs on the backs of her hands. Even though they were still young hands then, she remembered thinking how old they looked, all bone and loose skin; her wedding band drooped right down to the middle knuckle of her finger.

Des would get up some nights, say, 'Grace, come back to bed.'

'No, I want to stay here,' she'd tell him.

'Why?' he'd ask, never getting it.

'I'm keeping watch.'

Her sitting lasted months, and she came to sense something stir within those walls. If asked to describe what, she'd say it was as though the kitchen developed a will of its own; it became strong, committed, ready.

She went back to her bed then, but would leave a light on in the kitchen each night. She told Des it was for Claire, in case she needed to find her way there. It didn't matter to Grace that her daughter couldn't. Des never argued the point; he'd stopped arguing many points by then, especially those about Claire.

There was something about that night light that finally calmed Grace. It was difficult to recall how or why now, but at the time all she knew with any certainty was that, while it was on, the kitchen remained awake, vigilant, so that she might sleep.

When the sun came up in the mornings, Grace could keep watch herself while she cooked.

★

She looked across to the table, a pine rectangle now, not Formica, its top equally scarred with everyday use. She pictured her family seated there. She could see them as they cleared food from their plates, and sometimes not; grumbled over schoolyard injustices, real or imagined; or sulked, chin in palm, until someone gave in. She could see homework books open, letters being written, friends sitting, hands cradling mugs, gripping glasses, tissues. She had visions of eight or more teenagers squeezed round that table, then at other times a solitary person taking a solitary meal, and recently two together. If the things that had occurred around her kitchen tables over the years were etched as words onto their surface, then their tops would be covered with the tiny print of dictionaries and bibles, just to fit all the stories there to tell.

Now Grace would've liked to spend some time at that table, alone, reading those stories with her fingertips for meaning as she used to. Instead, she picked up the carving fork from the bench, opened the oven door to a blast of heat and poked the long tines into the thickest part of the lamb. She watched as its juices ran clear from the two holes. She took the joint from the oven, wrapped it in foil and allowed it the liberty of rest.

Then Grace returned and placed a different dip on the patio table.

'What d'you call this one?' Peter asked.

'Baba ganoush,' Grace said.

'Baba-who?'

'Ganoush, you goose,' Jane jangled, like a cereal ad.

'It's Middle Eastern, Mediterranean – somewhere like that,' Grace said. 'Made from eggplant, plus a bit of garlic, olive oil, lemon and a few other things you wouldn't know. It's lovely with this dipped into it.' She held out a basket of flat bread cut into irregular pieces. 'Lebanese bread,' she said.

'Turkish, isn't it?' Jane asked.

'The packet said Lebanese.'

'They're much the same thing, Jane,' Susan said.

Peter grimaced at the taste. 'At least I know now what Dad meant when he said you had a weakness for foreign things.' He rinsed his mouth with beer.

Grace put the bread on the patio table, away from Peter, and sat down. She felt tired, and it wasn't because of the early start she'd had. This was a deeper fatigue. It grew from being on guard; wary of what might be said next. But she wasn't prepared to be silenced by it.

'Some choices are only a weakness in the eyes of some people, Peter. To others, they're just right.' Grace took a large piece of bread and pushed it deep into the dip. 'And your father was never the best judge.'

'I think you're being a bit hard on h—'

'Coo-ee,' rang out from down the side of the house.

'Kath,' breathed Ada.

★

'Here you all are!' Kath rounded the corner. 'I've been banging on your front door for so long, I was starting to think you decided turning seventy wasn't worth the effort.'

In winter, when her mountain was cooler, Kath wore an assortment of colourful berets. Today, in the heat, it was a wide-brimmed camel-coloured hat that dipped and folded with every step, partly obscuring her view of the uneasy faces around the table.

Grace got up and Kath lifted the brim of her hat to kiss her.

'Turning seventy's made you peaky,' she said, looking at Grace. 'Come on, it's not that bad. Here, this is for you – should cheer you up.' Kath handed over a large wicker basket. 'A birthday hamper – with some of your favourites.' With the other hand she flicked open an old black-handled fan in one quick motion like a bird opening its wings, to reveal a spray of pink cherry blossoms. 'I'm overheating with all the excitement,' she said, fanning herself.

In the basket there was a big bunch of rainbow chard and two jars of crimson jam Grace knew would be rosella. An old Danish butter biscuit tin she guessed might now hold homemade biscuits, possibly her favourites, Melting Moments. And there was a bottle of red wine, which Grace picked for a Shiraz even before she turned the bottle round to read the label.

'I picked the chard just before I left. Probably still growing.'

'Thanks, Kath. It'll be delicious.'

'Full of iron, without the metal filings, Grace,' Richard said.

'Another of nature's hard-to-swallow medicines?' Peter asked Richard.

'You could say that. But seriously, Peter, if you can't stomach the oily fish, have you considered taking a supplement?'

Safety, Grace decided, came in the most unexpected places.

She touched the dark leaves of the chard, admired its stalks, as colourful as any floral bouquet – yellow, orange, red, hot pink.

When Grace was a girl, she'd imagined men calling on her with a bunch of flowers in their hand. She would see herself press the blooms to her nose and close her eyes with a swoon as she caught the heady mix of roses or carnations or lilies. She'd smile at her beau with promise and he'd smile back, pleased with his clever foresight.

Des never brought Grace flowers when he called; he brought meat. He brought it wrapped in butcher's paper and secured with brown twine. Sometimes the paper would have a bloodied brown corner. At others, there'd be a pencilled tally of numbers or, if he'd taken the time, a love heart, always pierced with an arrow, and with Grace written inside. Sometimes the package would be large – a roasting joint of pork, the skin slashed in perfectly spaced lines, or a pearly heel of corned silverside – and at others it would be small, containing thick, lightly marbled medallions of beef eye fillet. Des's courting gifts were always succulent and tender, the best cuts.

Mother had looked on with a relaxed smile when Grace married Des, the butcher's legacy evident under his fingernails as he slipped the gold band on her finger. *At least my daughter won't know hunger*, her smile said. Pa's warnings had been more cautionary, and revealed an insight she wished she'd possessed back then. *A good cut of meat's only half the meal, Gracie. I hope he can give you the other half as well.*

Looking back, Grace supposed that what started as gifts of meat was always going to lead to marriage, because in accepting and cooking them for him she had already signalled her role as his wife. Back then, women weren't so worldly about their choices, if indeed they had that many to be worldly about. Grace envied young women today. She didn't think they'd be so easily swayed by a good meal, and neither did she think they would accept a plate only half full.

Grace lifted the chard to her nose. It smelt wholesome. 'As beautiful as a bunch of flowers,' she said to Kath. 'Only more edible.'

'Neuroprotection, Peter, supplements! We're talking the biggies here – Parkinson's, Alzheimer's – all the usual suspects that hit the elderly. How'd you like to keep those nasty players from your door, eh?' Richard said.

'Dad, are you pushing drugs again?'

'Only the good ones, Jorja. Only the good.'

Kath turned and addressed the table. 'Who's in charge of the wine round here?' she said, snapping the fan shut.

'That'd be me, Kath. We've got a lovely bottle of Viognier on the go. A little fruity, so perhaps not to everybody's liking but I think it's delicious.' Jane went round and topped up everyone's glass.

12

The kitchen was chaotic. The meat was rested to a stupor, the peas were at risk of losing their original emerald brightness, along with the broccoli – long stalks and all – and the baby carrots had moved just beyond al dente. The cauliflower au gratin had crisped to dark brown round the edges as had the roasted vegetables, an acceptable lapse given that was how everybody liked them.

But no one could argue: the aromas in the kitchen were good.

Grace could remember dinners smelling as good in Harvest, but not always as plentiful. Today's lamb was plumper than many she'd had in Harvest. Some years the roasts had left nothing to spare. During those years Pa's cows were as thin and rangy as a mongrel dog, their hip bones and ribs on show as though their hide had been neatly laid over a skeleton. To stroke the side of one was like running a stick along a picket fence. And their once-full udders, usually awkwardly crushed between their hind legs by milking time, shrank or dried up altogether. Some ended up in a big pit in the bush, which Pa had dug with a dozer blade attached to the front of the tractor, their legs poking out from their bloated bellies like knitting needles in a ball of wool.

Livestock wasn't the only thing that grew thin at these times. Mother's plate held less too, and she'd stitch fewer new seams and darn more holes. She'd do her clever hatchings over holes in socks and jumpers; pride made sure they were close to invisible. Her stews got thinner, the desserts less sweet and the Christmas turkey shrank to a stringy chicken. Mother no longer whistled when she pegged out the clothes. Pa looked to the sky with a cheated face and Joe left school early. Dust ran higher up Grace's shins.

It was only years after the rains had come, washed the cobwebs from the rain gauge and filled the old-china cracks in the dams, that Grace recognised the changes drought had caused. As a child she saw only what each new day brought, not what the old one had taken away.

But there were also seasons of plenty, times when frugality wasn't a necessary virtue, and the Harvest Christmas table would be laden with food. And not just with those items that had made it into the freezer after the Show. There had been glossy baked hams the size of a car's wheel hub, the tops scored with

189

diamonds and the centre of each dotted with a red glacé cherry, and crispy-skinned turkeys with drumsticks as thick as a toddler's arm. The custards for the dense, fruity puddings were silky and yellow, with eggs aplenty again. And Pa had loved that there could be a tot of brandy in the cream.

Grace was grateful for this hindsight now, to recognise the highs and lows of a life dictated by nature's kindness. Without it, the smiles and sighs and frowns from memories past would never reach people's faces. They'd be lost like old recipes or locks of hair.

Grace knew there was no sure way to get a large meal to the table perfectly. So, unsettled by the unfinished conversation on the back patio, she took solace in getting the gravy just as she liked it. She added a ladleful of master stock from the pot simmering on the back burner, and stirred.

'Jane, could you put your glass down and give me a hand, please?'

'Sure, Susie. Which hand d'you want?'

'Both. The mint sauce needs pouring into a serving jug for a start. On second thoughts, I'll do it – it's boiling. Here, take these into the dining room.' Susan wrapped the new carving knife and Grace's worn, horn-handled fork in a tea towel and passed the package to Jane.

Susan probably thought the blackened steel of the

fork looked shabby beside the bright new blade of the knife, maybe even made a mental note of what next to buy Grace as a gift.

But Grace didn't need a new fork any more than she'd needed new knives.

'Only need one hand for that job.' Jane picked up her glass again and tapped out of the kitchen.

'Watch you don't trip on the hall runner on your way,' Susan called.

Grace thought Susan should have stuck with teaching – there would be fewer scrapes and tears in any school ground where she worked.

'The heels only look dangerous,' Jane called from the hall.

'I wasn't thinking about the heels,' Susan mumbled.

Peter and Richard were conspicuously absent. They'd remained outside to tend the elders, as Peter put it. And Jane, even Grace had to admit, was more a liability than a help. The children, whose feed-o-meters had been grumbling for the past half-hour, kept coming in to ask that age old question: *Is it ready yet?* Nick placated them with a game of British Bulldog in the backyard. Grace could see through the kitchen window that he was making a show of not being able to catch the younger ones.

Susan decanted the mint sauce from pot to jug, spilling a good measure on the bench in the process.

'Shit, I should have used the one with the wider opening. I bet we won't have enough now.'

Grace ripped squares of paper towel from a roll hanging on the wall and passed them to Susan.

'Here,' she said. 'We can always wring them into the jug if we're short.' She was only half joking. She went back to scraping the sides of the baking dish with an old tablespoon, worn flat across the top from years of metal on metal. 'Besides, we're all family, Susan, so nobody's going to criticise our efforts. They'll all say it's lovely or delicious followed by thank you – don't worry so much.' Grace dipped her finger in the gravy and licked it. She liked it thinner and it needed more salt.

'If it's worth doing, it's worth doing well,' Susan said.

'It is done well.' *Some of it probably a little too well,* Grace thought.

The kitchen was at its hottest and the benches were covered in dirty pots and pans.

Grace ladled more stock into the dish, stirred some more then sampled the gravy again – it definitely needed more salt. She got the Saxa and sprinkled it across the gravy.

'Given the family history you'd do well to go easy on that.'

'Given the family history you'd do well to relax.'

'Maybe I would've relaxed if we'd gone out to celebrate.' Susan mopped the last of the spill with brisk movements and tight shoulders.

Grace was tired of that old chestnut. 'Any medical book will tell you we all need salt – just ask Richard.

It's when you add extra to your plate that the damage is done. Even cows have salt blocks to lick, you know.' Grace dipped her finger in the gravy again. This time she was satisfied.

'We're not cows,' Susan said, exasperated. 'And all you're doing is giving the kids bad habits.'

'You've got a vegetarian daughter descended from a butcher's family. So tell me where my bad habits have influenced that?'

'That's just a fad she's picked up from some stupid girl at school. It'll pass.'

'Can you still call it a fad if it's lasted more than a year?'

Then Grace wished she'd curbed her tongue. Susan opened her mouth to say something – but Jane tapped back into the kitchen.

'Love your plates, Grace! Such fun having all different ones. Did you pick them up at antique shops?'

'No. Life shops.' Grace worked briskly at the gravy. She imagined the spoon wearing down a year's worth of metal all at once.

'I've never heard of Life Shops. Are they anything to do with Lifeline?'

'Sort of.' Grace banged the spoon on the side of the baking dish. 'It's ready.'

'I'll get everybody in.' Jane went to the back door and yelled, 'Come and get it!'

'Classy,' Susan mumbled.

Grace looked at her daughter, disappointed. She thought sarcasm cheap currency.

'Hands, everybody,' Jane said to the children as they filed past, holding the screen door open at her back – and baptising everyone with a little wine from the glass she was waving overhead.

Richard and Peter helped Ada up the back steps next, followed by Kath and Nick. Kath had linked her arm through Nick's as though she'd claimed him as her beau.

In the dining room Grace began to place people at the table. Ada had just found her seat – when shouting broke out across the street.

'Oi, you. Bugger off.'

'You own the bloody nature strip, do you?'

'A good whack of it, yeah, I reckon I do given it's in front of my house.'

'That's bullshit. The useless council owns it which means I can do what I fuckin' well like on it—'

'Oh, for goodness sake,' Susan said. 'Do we have to listen to this?'

'Language alert.' Jane tried to clamp her hands over Meg's ears, but the fair head ducked and weaved out of her mother's reach.

'Everybody knows the f-word, Mum,' Tom said. 'It's part of the school curriculum.'

'Just ignore them. They'll move on,' Grace said.

'I'm moving them on right now.' Peter turned to go out.

'Leave it, Peter.' Grace caught his arm. 'People's tempers are frayed by the heat and mess. Let it go. They'll give it up soon enough.'

Grace watched Peter pause in the doorway. The tight fists he made of his hands. When territories were threatened, Peter's father had been like this, just as determined to reassert the boundaries.

Grace could still remember the smell of the dance hall that night as she and Bev walked in – it was ripe with cheap perfume, sweat and opportunity. The band was belting out a good likeness of Ray Charles's 'Hit The Road Jack', which struck a rhythm deep in Grace's chest. She looked across the sea of heads, trying to spot Des's among them. It was impossible not to be caught up in the pulse of the crowd.

She and Bev walked the perimeter, each gripping the other's hand so as not to be separated. Men shimmied in front of them as though acting out some kind of mating ritual, which Grace supposed in a way they were. She and Bev edged round them and continued the search, laughing. But after two circuits of the dance hall, Grace still couldn't see Des.

'Bev and I aren't off till late tonight,' she'd told him on the phone.

'You're always off late. Can't you just leave?'

'No.'

'Why not?'

'Because we're talking about sick people not dead animals.'

There was silence on the other end of the phone. Grace imagined him scheming ways for her escape from ward and duty, or maybe he was taking time to compose himself.

'I should be finished by ten,' she said.

He could meet her and Bev at the nurses' quarters, then they'd all head to the dance together by taxi.

But now Des had other plans. 'I guess I'll see you there then,' he said.

'How will I—'

He'd hung up.

'Do you think we should keep looking for him?' she asked Bev.

'We've looked enough. It's his turn to try and find you – if he's here at all.' They found a seat up on the terraced balcony running round the sides of the dance floor.

Two girls – two leggy girls – without partners at a dance didn't go unnoticed. The offers to dance from eager young men kept coming but Grace gave each a polite *No*. Bev's face, full of cheery enthusiasm when men approached, was dashed to disappointment as they were sent away.

'You dance.' Grace was conscious she was setting up an untouchable barrier around them. 'I don't mind,' she lied.

'I'm not going to leave you sitting here on your own.'

Grace was grateful. She was fragile enough with her chaste waiting, searching the crowds for the tall and familiar, but to be left sitting alone would feel like abandonment.

'Thanks, Bev. He'll turn up soon, and then we can all have some fun.'

Grace's mood changed as the band moved through its mixture of slow and fast melodies. Roy Orbison's 'Only The Lonely', too poignant in its title and theme, allowed her to wallow in calm and diligent waiting. Toni Fisher's 'The Big Hurt' sanctioned her right to feel the victim of thoughtless neglect. When Bobby Bland's 'Let The Little Girl Dance' came on, Grace saw it as a sign.

Angry indifference took over.

'Come on, this is silly. He's probably not even here.'

At the next song, they caught the eyes of boys Grace had turned down, and the two girls were soon up and on the dance floor – where they stayed.

The young man Grace danced with was powerfully built but not as tall as Des. He was a confident dancer and Grace had relaxed into his lead much the same way she did with Des. Years later, she'd speculate that Des had known where she was all the time, but remained out of sight, watching her, waiting to see what she'd do.

Maybe it was Grace's easy comfort that Des recognised and felt threatened by. Or was it more to do with the fact that Grace hadn't stayed seated, waiting for him to find her? Whatever started the scuffle – one man trying to push in and the other in no mood to let him – soon led to the throwing of fists. A space cleared around the men as they fought. But Grace didn't see till she was older that it was over little more than their own masculinity.

'Des, please. It was nothing,' Grace tried, to little effect.

She wanted to wade in and pull them apart but Bev pulled her back. 'Are you crazy? You'll cop one.'

She gripped Bev's arm and winced with each punch that found its target. Perhaps Des hadn't anticipated the strength or skill of the other man. His fists were making contact more often than Des's.

'Where're the bouncers? Why aren't they coming to break it up?' Grace's need for the hurting to end made time drag.

But barely a minute had passed before the men were pulled apart by two broad bouncers.

Grace followed Des's flailing arms as he fought his undignified exit from the building. Outside, thrown to the ground, he slumped, spitting blood.

Grace knelt on the rough gravel in front of him, not caring about the ladders she was putting in her expensive nylons. She dabbed at his lip with her handkerchief. But he wasn't ready to be soothed, not yet. He brushed her hand away.

'You're my girl,' he growled, spitting more blood.

At the time, Grace thought this was chivalrous, and enchanting.

'Of course I'm yours,' she soothed.

'I thought you loved me?'

They hadn't talked about love, despite spending all their spare time together, laughing easily. Perhaps he thought it was implied by their long kisses, by his hand sliding sometimes too high, or low, from her waist.

'I do,' she said. She pushed his hair from his forehead to expose a small graze. She dabbed at that too, and he let her.

She couldn't deny she liked the sense of menace that surrounded Des. He was a bit wild, intractable, hard to control, but all the more exciting for it. Perhaps she saw herself as someone clever enough to get the kind of behaviour she wanted from Des. Or was it more that she was determined to find love in the city where she'd failed at it in the country?

Grace tended his wounds and whispered, *Of course I love you* in his ear.

They slept with each other for the first time that night. She tasted his blood on her tongue when they kissed and in some ways this sealed her commitment to him.

Des seemed determined to cement his ownership over her too. At his flat, there was no gentle coaxing of her into the small bedroom; she was led. And there was no slow undressing of one another; each attended to themselves. Face to face across his narrow bed they dropped their clothes to the floor, proving their readiness to reveal their bodies to each other.

Des followed the routine. He caressed as he should, kissed as he should, but never offered the same commitment to her pleasure as she'd experienced in the past. Grace wished she'd not known anything else; that she could lie there believing this was the best of it. As it was, she knew she'd be party to a lie.

'All right?' he asked, pushing her legs apart with his.

She nodded but couldn't meet his eyes.

Grace didn't know if he noticed, though his earlier tentativeness soon gave way to the deep thrusts of experience; movements that told her the façade could be dropped, or that he didn't care about fragility.

She dared to look at him then, and was unnerved to see him staring at her. Defiant, even during this most intimate act, she didn't look away, daring him instead to fuck her like a prostitute if he must.

I do, she'd said. And she believed at the time that she'd meant it.

Gently, Grace placed her hand on Peter's arm again.

'Come on,' she said, choosing her words with care. 'Let's sit down. They'll stop.'

Poor Peter, he worked his fists a few more times.

'They better,' he said, finally, and returned to his seat.

Grace wondered what her life might have looked like at seventy, had she chosen her words better and not said *I do*, twice. But she reminded herself that this was her life now, so there was little point trying to imagine a different one.

13

Seated between her friends along one side of the table, Grace faced Jane, Peter, Susan and Richard. Meg sat with the older people, beside Ada, and was busy telling her of the benefits of Caran d'Ache colouring pencils over K-Mart specials.

Ada listened with the patience of a grandmother.

Grace had not had twelve people at her table for a while. Theirs wasn't the kind of family who shared regular Sunday meals. A certain level of commitment to one another was required for that, a commitment Grace conceded that as a family they'd never quite achieved. Past events hadn't helped, she supposed. History had a way of reorganising the future in unsatisfying ways.

Grace looked at the two tables she'd had to push together for the day, one a drop-leaf table that she and Jack had manoeuvred in from the lounge room the day before. She liked the irregularity of the two, the way one was narrower and taller than the other, forcing a central ridge in the cream damask tablecloth.

None of her wine glasses matched – some were cut crystal, others plain, the length of the stems varying as much as the size of the glass. And neither were the chairs all the same. Several had barley twist legs to match those of the dining table, others were of chromed steel, and she'd brought two moulded plastic ones in from the patio. The cutlery was a mishmash of bone-handled, stainless steel and worn silver alongside the confusion of plates.

Large serving bowls dotted the length of the tables. The roasted potatoes and parsnips were crisp and golden with little trace of the oil that had allowed it. The broccoli looked remarkably green under a sprinkling of toasted almond flakes and the baby carrots glistened with the honey Grace had drizzled over them. The cauliflower au gratin still bubbled from the oven, and the peas, Grace's favourite vegetable, were an army of minted emerald. There was a gravy boat here, the top flecked with the brownings from the roasting pan, a jug of mint sauce there, and baskets of dinner rolls at either end. Wisps of steam escaped into the air, which was sucked up by the steady orbit of the ceiling fan.

The leg of lamb reclined in its own glossy juices on the serving platter in front of Peter. The fat across the top was now crisply caramelised all the way to the knuckle. The marrow – the *coin*, Des called it, and something he'd dig out with a pointed knife, spread on a square of bread and sprinkle liberally with salt and pepper – was a chocolate-coloured dimple at the bony end. It was a plump joint, the prize of the table, except maybe to Jorja.

Grace felt confident it would feed them all, perhaps with a little to spare.

Grace had put Nick and Jorja at the head of the table, facing Tom and Jaxon at the other end. It would have been a squeeze to fit two adults along these shortest sides of the rectangle – and anyway, she wanted to break the tradition of the senior man overseeing a meal as though he were king.

When Grace was a child the carving of the Sunday roast followed a well-worn and traditional path. Mother would bring the joint to the dining table on her good oval platter. The beef or pork or lamb would ooze its juices onto the plate's design so that the blue Spode figures drowned in the flood. The table would be set with the best of everything the buffet offered, in the way of linen, crockery and cutlery. There'd even be a small posy in the table's centre, snipped that morning from the garden with Pa's well-sharpened secateurs. Mother would hand the platter to Pa, seated at the head of the table, and then she would sit to his right ready to receive her plate.

Pa always served Mother first. He would slice her off the first cut – the flavoursome, crispy skin coveted by all. 'There you go, Mother,' he'd say, 'the cook's reward.'

'Thank you, Frank.' On Sundays, Mother's voice could be gentle.

He'd then cut slices for Grace, then Joe and last of all himself. He might stop between Grace and Joe if a slice looked a particularly nice one – not too fatty – and he'd offer it to Mother as well, balanced on the flat surface of the knife's blade.

This exchange taught Grace about the division of tasks when life was tied to the soil. There were those who toiled inside the home and those who toiled outside and each respected what the other did. In this way Grace grew up believing the cook was valued in a household.

But then, Pa was an exceptional man.

Des too would carve the Sunday roast. He'd sit at the head of the table just as Pa had and Grace would sit at the other end, the three children between them. Unlike her mother, Grace liked to set the table casually with an easy-care tablecloth and pretty paper napkins. Des liked the stiff white linen, which never fell well at the table's corners and required laborious restarching and ironing each week. Early on she'd set it to please him. Later, she set it to please herself.

He'd carve the joint more deftly than Pa. Des knew how to wield a knife. But where Pa served Mother first, Des served Grace last and he kept the first slice back for himself. The children, more outspoken than when Grace was a girl, would dare to challenge him.

'You've got more crackling than us,' they'd chorus, or, 'That's not fair, you always get the parson's nose.'

'Who brings the meat home round here?' he'd say, and gobble the crisp, greasy treat down in front of them, while they sulkily looked on.

Today, Peter stood beside the table to carve the lamb. He wasn't as experienced with a knife as his father but he took to the job with the same earnestness; the tip of his tongue poked from his mouth as he concentrated on the task.

'Bagsy the first slice,' called Tom.

'Adults first, Tom,' Susan said to her nephew.

Peter put the first slice to one side on the platter. Grace knew why.

'The birthday girl gets served first, champ.' Peter placed the second slice on Grace's plate and passed it to her.

Watching how silently the new knife moved through the meat reminded Grace of an electric one she'd owned that had moved well enough but not been so quiet. It was a General Electric brand from memory, bought sometime in the late seventies. It was weighty to hold and noisy, but efficient. The action of its dual blades allowed the thinnest of slices to be carved from a joint. Des hated it. But that didn't stop Grace from laying it at the head of the table beside his plate each Sunday, daring him to use it or admit failure. She even kept a short extension lead in a drawer in the dining room, just for the knife. She enjoyed watching the foreign and unwieldy thing in his hands; she liked that it spoilt his masculine performance. She fancied that its intrusive buzzing was like an alarm bell signalling uncertainties and confusion in the normal hierarchy of the household.

Jorja silently winced at the carving process, especially once pink started to ooze from the flesh as Peter neared the bone. She followed the journey of each slice from plate to plate – making sure, Grace supposed, that no blood dripped onto the vegetables.

Peter cut a piece from near the knuckle and put it in his mouth.

'Delicious,' he said. 'Could have been hand-selected by Dad.'

Grace bristled. She'd had a lifetime of hearing the butcher praised above the cook.

'Oh, I don't know. Let's give the final credit to the pasture that helped the lamb get fat.'

'Or a good killing,' offered Nick. 'I read some-where that some abattoirs play Bach to calm the animals, thinking it helps keep the meat tender. You know, not … scared … stiff.' Here Nick did a fine impersonation of a terrified animal, arms and legs convulsing in front of him.

Jorja went pale. Grace was encouraged. It proved her granddaughter's vegetarianism wasn't just a fashion accessory.

Nick, remembering, said, 'Oh, sorry, Jorja.'

Richard spread his hands wide like Jesus at the Last Supper and addressed the food at the table.

'Can't see too much other protein on the table, Jorja. So where are you going to get it from this time?'

Jorja reached for the bowl of peas beside her plate. 'These,' she said to him. 'You're the one always selling the benefits of green.'

'Don't manipulate my ideas about clean energy to suit your imbalanced food pyramid.'

'There's nothing wrong with my food pyramid. Besides, vegetarianism's as much about clean energy as it is anything else.' Jorja's veil of hair was well back from her face as she looked at her father.

'Maybe I should heat up some baked beans for you.' Susan put her napkin aside and looked set to get up from the table.

'Don't give her baked beans again. They make her fart.'

Jorja flashed green eyes at her brother. 'They do not. You're the family stinker.'

'Now, Jaxon. You know wind's a normal part of bodily function. It's where we choose to release it that leads to social problems.'

Jaxon rolled his eyes at his father.

'And for him it's, like, everywhere,' Jorja said.

'So does Tom.' Meg nodded her head up and down fast, in cahoots with Jorja.

Tom was quick to defend himself. 'The gas poisons your blood if you don't let it out.'

'And poisons your sister if you do.' Jaxon accepted a triumphant high-five from Tom.

'Is there any chance of changing the subject?' Susan took up her napkin again, held her plate out to Peter and he placed a slice of lamb on it.

Meg obliged. 'Did Mummy tell you I'm learning the violin, Grandma?'

'No. She didn't.'

'I was leaving it for you to tell Grandma the big news, sweetie.'

'And I'm learning the trumpet,' Tom said.

'Which sounds like a bag of spanners when he gets it going.'

'Oh, Pete, it does not.'

'Better than her violin – it sounds like a cat getting neutered.'

'Now, son, watch your mouth.' Peter raised an eyebrow at Tom.

'What's neutered, Daddy?'

Richard saved Peter from having to answer Meg. 'Give me an acoustic guitar any day,' he said, plucking the air.

'Nup. Percussion.' Nick played a riff on the table with the index fingers of both hands.

'I played a mean triangle when I was younger,' Kath offered. 'I always timed the ting just right.'

Grace's favourite instrument was the harp – an

erotic instrument, she thought: to see one played well was like watching lovers. That was how Filip had played her body. He embraced her wholly as though she was that grand instrument and she allowed his fingers, encouraged them even, to whisper across her skin.

'Would one of your Macedonian girls do this?' It was fear that had prompted the question; fear she was no better than any of the girls Mother had helped stare out of town.

'Never,' Filip said, and he guided her hand a little lower.

'Never?' Her fear escalated.

'No. But only because they are not permitted to leave the sight of their parents.' He laughed then, and she relaxed.

They were lying under their favourite tree, a wide and droopy old willow whose branches swept at the ground like the hem of a long skirt. There was a creek below the tree's feet but it hadn't run since the previous winter. Transparent-winged dragonflies and water striders hovered or skated over the stagnant pools. Occasionally a bullfrog broke the surface, snatched at one that lingered too long, then plopped back underwater with a satisfied croak.

Grace propped herself up on one elbow and looked at Filip. She traced a finger along the soft line of his jaw to the small cleft in the centre of his chin. There, she felt the tiny cluster of bristles that hid in that hard-to-shave dip. He ran his hand up and down her back, slowed as he passed the two small raised moles near her shoulder and circled them with a finger in a figure of eight before his hand moved on.

'Do you ever feel guilty about us?' she asked.

'No. Guilt crushes the spirit, where love nourishes it. So let us feel only love.'

'I feel guilty sometimes.'

'That is because you have lived always in this small town. Here, guilt is used as power over others.'

'I don't have much choice but to live here.' Grace rolled on to her back and looked up through the mosaic of leaves.

'There are always choices, but not always enough courage.'

Grace couldn't see that there were too many choices open to her. Or was Filip right, was it only courage she lacked? Could that be Harvest's secret in keeping generations trapped in the town – a collective mistrust and fear of anything beyond it?

'So what brave choices have you made?' she asked.

Filip turned on his side and faced Grace. 'To teach in a town where people call me dirty wog behind my back.'

'I don't,' she said, hurt for him.

'That is because you do not fear things that are different.' He ran his finger along the V of breast above her bra. 'Or that give you pleasure.'

He kissed her on the forehead, as Pa had when she was a child.

'Do not listen if people try to control your life through guilt, Grace. Listen only from here.' He flattened his hand across her chest to cover her heart. 'It will show you a better life.'

Afterwards Grace would question whether she should thank or curse Filip for the things she'd learnt under his touch. Much later, when she was married to Des, she often cursed Filip. Partly because she didn't want to be reminded such touches were beyond her reach, but more because Filip had been proved wrong: sometimes guilt *made* you act.

'I prefer the saxophone, myself,' Peter said. 'It takes a big fella to get enough *um-pah* to blow a horn that size.' He did a phallic thrust of his forearm.

'Oh, darl,' Jane squealed.

Susan rolled her eyes.

'But because you can't play the saxophone you drive a big flash car instead?' Nick rocked back on the hind legs of his chair with a satisfied smile.

Peter ignored him. 'Now, Jorja, are you going to try some of your grandma's lamb?' He cut a slice off the diminishing leg, a thick cross-section of fibrous muscle, stabbed it with the carving fork and poked it towards her. It dripped pink onto the tablecloth. 'Get a whiff of that. Don't ya just love it?' He moved the fork backwards and forwards in front of Jorja. She reared back.

'Dad! Not cool.' Nick rocked forward on his chair with a thud and pushed his father's hand away from his cousin.

Peter shrugged and added the slice to Richard's plate.

'That'll probably do me, thanks Peter. Got the coronaries to think of, you know, and it's all about moderation when it comes to those little fellas.' Richard tapped his chest with an index finger.

'If I couldn't have meat – good meat – I reckon I'd starve,' Peter said. 'Coronaries or not.'

'I'd rather starve,' Jorja said.

'Is it the flavour you don't like or the killing?' Nick asked.

'Both. Plus I don't like the thought of eating anything with a face.'

Jaxon and Tom set up a chorus of distressed *baa*-ing down the other end of the table.

'*And* ...' Jorja scowled at the two boys, 'I'm bothered about what livestock does to the environment. Not that I'd expect you two cretins to understand anything about that.'

'Not wind again!' Peter looked to the ceiling and the fan ruffled his hair.

Jorja's fringe started to slip.

'Can everyone, please, just change the subject.' Susan snapped her napkin out flat and laid it across her lap.

Kath reached over and gripped Jorja's hand. 'At

least you're true to your beliefs, Jorja. It's admirable. Maybe we could all take a lesson from you.'

Grace admired Jorja's stand as well. For a young voice to remain strong in the midst of what was proving a hostile, meat-eating majority showed real commitment.

'You know, Peter,' Grace said. 'I might just pass on the lamb today too.' She poked her fork into the slice on her plate and placed it back on the serving platter. 'There's plenty of other goodies on the table to keep me alive, and healthy.' She winked at Jorja, who tried hard to hide her pleasure.

'Don't encourage her, Mum. She'll tell us she's going vegan next.'

Grace ignored Susan and thought of Pa instead, of the lambs he'd slaughtered in the barn. She felt his old bones turn in their grave.

'You know what, Gran. I might join you.' Nick passed his meat back too.

'Looks like there's mutiny in the Meat Works,' giggled Jane.

'Great. All the more for me.' Tom licked his lips.

Peter had sat down, burying the carving fork in the lamb, where it stood upright like Excalibur's sword, and clattered the knife onto the platter.

'So is everybody going to hand back their lamb? I needn't have carved at all!' He crossed his arms, daring other dissenters.

'I'm rather partial to roast lamb and I don't have

it often, being on my own, so I'll keep mine, thanks, Peter. But I'll eat respectfully after what you've had to say, Jorja.' Ada saluted Jorja with her glass.

'Thanks, Aunty Ada.'

'Ditto,' Kath said, also raising her glass.

'You other three just aren't true Bakers.' Peter took up the carving knife again and used it to hold down the joint as he extracted the fork.

The three dissenters laughed. 'Maybe that's where you're wrong,' Grace said, 'maybe we're more baker than butcher.' She reached for the basket of dinner rolls, took one and passed it along.

Pulled apart, the roll revealed a soft, white centre. Against all the dark meat on plates around the table the bread looked pure, a symbol of goodness among the blood. Des had used bread to mop up such juices on his plate; it would end up sodden and soiled. Grace tore a small piece from the roll and put it in her mouth. It tasted innocent.

When the bread basket made its way to Susan, she refused it: 'I'm trying to cut back on the evil white carbs.' And she passed the basket on to Peter.

Quiet came over the table. It was broken only by *Could I please have* or *Would you mind* passing requests and the clatter of serving spoons as people helped themselves to vegetables and sauces. The long wait for the meal meant appetites depleted the piles quickly. Jorja shared her vegetarian gravy with Nick and Grace. She passed it to each without request or show.

Strangely, Grace didn't miss the colour of meat on her plate. Nor the taste, which sometimes smelt so strongly of earth, grass and grain that she imagined the animal's last meal still making its way through the fibres as she chewed. She'd always taken meat in small quantities anyway and had cringed at the way the juices soaked into mashed potato, tinging it pink, or bathed lettuce in a dressing of animal fat and blood. As she added the various vegetables to her plate from the bowls that came her way, she imagined again how Pa would be turning in his grave, but she could also see Des's bony knuckles rapping on his coffin, demanding he be let out to put a stop to her tomfoolery. She smiled at his powerlessness.

'Joke to share, Grace?' Richard had taken one of his regular pauses between mouthfuls, knife and fork neatly crossed in a space he'd created on Bev's fine white china plate – he was the only person Grace had trusted with its care.

Grace looked at her son-in-law, momentarily caught for what to say. She didn't think Susan and Peter would appreciate their mother smiling at thoughts of their long dead father made powerless by the grave.

'I was thinking of a patient I had once.' The man who sprang to mind justified her smile. 'He was a funny fellow. An old headmaster or government official – I can't remember exactly which now. Anyway, he took issue with the meals at Moreville.'

'I can imagine most people taking issue with the meals in a nursing home.' Richard took up his knife and fork again. 'The one hospital meal I ever had, when I had the old snip-o, smacked of cheap cuts and mass production.'

'Well, if you'd had it done under a local anaesthetic like everybody else then you wouldn't have had to stay in overnight.'

'Some acts on the body are best experienced subliminally, Susan.'

'Like to hear you say that on a labour ward.'

'This man's issue,' Grace continued, 'was more to do with the colour of the foods. For some reason he couldn't stand green anywhere on his plate. He'd eat the greens if they were served on a side plate, but not if they came out on the main one.'

'He sounds just like me. I can't stand greens on my plate either but it doesn't stop Mum putting them there.'

'And I'm glad she does, Jaxon,' Richard said, 'green foods are nature's special little powerhouses.'

'Reckon they're Devil boogers,' Jaxon said.

Tom, quick to add visuals, picked up a pea from his plate and placed it inside his left nostril. 'Beware the Devil booger,' he growled.

'Tom – you are such a pig.' Meg scowled at her brother.

Tom closed his right nostril off with a finger and snorted the pea in his left back onto his plate.

Peter's laugh was loud, hearty.

'Well, for this man, peas were a no-no, as were broccoli, cabbage, beans.'

Jaxon's head looked set to nod off his shoulders.

'Well, one day cook had made parsley dumplings on top of a braised steak dish.'

'Braised because they were cheap cuts.' Richard nodded knowingly round the table.

'The trouble was you couldn't really see there was parsley in them until they were cut open. Well, when he did. *Nur-rse!* he bellowed, fit to wake the dead. *Let me remind you of the rules.*'

'Must have been a headmaster,' Tom said, with some authority.

'He banged his knife on his plate,' Grace rapped hers for effect, 'until I thought it was going to break. All the other residents were watching by this stage, mouths open in a great show of mashed food. No greens on the Governor's plate, he yelled, and turned the whole lot upside down on the table and stormed out with as much dramatic effect as a walking frame permits.'

Jaxon nudged Tom. 'I'm gonna try that.'

'What about green jelly, Grandma, did he eat that?'

Grace laughed. 'You know, Meg, I think he did.'

'So it was a control thing,' Susan said.

'Psychotropic drugs are my guess.'

'Or maybe he was just plain angry,' Kath offered, 'about where he'd ended up.'

'Nah – just another old kook if you ask me, like most of them in that place.'

'That's not fair, Peter. A lot of them weren't kooks.' Many had been forced into Moreville by circumstances other than broken minds.

'Not as unfair as you having to work at a place like that aged fifty-something.' Peter reached for the gravy boat and poured more over his meat. He wiped the spout clean with his finger then licked it.

'Only fifty. And besides, I didn't have a choice.'

'I wish I'd been in a position to help you out,' Peter said.

'It wasn't your job to help me. It was mine. And it's something I wish I'd done sooner.'

The prospect of losing your home is a powerful motivator, Grace had learnt.

Peter took up his wine glass, sat back in his chair and looked at Grace. 'But it was a miserable place to work. The few times I went there it smelt so bad. People called out all the time. Strapped in chairs. Made me think of POWs.'

'I admit it was no five-star resort.'

But neither was ageing a five-star experience. Some days when Grace entered the facility, she felt as though a crystal ball was pressed up close to her face, demanding she look into it, closely. The future could be a painful place to spend too much time.

'He should have provided for you better. It was his job.'

Peter's comment surprised Grace. It suggested a rub she didn't know existed.

'He probably thought he'd be around long enough to do just that.' Susan rounded on her brother. 'Dad didn't have the benefit of the big income you have now. Money to throw here and there on trinkets and cars.' Susan flipped her hand in the air as though tossing gold coins.

At least Peter had something to show for his spending, Grace supposed. Des had thrown his money away on sure bets and hot tips. But Grace decided to be kind.

'Maybe you're right, Susan. Maybe that had been his hope.'

Peter shrugged, unsure or unprepared to commit either way. But his face looked troubled as he brooded over the possibilities.

'And they weren't all like the man who had a thing about greens. I met lots of nice people too – ones who really appreciated what I did for them. Some even became friends, so it wasn't all bad. In fact, Peter, a lot of it wasn't bad at all.'

Peter looked at Grace over his glass, still not convinced.

'Did you meet any boyfriends, Grandma?'

'I made lots of friends, Tom, some of them boys.'

'Ooh, Grand-ma's got-a boy-friend,' Meg sing-songed.

'That'll be enough, you two!'

There was another rub. This one Grace knew about.

'Never would've said anything like that when I was a kid.' Peter brought his glass to his mouth. 'Never would've had cause,' he mumbled into it.

Grace had never expected to find a lover either, long after she was forced to find the job. Not that she'd ever described Jack using such a word. She considered it a term best left for young girls. She'd declared to Ada and Kath, 'I have a new companion.'

Kath, sharp when it came to matters of the heart, and loins, said, 'Companion, eh? Does that mean you haven't slept with him yet, or that you have and he was crap so you plan on sticking with just going to the movies together?'

Grace blushed like a girl, which she supposed answered the first part of Kath's question. 'I feel stupid calling him my lover. I'm too old,' she said.

'But not too old for the sex?' Kath's laugh was rich, dirty.

'Well, you're looking better for it.' Ada had nodded approval. 'It was getting so I could barely see you side on. You're looking womanly again.'

And she felt it. She had thought she'd seen the last of that sexy woman, even before Des had died; the one who'd once kissed her way round a man's body. Neither Grace nor Des had ventured a hand across the chasm that existed in their shared bed for several years. She'd wake in the night sometimes with an ache, but knew Des wasn't the man she wanted to soothe it. She'd roll away from him and pretend desire no longer existed. It was good to roll into a man again.

They'd met over a broken backrest on a bed. It was a pain of a thing, as Grace remembered it. She'd prop a patient up to feed them, or give them a view other than upwards, and without warning it would snap down flat again, giving the patient a terrible jolt.

'It's the sixth time it's been fixed,' she said to Jack, when he arrived on the ward to repair it. 'What have I got to do to get the job done properly?'

'Wish I'd been employed here sooner then you could've got me to come and fix it the first time,' he said.

'So you're the man to call?'

'I am now,' he said, and gave her a wink.

He reminded her of Pa, with his timber carry box of meticulously maintained tools. He set the box down carefully on the speckled grey linoleum and lowered himself onto one knee. One tattooed forearm on the mattress held him steady as he poked his head under the bed to look at the mechanism.

'It's got the same complaint I've got,' he said, bringing his head out again.

Grace looked askance.

'Dinosauritis.'

It took her a moment to get it, but when she did, she laughed. 'That's a common complaint around here,' she said, 'and not easily treated.'

'Luckily the bed's not terminal with it.' Jack took a number of tools from his box and put them to work on his patient.

And he was right – he should have been employed by Moreville sooner. Not only did the bed never play up again, but she could have met him when she was younger.

He gave her his direct number to the nursing home's workshop after that. Hate to see a woman disappointed, he said. She was only a year off retiring, so she didn't get to use it much. But eventually she allowed him to fix things in her home.

There was a sense of permanence to Jack's presence now; they saw each other once or twice a week. Equally permanent was Susan and Peter's resistance to him. But Grace looked upon this in much the same way she saw Jack's tattoo: something to be lived with.

His tattoo listed the names of his ex-wife and two children, their birthdates directly under each. The letters and numbers were distorted with age – the M in Marion a crushed accordion of vertical lines, but still readable. His wife had left him, *passed me over for something better*, he said. Grace's image of this other woman was of someone fussy, but courageous. Jack said she had it all wrong, that his ex-wife was simply a slut. Some nights Grace slept with those names and dates around her. She eventually got used to their company.

It was hard to imagine Susan and Peter ever doing the same.

Grace watched Peter as he studied the contents of his glass. She could see his anger by the way he gripped the stem, in a fist. Susan flicked at the thickened corner of her napkin with a fingernail, face impassive. As usual, what her daughter was really thinking was out of reach to Grace.

So many years had passed since Des's death, and still Peter and Susan looked to the door for his return. What business was it they needed to finish with him? One more *Good girl* pat to the head; another firm handshake, the words *You do your old man proud*? Grace had been dulled by Des's shadow, while Peter and Susan had always shone beneath it.

'Peter, would you mind carving me off another slice of lamb, please?'

'Oh, yes, please. Me too.'

Kath and Ada's plates still had meat left on them.

Peter put down his glass and took up the carving knife and fork again. 'Anyone else want seconds?'

Most agreed they'd had enough.

14

'Are you really seventy-six now, Kath?'

'As far as my birth certificate can be trusted, Susan, I'm afraid I am.'

'You look good for it.'

'Dare I say, perhaps a husbandless life has had its advantages!'

'Dare I say, you might be right.' Susan laughed.

Grace wondered what Susan saw when she looked at her now seventy-year-old mother. That she looked good for her age? The last time Grace had seen her own mother she was struck by how old she had looked. Mother had been not much older than Grace now, yet surely her mother's neck had been more pouchy, like a tortoise's, and she remembered how the face-powder gathered in the liver spots on her cheeks, accentuating them like lichen on pale wood. Her mother's eyes had almost disappeared into the tired folds surrounding them and her voice had lost some of its authority. By then, she only moved with joint-creaking reluctance, whereas every crisp step had previously been as much the purpose as the destination. She no longer saw or tasted the ants in the sugar bowl that made their way into her tea on the sugar spoon, and yet she still pegged her underwear to the inside of the line in case someone should call round.

Grace was yet to recognise those same features within herself, those telltale signs that suggested she'd started the slow surrender to age, yet she suspected Susan had. And if she had, Grace wondered how her daughter interpreted them. Did she see only the physical changes – incapacities to be feared or suffered in her own future? Or did she focus on how that surrendering might hint at something else – the lost opportunities, the disappointments and failings that could lie ahead? Did Grace remind Susan that you could reach seventy and still have things uncompleted, things not started, things that would never be started? That at seventy you could have a head full of words that no one wanted to listen to, memories no one wanted to live, sadness no one wanted to feel?

Grace supposed there were few people who comfortably looked into their future. Looking into the past was bad enough.

'How old are you, Aunty Ada?' Meg asked.

'Seventy-five.'

Meg looked at Kath then back to Ada. 'Oh.'

Honesty sat comfortably on a six-year-old's face, and Ada smiled.

'Getting hit by a truck has a way of ageing you, dear. Maybe when all the bruising's gone away, Kath can look like the *old* girl again.'

Normally Kath would have been quick with a retort, something like *Older, but naturally brunette at least* or *Wisdom comes at a price.* Today she remained silent.

Grace looked from one to the other and worried her friends were accepting the order in which they might head to their graves, taking their numbers – one, two, three – like tickets in a deli queue. Her thoughts leapt back to all that talk earlier, on the patio.

'All the worry over what's in the backyard, Peter,' she said, thinking out loud, 'maybe what it's really telling us is to be mindful of what we throw away. To think twice before letting something go.'

'Who needs to think twice about throwing away rubbish?'

'Mum's using a metaphor, Jane.' Susan held her hand out to her sister-in-law who handed her plate over at an angle, the knife and fork almost sliding off and onto the tablecloth. Susan righted it just in time. 'Do you want me to take your glass while I'm at it?'

Jane wrapped her fingers round its stem. 'No, thank-yup.'

'If we were all as mindful as you, Mum, we'd have backyards that were just as unnavigable,' Peter said. 'You never throw anything out.'

'I do throw things out, just not the things you think I should. And my backyard is navigable. You've just got to steer your path through it.'

'And that's where choosing the right way starts, kids. Right here at home.' Richard tapped the tabletop with his finger several times, leaving a cluster of dents in the damask cloth.

'Argh!' Jaxon collapsed back in his chair, arms hanging straight at his sides, feigning exhaustion. 'Dad's gonna give us one of his don't stray from the path lectures.'

'Well, Little Red Riding Hood did and we know what happened to her.' Meg looked earnest. 'Gobbled up. Just like that.' She tried to click her fingers but had yet to develop the strength to do it properly.

'I expect we've all thrown things out we wished we hadn't,' Ada said. 'I can remember things from my childhood that ended up in the bin – letters, dolls, trinkets – things I'd like to have back now, to remind me of the person I was then. So don't criticise your mother for taking her time to decide what's worth keeping and what's not. A decision made in haste only frees up time for regret later.'

'I'll keep that in mind, Ada,' Peter said, 'when I'm *mowing* – then regrettably digging out the several rolls of chicken wire buried in the long grass down the back and snagged into the mower.'

'You won't ever throw that picture of us out, will you, Grandma?'

Grace followed Meg's finger to the portrait of her five grandchildren on the china cabinet behind her. It was an outdoor shot. The three youngest were lying on a lawn on their stomachs, Meg with her chin cupped in the palms of her hands; Tom and Jaxon rested on their forearms either side of her. Nick and Jorja were sitting back to back behind them, like bookends.

'No, Meg, for as long as I'm alive you'll always have pride of place, looking over my table,' Grace said.

She always felt those grandchildren at her back as if she was in the foreground of the photograph looking out – and the younger generation, with their smooth faces and perfect teeth, were gazing over her shoulders. She was comforted by that youthful legacy. While they existed even the dead were never completely gone.

The feel of cold, pink lamb under the hand, the taste of mango, the healthy perfume of fresh chard – Grace wondered what would spark her family's recollections of this day in the future. Would it be the touch of real linen napkins, soft and pliable with age, as they pressed them to their lips? The sharp taste of vinegar reminding them of her freshly made mint sauce? Or maybe it would be the sight of rusting corrugated iron that would return them to this day, years from now.

It was the turpentine smell of camphor that always reminded Grace of why she'd left Harvest.

At seventeen she had missed a period. Before the due date for the second had passed, morning sickness also told Filip that Grace had a secret she could not keep.

Filip's prior gentleness was unravelled by this sudden understanding. Grace flinched as he lashed out. Once, twice, three times he dented the fibro of his living room wall, before he slumped into a chair, defeated.

'How?' he asked, over and over, head in hands, knuckles bloodied.

His self-pity made Grace see a different man.

'You're the science teacher, how d'you reckon?' She paced his lounge room, unable to settle.

'Of course I know how it has happened. But we were always very careful.'

'Not careful enough.' She kept pacing, arms hugged round the telltale swelling of her breasts.

'*Ebam!*' Filip brought his fist down on the arm of the chair and Grace heard the timber give a little.

She knew no Macedonian but some utterances were universal.

'I cannot marry you.' He wouldn't face her. Instead, he spoke to his shoes.

'*What?* But you said you loved me.'

'And I do, but I am to marry someone else. It is all arranged.'

'Arranged? When was it arranged?'

'A long time ago.'

Reality slowly dawned on Grace. 'And you never bothered to tell me? What was I then – just something to pass the time with?'

He looked up at her but said nothing. Years later she'd understood that look, of a damned man. He might have to honour his old-country traditions but he'd sold himself short in doing so.

At the time, though, she cared nothing for his honour, only hers. She stopped pacing, picked up an ashtray from the coffee table and hurled it at him. He didn't flinch as it whistled past his head and smashed against the wall beside the dents made by his fist. His face, his body – one Grace knew the surfaces of intimately – said something more hurtful: *Do your worst, so we can end this.*

She knew then she couldn't marry him either, not even if his arranged bride was to drop dead that very day.

'After all your big talk,' she said, 'you're just a bloody coward like the rest of us.' And left him with his shame.

Outside, she stood a while in the hot Harvest sun. The whispered stories from girls about hot baths, empty gin bottles and knitting needles terrified her, as did those of lying on sheets stained with the blood of the three or five girls before in a backyard abortionist. But at seventeen, and with no husband, she wasn't brave enough to walk the small-town streets of Harvest with a growing belly. And neither did she think her spirit could withstand several months of hiding out on the farm under the scrutiny of her mother's damning eyes.

She looked left then right down the dusty, sleepy street as though choosing a direction. She turned left, towards home.

As it turned out, it was Mother who decided. Fierce Mother. Pious Mother. Mother of little love but much practicality.

'Drink this,' she said to Grace.

Grace saw her mother as one of Macbeth's witches then, or Snow White's stepmother, but she had to trust in that foul-tasting drink. But while she drained the cup, and many others like it over the next few days, she never doubted that her mother would just as happily kill the mother-to-be as the foetus, in order to rid herself completely of the shame.

When the cramps started that's what Grace thought her thin-lipped mother was doing with each silent drink – until the blood and clots came away, soaking rag after rag, which Mother tossed into the fiery, secretive mouth of the wood stove.

So it was that, with the herbal camphor smell still in her throat, she recalled the photograph of the smiling nurse in the magazine, and soon after followed the path towards a nursing career and away from the disappointment permanently etched on her mother's face.

Jane, hand still firmly gripped round the stem of her wine glass, let out a plaintive, 'Oh, Grace, don't talk like that. You make it sound as though you're not going to be around much longer. You know I'm emotional at the best of times, let alone after a couple of wines.'

Susan rolled her eyes. 'And then you're emotionally incontinent.' She leant across to take Jane's glass from her, but Jane moved it out of reach with surprising stealth.

In an extraordinary show of sobriety, Jane said, 'At least no one can ever accuse me of being a cold fish.'

Startled, Susan opened her mouth to say something, but then thought better of it.

'I never told your Pa,' Mother had said into her cup, 'about that incident – before you left Harvest.'

Grace had been back on one of the few visits she made to her childhood home, three young children in tow by then. Joe was running the farm and Pa had been laid to rest deep in the cemetery soil. For all Grace knew the tufts of grass from his land were still caught between his bony fingers. She liked the idea of that.

Mother was sitting, still at the old red-and-white flecked Formica table, finishing one of the many cups of tea she had in a day. Grace was preparing food for their dinner, ready for Joe's return from the dairy. It was a quiet evening, except for the clack, clack of the ceramic milk saver in a saucepan of milk she was heating for custard.

She had stopped turning the key on the tin of ham she was opening when her mother said those words, but she couldn't look at her. The topic had remained unspoken since Grace took that first drink. To hear it reduced to an incident all these years later, didn't take away any of the fear and hurt and guilt that had come before or after.

'I thought you should know that. In case it was important to you.'

Grace placed the tin carefully on the table, not trusting herself to open it any further without cutting herself. The narrow ribbon of tin that had gathered round the key hissed a little as it uncoiled. She sat down opposite her mother but still couldn't look at her.

'It is important to me,' she said. 'Thank you.'

'You were lucky it worked, you know.' Mother drained the last of her tea and clattered the cup into place on the saucer.

Should she express gratitude? Grace wondered. Was that what her mother expected? It was never a word she could associate with what they'd done.

'I didn't expect it to,' her mother continued. 'I wasn't sure of the quantities. Guess work, really.'

Grace looked at her mother then. 'And if it hadn't worked?'

But her mother looked away. She sighed into the dusty-lavender sky beyond the kitchen window. 'I've thought about that a lot over the years. At the time I figured I'd have taken you to the city and found a doctor to finish off what I'd failed to do. Later – years later – I wasn't so sure. But it's enough to say I still feel the weight of that decision every time I go to church.'

Grace saw then that shame was more powerful

even than God. But maybe she'd got it wrong. Maybe they'd both got it wrong.

'Still, what's done is done. No undoing it now.' Mother slapped her hands on her thighs, then pushed herself up from her chair. She gathered the dirty cups and saucers from the table and took them to the sink.

The table was scattered with pale cake crumbs, left over from lunch. Grace gathered them together with the edge of her hand and pushed them into a pile. She imagined the mound as equal to the size of a seven-week foetus. Given the smallness of the cluster, could it be considered such a big sin?

But the question of whether she'd sinned had already been answered, first when Peter was born and she held the fully formed reality of what she'd got rid of in her hands. And many times since, even just then as Claire ran through the kitchen, two ponytails flapping at the sides of her head like the ears of a Bassett Hound.

Grace had scooped the crumbs into her cupped hand and tossed them in the bin.

Eventually, she'd stopped her mental tirade at Filip and in some ways she even felt obliged to respect his loyalty. Because where Mother had readily put aside the teachings of her church, Filip had remained true to his cultural ones. And while none of that loyalty had been extended to Grace, she never doubted he still carried the burden of his betrayal.

No amount of wine or close friendship had ever allowed Grace to share this part of her life.

15

When Grace was a girl, dessert was called *pudding*. Mother had served it after their evening meal as religiously as Father Donnelly had placed the sacrament on the tongues of the confessed every Sunday. But where his dry wafer was a tasteless puritan gift, Mother's puddings had shown no constraint.

They could be complex dishes, like choux pastry made from scratch or a five-tiered trifle, the jammy Swiss roll at its base drunk with sweet sherry. Mother would add layers of preserved fruit, vanilla-infused custard and red jelly, then top it off with thick whipped cream and a sprinkling of crushed nuts. The curd in her lemon meringue pies oozed a sticky syrup that soaked right through to the pastry and each spoonful made the cheeks dimple with the lemony tang. The pie's lightly browned meringue peaks – two or three inches deep at their highest point – dissolved on the tongue. And the crunchy-oat cobbler on Mother's crumbles topped sweetened, poached fruit – apple, rhubarb, apricot, peach – which bubbled up in the oven through the gaps and cracks of the crust like lava. Grace remembered how later – when Mother was out of sight – she and Joe would put the empty, deep pie dish between them at the kitchen table and each use a butter knife to scrape at the caramelised sugary sides.

There were simple puddings too, for those times when Mother was busy helping with the hay harvest or calving season. Then, she'd quickly make junket or jelly in the morning before leaving the house and serve it that evening with tinned cherries – one of the few preserved fruits she bought – and cream, scooped fresh from the top of the milk in its can at the dairy. But there would still be a shortbread or Madeleine biscuit in the tin for them to have with their hot tea afterwards.

As a cook, Mother's puddings attracted her greatest praise.

Grace imitated her mother in this way: she too presented desserts to her family like a gift at the end of a hard day's work. But it was a tradition that had stopped like a dying man's heartbeat in the generation that followed hers. Nowadays desserts were served only at special occasions, or taken on the hop from a tub or packet or cone, often with guilt.

One thing remained unchanged. Sugar, in all of its ingenious guises – meringue, chocolate, pastry – could reveal much about the person who consumed it.

Mother had taken hers in small, measured quantities, not denied altogether but meted out to prove she was capable of sacrifice. Pa and Joe had adored the sweetness of Mother's puddings and cakes and devoured them without regret or guilt. Sugar had proved a seductive poison for Des; for her grandchildren it was the prize for eating their vegetables. Susan took hers in small amounts like Mother, but it was more about restraint than sacrifice. Peter shifted between gluttony and abstinence according to his willpower. Richard's sugars were limited to those found primarily in fruit. Jane declined it, but with saliva on her tongue, and blind to the sugars in the wine.

For Grace, sweets were the reward of patience. With the weight of meat and the goodness of vegetables taken like medicine, the taste buds were allowed to relax around the simple pleasure of pudding.

Today she'd try to satisfy the sugar habits of all those around her family table. There was mango for the health conscious; cookies-and-cream ice cream for the children, because she could never deny a child their favourite; and then there was a simple, old-fashioned pudding from her past – baked custard. Mother would have thought this dish an ordinary one for a celebration, a pudding that showed little effort. Grace had chosen it, first, because it was one of the few she could still make from memory. But more importantly because of its simplicity, not just in preparation, but ingredients as well. Yesterday, she'd considered opening one of her recipe books to a page for a torte or flan or a fancy gateau, which some in her family might have preferred. But in the end she decided the modern tongue was rarely given the delicate pleasure of just three basic ingredients – egg, milk, sugar. Today's baked custard paid homage to a lost era.

She thought of Pa as she placed the baked custard on the tray. He would have called it dirt pudding because of the nutmeg sprinkled across the top. She must tell Tom and Jaxon; they'd get a kick out of that.

Nick and Jorja were in the kitchen with Grace, rinsing the dishes Susan had cleared.

'You'll have to go and see them. They're awesome,' Nick said.

Their voices were a pleasant background noise after the orchestra of sound at a table of twelve. There, the falsettos competed against the baritones, and Jane's alcohol-induced caterwauling periodically cut across them all like a cymbal.

'Mum won't let me go to concerts. Not until I'm sixteen.'

'She's probably right. But, hey, when you are, I'll take you to see them.'

'Sweet.'

Their talk moved next to the latest movies they'd seen. Grace started to polish the dessert spoons, content to remain on the outskirts of their conversation. It was a steady stream of popular culture, which required words like *awesome* and *sweet* to describe;

modern derivatives of her children's *groovy* and *cool* or her own *beaut* and *bonza*. They let their guard down with their parents absent from the room, and allowed the odd *bullshit* or *wanker* to slip into their talk as well. Maybe they thought she was *awesome* enough not to mind what they said.

Grace ran the tea towel over the curve of the next dessert spoon. She was pleased to see the metal could still be brought to a shine after the number of desserts it had brought to the many tongues that had licked it clean. She set the spoon on top of another on the tray, allowed the handles to spread out like Kath's open fan. She took the next one from the pile on the bench and started to massage its curved surface between thumb and fingers with the cloth.

Like Nick and Jorja now, when Grace's children were small they could easily ignore an adult audience, as they brought to life the fantasy worlds their imaginations created. They'd invited imaginary friends to staged tea parties, set up hospitals under bed-sheet roofs, or created jungle wildernesses behind potted plants. Claire had been the best at it. She could free up her inhibitions as readily as any actress on a stage, and provided the perfect voiceover for her make-believe friends and toy animals, granting them varying degrees of bliss or peril at a whim.

Watch out, there's a hyena after you, she'd say to a plastic monkey as her small hand made it lope across the carpet, plastic dog chasing it in the other hand, or

Quick Alice, hide! she'd breathe urgently to no one over her shoulder.

Grace listened to these adventures being played out as she went about her work, as keenly as she had listened to *Blue Hills* when it was broadcast on the radio. Staying tuned, as it were, for the next instalment of a young and creative mind happy to escape reality.

Grace had loved this motherly invisibility.

And she too knew an imaginary place, a dark and comfortable refuge she'd created, where she would breathe deeply of Claire and pretend she always could. To think of this place now, right or wrong, reminded her of Des.

One day their journey home from the beach was particularly hot, slow and uncomfortable. Each had salt-crusted and sunburnt skin that stuck to the vinyl car seats. Des hunkered over the wheel, muttered at various speeding drivers and braked regularly. Grace quietly drummed her fingers on the door's armrest, the only outlet she had for her frustration. Searching for a new station on the car's radio or increasing the volume was taboo, as was playing a game of I Spy. About the only game Des allowed was the one where each competed against the other to see who could make their boiled lolly last the longest – a dull but quiet distraction, intended as much to keep the lolly tin full as to create calm.

Claire sat in her usual spot in the middle of the back seat. They each had an ice-cream cone, bought from a van before they left the beach. Peter had finished his quickly then kicked at the back of Grace's seat as he fidgeted about, trying to get comfortable. Susan stroked her father's shoulder as she licked hers. Claire, who declared ice cream her favourite thing of all, even though the icy cold gave her a headache, ate hers slowly. Watery trails of melted ice cream travelled down her cone. She tried to keep up with the flow, but in the heat of the car was hard pressed to do so.

The car laboured uphill and Des crunched the column shift down a gear, then turned to check his outside lane.

'Claire, you're making a bloody mess with that thing.'

'I'm trying not to. But it's melting quicker than I can eat it.'

'Just hurry up and finish the thing or I'll throw it out.'

'But it makes my head hurt if I eat it quick.'

Grace rummaged round for a handkerchief in her bag but for once couldn't find one. Claire licked fast like a kitten but still the melting ice cream beat her down the cone. She cupped it in both hands to stem the flow. Des cranked up a gear again, and risked quick looks into the rear-vision mirror from time to time to check her progress. 'Finished that thing yet?' he'd ask.

'Nearly,' she replied, but Grace could see she was a long way off.

Despite their ice-cream treat, Peter and Susan were tetchy in the heat.

'Claire, keep your legs on your side.'

'I can't. Peter's got his spread wide.'

'Have not.'

'Have so.'

'Have n—'

'That's enough,' Des bellowed.

'Why don't you let me drive, Des?'

'Bloody women. Always tryin' to put their men in the back seat.'

'I'm only thinking of how tired you must be after the big day.'

'I'm fine. Now quiet. I'm concentrating on the road.'

'Cla-ire, shift your legs.'

'I can't.' Claire took one hand off her cone to budge Susan's leg back.

'Get your sticky hands off me. And look you've dripped it all over the seat now. Da-ad, she's making a mess.'

'Am not.' Claire clamped both hands on the cone again and wiggled her bottom across to hide the drips on the seat.

'You have so. Look – here.'

'Give it to me.' Des risked a hand off the steering wheel and held it out to Claire.

'Oh, Des. She's trying to eat it as quickly as possible. It's hot. Let her have it.'

'Not if she's makin' a mess in the car with it. Come on – give it here before you cause an accident.'

Claire fought back tears as she passed the soggy cone to her father.

'Here,' he said, and thrust it towards Grace. 'Wind your window down and throw it out.'

'I'm not doing your dirty work.'

'Well, I can't. I'm drivin'.'

Grace took the cone from him, turned and handed it back to Claire. 'I won't throw a child's ice cream out, not when they've done nothing wrong.'

Des mumbled something about who'd be cleaning the seat and hunkered back over the wheel. Quiet took hold in the car after that, leaving Des to focus on little more than his nerves.

Half an hour into the homeward journey and it was time for the first smoko stop. Grace was hopeful as Des pulled into a shallow lay-by off the highway that, having got this far, he might make it home without a second stop.

'Can we get out, Daddy?' Susan asked. 'I've got sand in my togs.'

'So long as you don't bug me while I have me smoke.'

'Keep on my side of the car,' Grace called.

All three children filed out from the back, leaving lines of sand in the seams of the seat, which Grace thought made the ice-cream drips inconsequential. The children milled around Grace's window, un-sticking swimming costumes and hooking sand out from seams and folds with their fingers. Des took up his post on the bonnet, tobacco tin on the hood beside him. With his back to them all, he gazed off into the scrub, plumes of smoke rising above his head. Grace wound down her window and turned up Elton John's 'Rocket Man' on the radio. She rested her head on the seat back and hummed along, eyes closed. The children's chatter and the passing of cars merged into white noise as she dozed.

'In the car!' Des called.

Grace was startled from her lull. She pulled herself upright.

Susan, shrewd enough to notice before he called that her father had almost finished his cigarette, was already at the car door.

'I'm sitting behind Mum,' she taunted, and got in behind Grace. She slammed the door on her victory and pushed down the lock.

'That's not fair. I had the sun on my face all the way to the beach and I'm not gonna have it all the way home as well.' Peter stood beside Susan's door, banging on the glass. 'Lemme in.' His fists worked at the glass. 'Let – me – in!'

Susan poked her tongue out at Peter.

'Come on, Peter. Hop round the other side, there's a good lad. It's not long now and we'll be home.'

Peter ignored Grace, stood his ground, banging on the glass.

'Come on. You can have first pick from the lolly tin. How's that sound?'

'I don't want a lolly. I – want – my – seat!'

Claire stood on the driver's side, ready to get in. 'You can have the middle if you want, Peter.'

'Don't want the middle. Wanna sit behind Mum.'

'I've had about as much of this as I can stand.' Des got off the bonnet with more speed than Grace had seen in him all day.

Too quick for even Peter to rethink his tantrum, he got to the boy, grabbed him by the arm and man-handled him round the back of the car to the other side.

'Out of the way, Claire. He can sit in the bloody middle now. That'll teach him a lesson.'

Peter, whose indignation was poorly controlled at the best of times, thrashed about trying to wrench himself free from his father's grip. Claire, seeing the tumultuous lashing of arms and legs coming her way, stepped back from the car to avoid being caught up in the fray.

Grace craned her neck round to follow the spectacle. 'Des, just let him get in on his own,' she pleaded. 'And you can take that smirk off your face, young lady. You're no little Miss Innocent in all of this.'

'He deserved it. He's a big bully.'

'Dad's the bully,' Claire yelled at Susan. 'And you're a nasty girl who starts fights.'

'Shut up, Claire,' Des roared.

'Yeah, shut up, Claire,' Susan mimicked.

'Des, please. Let him go.'

Tears of rage and frustration streaked Peter's red face and snot bubbles glistened at his nostrils. But he never faltered in his determination to break free – equalled only by Des's determination to best the boy.

'Des, please. Claire, come back from the road.'

Almost to the open door by now, Peter gave one final frenzied scrabble, and lashed out with his un-pincered arm against Des's grip. Des, losing any sense of control he might still have had, and with the superhuman strength of the enraged, swung Peter round by the arm, legs flying out as they did when he'd swing him by the hands, playfully, in the back-yard. Grace, terrified, thought he meant to slam the boy into the side of the car.

'Des! Stop it!'

Peter's feet went wide and struck Claire full on in the chest, sending her reeling backwards. Her little face looked stunned by the blow as she stumbled back on unsteady legs towards the road. Des and Peter were oblivious, so intent was each on victory, but Grace watched it all as if in slow motion.

Claire had no time to recover from the blow from her brother before she was hit by the oncoming car with such force that she was ripped from Grace's view in an instant. Grace turned to watch her youngest child tumble and roll down the bitumen like a rag doll thrown from the window of a passing car.

'Claire!' she screamed, though she couldn't hear herself, only the sound of blood pulsing in her ears.

In that moment Grace became two people – one who acted and one who observed as though from above. She saw herself scrabbling to open the car door and then slipping in the gravel in her flimsy sandals as she rushed to get to Claire, a misshapen bundle fifteen yards up the road. Grace the nurse ran but the other Grace, the one watching, didn't want to arrive at her destination.

When nurse Grace got to her twisted and bloodied child, she knelt in the dust, felt for a pulse and put her ear close to Claire's torn mouth to see if she was breathing. This Grace stuck a finger inside the bloodied cavity, hooked a tongue forward and cleared away tiny broken teeth.

The watching Grace was fearful to touch her child. She could see she'd already suffered enough pain and to lay a finger on her now, to hold her, would only add more.

Nurse Grace alternated between compressing the child's chest and forcing short, sharp breaths into her damaged mouth. This Grace, the one with wide pupils and a clinician's nerve, ignored the salty taste of blood on her lips.

Watching Grace knelt too and placed her hand on the crown of her child's head, flinched at the boggy scalp she could feel under the blood-wet hair. 'Claire?' this other, watchful Grace whispered. 'My beautiful little girl. What have they done to you?'

Nurse Grace kept working at heart and lungs as an uneasy and assorted collection of legs and shoes gathered around her to witness this pain between mother and child.

'Has somebody gone to phone an ambulance?' Grace demanded between frantic breaths and compressions.

'Yes,' the owner of one set of shoes answered. 'A bloke's run to the house up the road.'

'God, she just came out of nowhere. Nowhere.'

'Poor little mite.'

Watching Grace wished they'd all go away, that she could have these moments with Claire alone to tell her the things she'd remember.

Nurse Grace didn't stop until she felt the touch of an ambulance officer's hand on her shoulder. His fingers curled around her bony joint and gripped it tenderly as a lover might. She knew then that what she was doing was pointless, probably knew it all along but couldn't stop while the decision was hers to make.

Grace became more like her watchful self then, though it would be years before the two could come together again and confront what had blown them apart. Tenderly, gently, she scooped Claire's small body into her arms and pulled her against her chest. She gripped her flaccid hand, pressed it to her cheek, her lips, and tasted the summer-sweetness of ice cream. She rocked her to and fro as she'd done when she was first born, until her sunburnt arms started to cool.

Des, never a brave man, rested his head on his arms on the bonnet of the car while two small terrified faces looked over him from the back seat.

After Claire's death Grace had started to turn her crazy circles and sit at the kitchen table trying to read the stories etched in its top while the moon shifted across the sky.

She wasn't sure now how long she'd retreated into this dark madness for, but it was long enough for Susan to start her period and Peter to learn to shave. Sure, she would have bought the sanitary napkins and the shaving brush and soap stick but any recollection of doing so was lost. Just as she couldn't recall cleaning the house during this dark time or washing or ironing or cooking, though she supposed the house had been tidy and her family ate.

Gradually, the lights had come back on. It started like a sliver of daylight forcing its way through the gaps of a closed door. Those gaps steadily became wider and wider as the door was allowed to drift further ajar.

Eventually Grace could see everything clearly again, though the terrain had changed. The first thing she noticed was that few of her clothes fitted her anymore, most hanging loose at the waist or shoulders.

The second was that her two surviving children had grown much taller than she remembered and that they were timid around her. The third thing she noticed was that Des had gone grey.

Now Grace took an involuntary step back, but continued buffing the remaining dessert spoon with the tea towel. The concave side of it was face-up. She was mirrored upside down there, the features of the room distorted around her. Flipping it over, she was the right way up again.

Nick was carrying the heavy dessert tray to the dining room. Grace followed him in as Meg called, 'Yummy! What's for dessert?'

'There might not be any,' Susan teased.

'There's always dessert at Grandma's house,' the three youngest chorused down their end of the table.

'That's right,' Grace said, gathering her voice up, 'there's always dessert at Grandma's house.'

What would happen when all the old-fashioned grandmas went the same way as the word pudding? Grace wondered.

Nick placed the tray on the table.

'Delicious,' Kath said. 'Baked custard. I haven't had one of those in years.'

'Yes, ageless appeal,' Ada agreed.

'Just the mango for me, thanks.'

'Of course, Richard.'

'I'll pass.' Jane sucked in her stomach and ran her hand down her front. 'Or it'll be a double gym session tomorrow.'

'A small serve, thanks Mum.' Susan nodded.

'With ice cream. And lots of it, thanks, Grandma.'

Grace dished out spoons of this and that to suit everybody's tastes.

With the last bowl served, she said, 'Before we start, I'd like to propose a toast.'

'You can't call your own birthday toast,' Peter joked. 'That's my job.'

'I'm not toasting me.'

'Who then – the Queen?' Susan joked.

'No. I'd like to propose a toast to Claire. I don't think she's ever received one.'

The table went quiet, except for Meg, who said, 'Who's Claire?'

Peter and Susan looked into their dessert bowls. Richard and Jane fidgeted with napkins or placemats. And the grandchildren looked from one to the other, unsure what was expected of them. Kath and Ada shared fond, thoughtful smiles with Grace.

Ada was first to break the silence. 'What a lovely idea, Grace.'

The three old friends lifted their glasses high. Richard and Jane followed, Peter and Susan were next – and the children, not really knowing what was going on, did the same with their tumblers of fizzy drink.

'To Claire,' Grace said.

A chorus followed, *To Claire.*

'And here's to you too, Grace.' Kath raised her glass again. 'Happy seventieth!'

Grace took a second sip from her glass, then picked up her shiny dessert spoon and allowed the metal to slide through the soft custard. There was no ice cream in her bowl, she hadn't eaten it since that day all those years ago.

'Who's Claire?' Meg asked again.

'A dead aunty,' Jane whispered. 'Let Mummy try a tinsy bit of yours, Meg.' Jane reached across the table, spoon outstretched.

Meg ignored her mother. 'I didn't know we had a dead aunty.'

Jane leant in and answered Meg so quietly, all Grace could hear was *busy road* and *accident.*

16

Any sweetness left in the day was lost. Susan stabbed at her baked custard. Peter ate his slowly, quietly, as if fixated on the task. When he'd emptied his bowl, he asked for seconds then ate it the same way. Maybe he wanted to make his way through all that was left.

Jane remained true to her refusal of dessert and hummed some invented tune. Richard, meanwhile, ate his mango slowly, in spoon-length portions.

The younger children grew restless at the table once the ice cream was back in the freezer, so Nick and Jorja led them outdoors for a game.

'I guess that's the eating over and done with.' Richard sat back, hands linked behind his head.

Susan flared. 'You make it sound like a chore.'

'Don't get me wrong, I enjoyed the meal. But you know me, eating's a means to an end.'

'A productive end, Richie?'

Susan was in no mood to laugh with Jane. 'I wish you'd let me know that before we put all the effort in to prepare it. I'd have given you a glass of water instead.'

Peter gave Richard a slap on the back, propelling his brother-in-law forward. 'Lucky we blokes have broad shoulders, mate.'

Abruptly gathering together the empty dessert bowls, Susan clattered one on top of the other, not bothering to separate the spoons from between each.

Grace felt sorry for Richard. She didn't think his shoulders would ever be broad enough for some of Susan's comments.

'Here, let me clear those, Susan. You've done enough today.' Grace took up Ada's bowl and put it on top of her own.

Susan didn't answer, kept stacking dirty dishes instead.

'Come on, I can do—'

'I heard what you said.'

'Ooh, some-one's get-ting tetch-y.'

'Oh, shut up, Jane. Here, suck on another bottle, why don't you.' Susan thumped the last unfinished bottle of wine in front of her sister-in-law. 'Wanna straw?'

Richard looked at Susan, shocked. Ada and Kath each made a labour of carefully folding their napkins. Peter laughed softly.

The sound of the doorbell cut across the quiet.

'Headline,' Jane said with a dramatic swipe of her arm. 'Family feud saved by bell.' She looked pleased with her joke, and she refilled her glass.

Susan started loading up the dessert tray while Grace went to answer the door.

Standing on the Welcome mat was Ada's son.

'Max – I thought you were going to ring first?'

'Sorry – I forgot. Aren't you done?'

'No. We haven't had coffee yet.'

'Close then.'

'Depends on how many cups your mother would like. You might as well come in.' Grace held the door open for him. She needed to busy her hands, which itched to reach out and smack him.

'Just for a minute. She might have to skip the coffee. I've got my instructions – one kid here, another there and Mum home somewhere in the middle of it.'

Scraps of time thrown about like bread crusts to birds; the noisiest, bossiest ones got the most.

'First on the right,' she said, letting him past. 'In case you've forgotten.'

'Hi all.' Max held his hand up to greet those at the table like a policeman stopping traffic. 'Sorry to disturb.'

'Oh. Is it that time already?' Ada said.

''Fraid so, Mum. I've got a lot of running around to do this evening.'

'Got time for a quick drink, Max, while Mum gets Ada sorted?'

'Sorry. Can't, Pete. I'm in a bit of a rush.'

Ada tensed under Grace's hand with the pain of movement as she helped her up from the chair. 'Don't rush, Ada. Time can stand still for a few minutes.'

'Good – I'm a bit stiff from sitting so long.'

Once upright, Ada stood as tall as she could.

'I'll start making my way to the car then. Bye, everyone.'

Getting up, Kath hugged her friend. 'See you soon. Lunch at yours next?'

'Do I have to wait for my birthday?'

'Definitely not.'

Susan came round and embraced Ada, but it was quick, distracted; her flurry of *There, there* pats to Ada's back conveyed little warmth.

'Hope you feel better soon,' she said, going back to stacking the tray.

Richard stood. 'Don't forget what I said about alternating those two analgesics. I think you'll find that'll work a treat.' He shook Ada's hand, encasing her smaller one in the two of his.

Then came Jane, who'd left her drink behind to enwrap Ada. She was almost tearful as she said, 'I think you're beautiful, even with bruises.'

Caught up with Max in talk of results from the previous night's game of cricket, Peter gave Ada a wave that looked more like a salute.

'Watch out for those mirrors, eh?'

Grace and Ada left the house as they'd entered it, arm in arm, down the front steps and onto the footpath. Grace cleared a juice box from their way with her foot.

'You didn't have to bring me all the way,' Ada said.

'I needed some air.'

Ada looked at Grace, eyebrow cocked.

'The day's been a strange one cooped up inside.'

'Turning seventy not what you thought it'd be?'

'I don't know what I thought it'd be.'

They stopped beside Max's car. As far as the eye could see, the nature strip on either side of the road was covered with mounds of rubbish.

Ada followed Grace's gaze. 'It's a neglected landscape, isn't it? Do you think people even see the mess anymore?'

Grace shook her head. 'I doubt it.'

'You've already got her there,' Max called from the front porch. 'For a couple of old girls you've got a half-decent spring to your step.'

'Do they not hear themselves?' Ada said to Grace.

'Not with our ears.'

The two friends embraced.

'Enjoy what's left of your birthday.'

'I'll try.' Grace opened the car door for Ada, helped her in.

Max got into the driver's seat. 'All tucked in, are we?'

'It's a car, Max, not a bed,' Grace said.

'Let's get Cinderella home then,' he said, and found reverse.

Grace closed Ada's door then stood back from the car as it pulled out from the kerb. Ada waved as Max drove away, her battered face small behind the glass.

Back inside, Susan was at the sink, back turned, rinsing the bowls.

'Thanks, Susan. You've been a great help today. But leave all of those now. I can clean up in here later when everyone's gone.'

Susan kept rinsing. 'I've started now.'

With the day growing long and Grace's patience growing short, she'd lost the energy to jolly her daughter along. 'Suit yourself.' She took a clean tea towel from the drawer and waited while Susan rinsed the last of the bowls then filled the sink with hot water.

Grace could see Susan was angry. She wore it in the ropey tightness of her neck and the muscular tic in her jaw, one of the many ways Susan reminded Grace of Des. There was a part of Grace that wanted to ignore her daughter's thin lips and rigid shoulders, her fierce pumping of the dishwashing brush inside a glass, four, five, six times more than necessary. The other part – the mother – thought she should try to coax her out of it.

'It's been a lovely day,' Grace lied.

'I'm glad you've enjoyed it.'

Grace picked up the glass Susan had placed upside down on the sink, stuffed the tea towel inside it. Susan started her pumping action on the next one.

'Maybe you're right though – a restaurant would have been easier.' Grace fished, cautiously.

Susan shrugged. 'Too late now.' She placed the next glass on the sink, set to work on another.

'Jane'll have a thumper tomorrow.'

'Oh, I don't know – she usually pulls up all right.'

Grace was quiet, unsure of what to try next. She put the glass she was drying on the bench, picked up the next one, forced the tea towel inside it, and twisted. She stepped forward to place it on the bench alongside the other and budged her sandalled toe up against something sharp near the kickboard. She looked down and saw it was a broken section from the donkey dish. The missing eye. A small drop of blood oozed from her little toe where she'd kicked it. She bent down and picked the jagged triangle up from the floor, held it in her hand a moment.

'Must be the last of it,' she said, and set it on the window ledge.

Susan stopped her pumping action inside the glass and stared back at that indignant little eye. After a moment she pulled her gloved hands from the water, flicked the suds from them, then took the broken piece of china from the ledge. She walked to the bin and threw it in. The lid slammed shut with a tinny crash.

'It is now,' she said.

Grace looked at her daughter, hurt. 'That's something your father would have done.'

'Well, he was a practical man too.'

'There's practical then there's heartless.'

'Heartless?' Susan turned on Grace.

Grace said nothing. She picked up the next glass and stuffed the tea towel inside. She turned it round and round until the tight ball of cloth started to squeak against the glass.

'You're the one who pulled the let's-make-a-toast-to-Claire stunt. Not me. I can't believe that after all this time you're still hell-bent on making us feel guilty. And you think I'm heartless.' Susan dropped a serving bowl into the sudsy water. It was an old one and Grace sensed the already deep crazing give a little more as it knocked against the metal sink.

Susan wasn't about to stop there. 'You weren't the only one hurting after she died, you know. We all lost something that day.'

Grace stiffened.

Susan added more hot water to the sink. She turned the tap on so forcefully it sprayed water up the front of her silk shirt.

'I had nightmares for months afterwards. I kept seeing the way you held on to her at the side of the road. It was almost as if you were trying to consume her, absorb her back into your body in some way. It freaked me out.'

Susan ran the dishwashing brush round and round

the bowl so fast that it started a whirlpool in the sink.

'I always doubted you'd hold me the same.' She made a sound that could have been a discordant laugh or a choked sob.

'Of course I would have.' Grace spoke automatically. Grace didn't see if Susan believed her because she couldn't look at her daughter.

'Nobody could get near you afterwards.' Susan set the serving bowl upside down on the draining board, took up another one, ran the brush round it more calmly, started on the plates. Grace kept up her own steady action of turning the dish she was drying between fingers and thumb, more times and with greater care than necessary.

'It was as though you'd left us too. If it wasn't for Dad, I don't know what we'd have done. He kept us safe – in here.' Susan tapped her head. Her finger left a small collection of popping foam on her hair. 'He hugged us. Talked to us. Told us we had nothing to do with what happened. But not you. You never said a word. Never tried to take the pain away.'

Grace remained quiet. She picked up a plate, started drying the face of it. What would people do without these mundane tasks to occupy them during such conversations? Where would they look? What would they do with their hands?

'I remember how some days I'd rush home from school to tell you about something that had happened and you'd go through the motions of listening. You'd stop whatever you were doing and face me, but you never listened with your eyes. Dad did though. He'd get down on one knee, just so I could see he was looking right at me. *Tell me, love,* he'd say. *Tell me all about it.* But you cooked. Boy, did you cook.' Susan's laugh was at odds with her tense shoulders. 'I'd come in from school and there'd be fresh biscuits or cakes on the table even though the lot you'd made the day before were still in their tins. There'd be soups or casseroles on the stove, pies or puddings in the oven and custard or sauces to go with everything. You must have been at it all day. It didn't feel like a caring, motherly act though. It seemed more like madness.'

Grace felt like an alien visiting her life, the way Susan was telling it. 'I think I must have had some kind of breakdown.' Grace's voice sounded old and feeble to her ears. 'Much of that time's a dark blot on my memory.'

Susan looked at her in a way that reminded Grace trust was a hard-won thing.

'It's the truth,' she said.

'Well, what I remember is how you'd pile Dad's plate up high with food and watch him empty it, and then you'd add more. I don't think he knew how to tell you he was full, like he didn't feel he could. He put it all down to you needing to keep yourself busy, so he went along with it, ate everything you gave him. I think he believed he was keeping you happy that way.'

'I was just doing my job,' Grace said.

'In spades.'

Grace looked away from Susan's gaze. She put the plate she was drying down on the bench carefully and took up another from the draining board.

'And the lock on Claire's wardrobe door – do you remember that?' Susan asked.

Grace nodded. That, she remembered.

'I'd stare at it and imagine you'd put her body in there and that one night the door would fall open and she'd come tumbling out. I'd lie awake for hours some nights thinking about what she'd look like.'

Grace had started to tremble a little. She put the plate on top of the last, barely dried, fearful she'd drop it.

'Part of me was desperate to steal the key to see what you were hiding. If you hadn't kept the damn thing round your neck the whole time I probably would have.'

Susan rested her gloved hands on the edge of the sink, looked right at Grace. 'You let her death ruin your marriage. How could you do that? He never understood it.'

'It was already on its way to ruin. He never understood that.'

'It was not.'

'How would you know? It wasn't your marriage.'

'You should have patched it up. Other women lose children and don't let their lives fall apart.'

'Maybe their children didn't die the way Claire

died. And nor did their husbands handle it the way mine did.'

'He had to do something. You weren't capable.'

Capable and grief – did they go together?

'You remember her sheets?' Susan asked.

'Yes – I remember her sheets.' Grace spoke quietly. She took yet another plate from the draining board with care, barely trusting herself to hold it but needing her hands to be busy.

'It wasn't fair. I could still smell her in the room.'

'So could I.'

She'd wanted to keep every skerrick that smelt of Claire. With Des, she scrubbed the place from top to bottom after he died, several times over, just to get rid of the smell of him – his stale tobacco, his old sweat, the California Poppy he used to oil his hair that left a grimy halo on his pillow. She washed curtains, blankets, quilts, and those things that refused to give up his scent – his pillow, his chair cushion, the clothes she couldn't give away – she burnt in the incinerator down the back. It seemed a just act.

'And I knew you slept in her bed during the day, even though you tried to hide it by straightening the covers again. I put threads across the bedspread because I had to know for sure. They were nearly always disturbed when I got in from school.'

Grace looked at the blue concentric rings that patterned the plate she was drying. Through moist eyes the colour blurred like a spinning roulette wheel.

She'd run a finger round and round the small blood spots on Claire's bottom sheet, from a scab she'd have picked. Most days they'd blurred too. Some were the shape of Tasmania, others were more like Britain. She'd loved the indelibility of those spots, even as they faded to a dirty brown, tracing their permanence while she breathed deeply of Claire's breath on the pillow.

'I needed something of her.'

'But what about us? Did you care what we needed? It was like sleeping in the same room as a ghost. If it wasn't for Dad letting me fall asleep on the sofa each night and carrying me to bed later, I'd have gone mad with my fear of that room.'

'Why fear? She was your sister – a child.'

'Mum, I was eleven. Ghosts aren't fond memories at that age. They're things with fangs and claws that jump out from dark places or suck the breath from your lungs while you sleep.'

'But I couldn't just give her up – not that quickly.'

'It'd been more than a year.'

'Only a year.'

'Dad did the right thing – getting rid of it all. It was time.'

It's time, Grace. She could still hear his words along with the splintering of the wardrobe. She'd clutched at the key on its chain round her neck, refusing, still, to give it up even as the crowbar did its work. And she watched as the clothes and shoes and drawings and books clattered to the floor when it sprang open.

'No, he did not do the right thing.' Grace slammed the blue plate on the bench. It broke in two. 'It was too soon. Much too soon.'

Nick was on the back patio when the plate broke. He came to the back door, stood with the flyscreen between him and the kitchen. Susan had her back to him; only Grace could see his troubled face.

'Everything all right?' he asked.

'Mum,' Susan's voice gentled, 'it was always going to be too soon for you, but it needed to be done.'

Grace closed her eyes to Susan and shook her head.

17

When Grace opened her eyes again she saw Peter had come into the room and that Nick now stood on the kitchen side of the screen door. Peter leant up against a wall, legs crossed at the ankles, hands dug deep in his pockets. He looked at the floor in a state of rare quietness. Grace was reminded of the insecure boy he could be. Nick seemed young, uncertain, caught in the crossfire of adult discontent.

'What's going on?' He looked from Grace to Susan and Peter. 'Gran?'

Grace reached out and gripped the back of a chair. She pulled it out and sat heavily. Years of fatigue weighted her bones.

'What have you been saying to her?' Nick came up to Grace, placed a hand on her shoulder. The weight of it was comforting.

'You're too young to understand what this is about, Nick. I suggest you go back outside to the others.'

'Do as your aunt says. Go.'

'There's no way I'm leaving Gran alone in here with you two.' Nick pulled out the chair beside Grace and sat down. 'What you say to her, you say to me.' He stabbed a finger in his father's direction then brought it back to touch his own chest. But all the while one leg bounced nervously under the table. Grace reached out and steadied it. She took strength from the action.

She looked from Susan to Peter. 'Your father had no right to do what he did. It wasn't for him to decide when it was time. It was for me to decide. What he did was wrong.'

Peter and Susan pulled themselves up tall, ready to disagree, Grace supposed, but she wouldn't be put off.

'And the only reason he did what he did was because he wanted to clear his conscience. By getting rid of everything that belonged to Claire he could pretend she never existed.'

'That's not true.' Susan snapped off her dish-washing gloves and threw them on the bench. 'He got rid of everything to give us all a fresh start.'

'You can't just strike a line under a child's death, Susan – write a new kind of beginning to suit yourself.'

'Granddad got rid of everything of Aunty Claire's?'

Grace nodded at Nick. 'Burnt it.'

Nick winced. 'Harsh.'

'Yes,' Grace said. 'Harsh.'

'It's not exactly as your grandmother says. Mum was a wreck, wasn't she?' Peter looked to Susan, who nodded. 'We were suffering. Dad made a tough call to help everyone get back on track.'

Susan added her pitch. 'And he thought the best way to do that was to clear the house of painful reminders.'

'Rubbish! It had nothing to do with helping either of you, or me. It was about helping himself.'

'Do you seriously think it was a decision he made lightly?' Susan asked. 'And he didn't get rid of everything. He left all the photographs. You still had those.'

But they weren't enough. They only showed Claire as a little girl in shades of grey, and she was every colour other than grey. They'd had no fragrance.

Des had wiped out Claire's scent.

'It was time for all of us to move on, Mum.'

'Yes. Time,' Peter agreed.

Nick looked confused. 'Excuse me if I sound a bit thick, but are there rules about this sort of thing or something? Did somebody write a book telling everybody how they're supposed to act when someone dies?'

'You're too young to understand,' Peter said.

'You had to be there,' Susan added.

'Young – yes. Ignorant – probably. But let's look at things the way I see it.' Nick wrapped his arms around salt and pepper containers, empty dip packets and a half-finished packet of Starburst sweets left on the table. He drew them in towards him. 'We've got Granddad here ...' he set the pepper mill out on its own, 'telling everybody *It's time.*' He added italics to the words with a matching pair of rabbit-eared fingers. 'Then we've got two kids siding with their dad ...' he shifted the salt pot and the empty baba ganoush dip container alongside the pepper, 'because, understandably, they're upset and want the whole thing to go aw—'

'This isn't some bloody game, Nick.'

'Leave him,' Grace snapped at Peter.

Nick looked at Grace. She nodded, and he continued. 'Then right over here ...' he moved the empty cream cheese container to the other side of the table, 'we've got somebody whose child has died ...' he laid the packet of Starburst sweets between the divided groups, 'being told to get over it.' Nick looked at the scene he'd created and shook his head.

For the first time Claire's death brought a faint smile to Grace's lips. Claire would love it that she'd been depicted by a packet of Starbursts. She'd always had an insatiably sweet tooth.

'You're interfering in adult business. Just leave, will you.'

'Excuse me, but I am an adult, Dad. And I'm not budging.'

'Why are you always threatened by people who don't do things your way – your father's way?' Grace fixed her gaze on Peter. When he didn't answer, she turned to Susan. 'And if it had been you and not Claire, I would have kept your sheets on the bed, your wardrobe locked and full of your precious things.'

Peter and Susan looked anywhere but at Grace.

'Nick's right. There's no right or wrong way to grieve, just as there's no *decent* amount of time for it to go on.' Grace copied her grandson's rabbit-eared fingers.

'Just as it's not decent to keep blaming us,' Susan said.

'I've never blamed either of you. You were children.'

'Dad then.' Peter said. 'You've got to stop blaming him.'

'Because that hurts us,' Susan added, 'given he was the only one trying to protect us afterwards.'

Grace didn't know that she could stop blaming Des. In a strange way she'd taken comfort from knowing who was responsible for Claire's death.

'Why's anybody blaming anybody?' Nick asked. 'It was an accident, wasn't it?'

'Yes, an accident,' Peter said.

'A terrible accident.'

'No, it wasn't. It should never have happened.'

'But it did, Mum,' Susan said. 'And we can't change that, only how we live with it.'

Nick looked from Susan to Grace to Peter. He seemed confused by this mixture of gravity and anger, and sensed, perhaps, there was more to it than his nineteen years allowed him to grasp, so remained quiet.

'It was such a long time ago now,' Susan continued, softly. 'You've got to let it go.' Her words hung in the kitchen.

But if she let Des off, declared Claire's death a tragedy of circumstance, it would reduce it to just another senseless loss. To be able to pinpoint the moment, the events, which led to it had kept Grace grounded all these years. The alternative would be to have spent a lifetime asking the air around her *How? Why?* which would likely have sent her mad permanently.

Nick spoke now, having thought his way to a new understanding. 'Maybe they've got a point, Gran. Anger's like a poison if you don't get rid of it.'

She studied her grandson's stubbled and studded face. Such a rough exterior, but inside so gentle. What if Des *had* still had something of this softness inside him behind his coarse, indifferent exterior? What if it really was a gentler man who'd got rid of Claire's things, genuinely believing he was doing everybody a favour?

Grace thought back to when each of her children was born. When Des first saw Peter, he'd looked at her, still exhausted and sore from delivering him, and said, 'You've done well, doll. He's a little beauty.' He then laid a gentle hand on her cheek, kissed her, allowed his face to linger against hers a while. She remembered how his chin was smooth and smelt of Sunlight soap; his palm soft, careful. He did the same thing three times over and each time that tender act offered a sweet release from the war of her labour.

Thinking again about the day he'd gathered together all the traces of Claire and carried them out of the house in a hessian sack like unwanted kittens ... there'd been wet streaks on his cheeks; she'd never seen that before. And they were still there when he came back in, some time later, smelling of smoke and looking older.

Grace sighed with the weight of such thoughts. Had she allowed herself to be poisoned by her anger, as Nick suggested? If so, then her children had allowed themselves to be also ...

'Have the pair of you been able to put your father's death aside, as you expect me to do with Claire's?' she asked. 'A fresh start is the ticket to recovery you say, but I wonder, does that apply to all of us?'

Susan and Peter didn't answer. But Grace knew her point wasn't lost: each of them shifted their gaze around the room.

She answered for them. 'No. I thought as much. There are two sets of rules – one for you and one for me.'

'But this is where we come to remember him,' Susan said. 'This was his home ...'

Peter went ahead: 'And it's not right his place being taken by somebody else.'

'Who's taken whose place?'

Grace reckoned she could answer Nick's question in a word. 'Jack.'

'Who's Jack?'

'A friend,' Grace said.

'A boyfriend?'

'I suppose you could call him that.'

Jorja came in and filled a glass with water from a jug in the fridge. She downed it in one. 'You coming back out, Nick? I'm getting slaughtered by those midgets.'

Nick was too distracted to answer. 'I never knew you had a boyfriend.'

'Who's got a boyfriend?' Jorja asked.

'Gran has.'

'Cool. What's his name?'

'Jack, apparently.'

'Is he handsome?' Jorja rested her elbows on the island bench, eyes bright with the prospect of gossipy girl-talk as she looked at Grace.

'Jorja,' Susan snapped, 'I don't think that's really relev—'

'At my age?' Grace cut in.

Peter tried to take charge. 'I think it's high time all children left the room. Now.'

'Oh, I get it.' Nick looked from stern-faced father to sullen aunt. 'You two don't like it.'

'Why wouldn't they like it?' Jorja asked. 'Grand-dad's been dead for years, hasn't he?'

'No bloody respect,' Peter blustered.

'Dad, when are you going to learn bullying us is a waste of time? Sooner or later we all end up ignoring you and you just sound like some old bleating sheep lost down the back of a paddock.'

Grace liked the analogy. So would Pa.

'Why isn't he here today, Grandma?'

Grace didn't speak, but Nick saw the answer.

'Because there are two sets of rules, Jorja.'

18

Neither of her children could look at her; Grace saw it in the brisk way they undertook tasks, and how they'd defaulted to over-politeness.

Nick and Jorja had gone back outside, though Grace wished they hadn't: their straightforward way of interpreting the past was refreshing.

'Paper plates would have been the ticket.' Peter slung a tea towel over one shoulder then stacked the last of the dried plates together. He looked as ungainly as Des would have on the end of a feather duster. 'Though I expect Nick and Jorja would've had something to say about that, now they've gone completely green on us. Which cupboard?' he asked Grace, lifting the weighty pile from the bench.

'They're from the china cabinet in the dining room. Leave them there. I can put them away later.'

'It's okay. Dining room it is.' He left the room with

the crockery, tea towel still in place, escape perfectly executed.

Susan carefully put some of Kath's biscuits on a plate, then poured the boiling water into the plunger. The ground coffee released its fragrant aroma like a freshly opened box of chocolates. Grace had drunk so many cups after Claire's death, giving her hands and mouth a distraction, when her fingers ached to curl into fists and her tongue to spit mean words. Perhaps she should have allowed these hands their freedom, let them punch the walls, scratch, claw; opened her mouth to scream at the moon. It might have given Susan and Peter permission to do the same.

Susan set the kettle back on the hob, then turned to face Grace. 'Can I ask you something?'

'Of course.'

'Why did you marry Dad?'

It was a good question. Not *Why did you marry Dad if he made you so unhappy?* but rather a simple enquiry about the early spark between two people. Grace thought for a moment. She made her mind go back, past the disappointments and complications, to her earliest, easier impressions.

'I guess because he made me laugh at first. As a young man he was very witty, very playful. Always ready with a joke.'

Her early cooking days, before she'd fully honed the skills acquired from Mother, had offered him scope.

'Bloody hell, doll. You're meant to pluck a chicken before roasting it.'

'I did, but not all the feathers would come out. I don't think I had the water hot enough.'

'Sit the next one in front of the radiator. She might take her coat off for you.'

It was only later that he stopped laughing at her mistakes.

'But at a deeper level, I was attracted to him because he was risky – dangerous even. I didn't want to live as my mother had – afraid to do anything that wouldn't meet with the town's approval. In many ways he was the opposite of what people in Harvest would want me to marry. That had a lot of appeal.'

'And love? Did you love him?' Susan took up a spoon and started stirring the coffee grind in the boiling water.

Grace thought back to the dance hall fight. That experience had taught her that love wasn't just an emotion that started as a dull ache in the pit of the stomach and spread to the heart; it could also start as an expectation.

'I thought I loved him. But what is love really but an alternative to living alone? You look at a potential mate and ask yourself *Can I live with this person for the rest of my life? Is he the best match for me?* When I was young, they were the sorts of questions I asked myself about love. What I didn't think about was how much we all change in a lifetime. It was foolish to think that match wouldn't alter as well. I'm not sure your father or I liked some of those changes.'

'He still cared for you, you know? He told me as much – not long before he died.'

Still? Even then? How was he so sure it wasn't just familiarity he felt?

Susan continued. 'He said you were a sparky one, but that he'd always loved that about you. He also said he'd never considered himself good enough for you.'

How was good enough measured? What defined it – words, actions, deeds? If those were the yardsticks then, Grace decided, neither she nor Des had been *good enough*.

Susan stopped stirring, looked thoughtful. 'I always considered him a man of his time,' she said. 'A bit arrogant. A bit chauvinistic. A man's man with not a lot of insight into female emotions. But I also believed he was being the only man he knew how to be, so we could forgive him his faults.' She gently tapped the spoon on the lip of the plunger before placing it in the sink.

'Perhaps we were all being the only people we knew how to be,' Grace said. 'Perhaps we still are.'

Susan put the plunger in position. 'Sometimes I struggle to know who it is we really are,' she said, and pushed slowly. 'And then there are times I think I know exactly and I don't like it.'

★

Kath turned an anxious face towards Grace as she entered the dining room. Maybe Peter had given them the heads-up when he'd carried the plates in. A little family tête-à-tête, he might have said, trivialising it, or perhaps he blew it out of all proportion with a *Man-o-man, am I glad I got away from that one.*

'Here we are.' Grace placed the tray on the table. 'Your biscuits look delicious, Kath. I hope everybody's got room for one.'

Peter was in his seat, tea towel still over one shoulder. Richard had pushed his chair back from the table, long legs crossed, the top one swinging idly. Jane's make-up had slipped a little further down her face, and her body down her chair.

Susan came into the room and stood behind Richard. She put a hand on each of his shoulders. He reached up, gripped the fingers of one. Grace thought it a comforting gesture to see. Her daughter would always have a safe home in Richard. Susan took Nick's seat, closer to Richard.

'Now, who's for coffee?' Grace asked.

'I'll have a big one. With just a dash of milk, thanks, Grace.'

'Coming right up, Jane.'

'White and one, thanks, Mum,' Peter said.

'Anything other than coffee in the shop?'

'We've made a pot of green tea for you, Richard,' Susan said.

'Don't you just love the way these ladies have looked after us today?' Richard announced.

'We aim to please.' Grace passed him his cup and pot.

'The usual, thanks, Grace,' Kath said.

'Nothing for me,' Susan said. 'It's too hot. I'll stick with water.'

'Why don't you share my green tea? Full of anti-oxidants – help with those tiny crow's feet you keep worrying about.'

'Here we go again,' Peter said, not unkindly.

'In that case, pass the whole pot here. Surely it's never too late?' Kath said, and Grace felt everybody relax a little as they laughed.

The children came back into the dining room Indian file.

'The heat's gone up as the breeze's gone down,' Nick said, sitting next to Susan.

Jorja slid into Ada's seat, beside Grace.

'Great. Biscuits,' Tom said. He and Jaxon took one each as they passed on the way back to their chairs.

Settling beside Peter, Meg rested her head against her father's shoulder and pulled the tea towel over her head like a veil.

'Your tea towel isn't very *manly*, Daddy,' she said. A new word, Grace guessed.

'Sometimes even manly people have to do girlie jobs. You're all hot and sticky. Why don't you lean up against your mum?'

'But you're squishier.'

'Translation – fatter,' Nick said.

Peter balled up the tea towel and threw it at Nick, who ducked in time to miss it. Nick used the same gun-finger action Peter had used on him earlier.

'What were you saying about reflexes?'

Families were like sand dunes, Grace decided. They shifted shape and position with even the gentlest of forces. Even a tiny puff – a shrug – could bring about change, move a handful of thoughts to a new understanding, a new authority. A gale, like today's, and whole dunes – lives and futures – were relocated, reimagined.

So much resentment had percolated undetected in this family for so many years. Each of them had failed to recognise the other's hurt, everyone had believed their suffering was more worthy. So what should they do about these feelings, now that they were out? Because it was clear that what had been said today couldn't be unsaid, or forgotten.

Abruptly, with the last of the coffee drunk, Peter slapped his hands on his thighs.

'Well, we better hit the road.'

'We probably should too, Susan. School day tomorrow. Can we drop you anywhere, Kath?'

'No thanks, Richard. I thought I'd see if Grace had a spare bed I could cadge for the night.'

'A big girl's sleepover?' Meg asked.

Kath laughed. 'Yes. We'll sit up late eating chocolate in bed, reading the Seniors Supplement and giggling about the boys we fancy.'

People filed out of the dining room and went in their different directions, gathering belongings.

At the front door Grace waited for them.

Susan came to her first. Grace wrapped her arms round her daughter and held her close and for longer than they'd normally embrace.

'Thanks for your help today,' she said.

Susan didn't completely relax inside her arms, but neither did she pull away.

'I love you,' Grace said quietly, so only Susan heard. They were words that were always awkward between them. She held Susan at arm's length and looked into her face. She could see that stern and determined child marked indelibly in the adult – in the frown lines that sat like thick commas between her eyebrows; the small muscles that pulsed either side of her jaw – her legacy from Des. Grace reached out, gently massaged the space between Susan's brows with her thumb until it was smooth, then looped a strand of hair behind her ear, just as she'd have done when she was a child.

'Will you come and see me for coffee next week?'

Susan paused a moment, visualising her diary, or considering her desires, perhaps. Then her face softened. 'I'll try.'

'Room for a small one?' Jaxon said, and slipped into the space between mother and daughter.

'Always,' Grace said as Jaxon hugged her.

He did the limbo out under their arms.

Next came Tom. 'And a bit bigger one?' He squeezed between them and hugged Grace as well.

By now Susan and Grace had clasped hands and created a bridge for each child to play the game, lowering their arms and capturing each as they came between them.

'And a teeny-weeny one?' Meg asked, taking her turn.

'A gorgeous one?' Jorja flicked her fringe back from her face and laughed as she hugged Grace.

'A tall one?' Nick dwarfed them both as he moved into the space.

'Anybody else?' Grace asked. By now the children were cheering and clapping the adults on.

Jane teetered through next, her breath sour but her embrace warm.

Then it was Richard's turn. He ducked in and wrapped an arm round the waist of each of them; kissed Grace's cheek first, then Susan's.

'Lovely meal, ladies. Thank you,' he said, and moved through to join the others.

Peter was the last to stand on the other side of the bridge. He looked reluctant, hoping it would collapse and he'd be let off the hook.

'Come on, your turn,' Grace said, and the chorus of those already on the other side repeated it.

He moved into the space and Grace lowered her arms as she'd done with the others. Confined, he was forced to stay and hug her. He was wooden, a man not used to public displays of affection. Grace kept her arms lowered for longer than she had with the others, in the hope he'd soften. Only his voice did, as he said, 'Happy birthday, Mum.'

Grace thought of the grains of sand in a dune and how big changes could also start with small shifts. A gentle voice would have to do for now.

At the end Grace and Kath stood side by side on the front patio and watched the departures. Outside was Sunday night quiet, light disappearing from the sky, snatched to the west as the sun dropped over the horizon. The streetlights came on, their glow orange and pale, not yet warmed up. The bags of waste on the sides of the road were grey silhouettes between each light pole – soon they would disappear from view altogether. A bottle tumbled free from a pile somewhere, likely upset by little more than a footfall.

Nick drove away first, sounding a playful tune on his car horn. Peter followed. Jane, Tom and Meg stretched their arms through their open windows and waved wildly. Richard went last with Jorja and Jaxon waving just as keenly from the back. Susan's face looked pale and small, just as Ada's had, as she drove away.

'There goes your future,' Kath said, as they waved them off.

And here stands their history, Grace thought.

EPILOGUE

Once Grace thought she'd seen Jesus in the barn. She'd spied him through a knot hole in the wood with a five-year-old's eye. He was strung up high, arms wide, just as he hung on the timber cross behind Father Donnelly's altar. But her Jesus was suspended from two large hooks.

The barn had been gloomy, but beams of light from other holes and cracks in the timber walls shot lines across his upper body; his hips and legs were hidden by a wall of baled hay. At the time Grace thought it must be the light of his attending angels or the ethereal glow she'd seen surrounding him in pictures at church.

Her eye had grown wide as she'd peered through that knot hole, taking in the scene of Jesus, bloodied and crucified in the barn.

Fearful, she'd run home to Mother, where she blurted in a breathless, unthinking rush: 'Jesus is hanging in the barn.'

Mother had slapped Grace hard across the face.

'Don't you make fun of the Lord,' she said, and sunk her fist into a mound of scone dough she was working.

Red-cheeked and afraid to speak of her vision again, Grace slipped away to a quiet spot in the shade and drew the image with a stick in the dust.

Sixty-five years later, this picture of Jesus had remained vivid to Grace. But she knew enough now to be able to laugh at the wild imaginings of a child. At the time though, even as Pa carried the buttery-coloured carcass of a lamb across his shoulder from the barn and placed it on the kitchen table for Mother to cleave into all manner of chops and roasts, Grace the child had failed to see what the adult eventually could.

Grace remembered this long ago incident after her family had left that day. And it had made her wonder: if a child could get something so wildly wrong, why not an adult? How could anyone's perceptions of an event ever be trusted?

Such thoughts had made her ask Kath: 'What was I like after Claire died?'

After the family lunch the two friends had sat drinking wine into the evening.

Kath, pushing and plumping a cushion at her back at the time, had paused, then resumed again, adjusting the cushion in small, considered increments, delaying her answer, or thinking about it, perhaps. She finally settled back.

'Troubled. Distant. Frightening,' she said.

Grace stopped stroking the corded fabric of the sofa. 'Why frightening?'

Kath considered the question, elbow on the armrest, chin cupped in hand and one long finger tapping at her temple.

'It was as though you walked a tightrope,' she said, 'balancing or teetering between madness and reason, calm and frenzy. Some days we had to watch you fall. That was frightening.'

Grace pictured this crazy woman Kath described as a cinematic cliché – dishevelled hair, wild-eyed, manic hands doing and redoing tasks, then at other times inert, vacant. She felt frightened of her too. But the fear grew not from imagining this Hitchcock re-creation but from not really being able to recall her at all.

What she could recall, though, before everything became dipped in darkness, were those two small, terrified faces in the back of the Belmont that day, hands clutching the seat in front of them. Grace had no memory of what those faces looked like for a long time after that.

'Maybe he did the right thing,' she said, 'getting rid of everything the way he did.'

Kath shrugged. 'The anger it provoked had a way of reawakening your spirit.'

'But what a way to do it.' Grace remembered how the incinerator smouldered for a full forty-eight hours.

Cremations were quicker, surely.

'Des didn't – how shall I say it ...' Kath looked briefly to the ceiling for an answer, 'show a lot of insight.'

Grace would have said it was compassion he lacked, but she could see that the word insight was one Susan would use too. She went back to stroking the corduroy.

'Nick says anger's like a poison if you don't let it go.'

'Now that's insightful, and he's probably right.'

For a moment the only sound between the two friends was the tick of the mantel clock. Grace was lost in her thoughts; Kath waited for her to find them. As the minute hand slid to a new block of time, Grace sighed deep and long.

'And I thought I'd got us all through it okay. Nobody starved. Each of them got through school. Married. Had families of their own.' Grace marked off the list against the fingers on her left hand. 'Job done. House in order. While all the time everything was a mess – still is a mess, as it turns out.'

'You weren't the only one responsible for keeping things in order.'

'But rightly or wrongly, it's sounding more and more like Des was the only one who did take any kind of responsibility. God knows what I was doing.'

'Grief's a personal thing, Grace. There's no perfect or right way to do it.'

'But I'm sure Susan thinks I acted like I did on purpose – trying to punish them for how Claire died.'

'Were you?'

Grace looked sharply at her friend. 'No.'

'So what are you afraid of?'

That, Grace thought, was a good question.

From the kitchen window Grace could just make out the length of her quarter-acre block in the almost dark. The remnants of the party were long gone. She'd just finished clearing up after another meal: a meal for two.

She smiled remembering Peter's suggestion that she lived on a large area of land. She had always considered it small. Yet she'd also considered the farm at Harvest small once. Grace remembered how she'd felt confined by those hills that surrounded it, just as she felt confined by the houses and units that were around her now. What a fool she'd been not to appreciate the space that stretched before her back then, all the way from the home paddock down to the river. Two hundred acres made a quarter of one look like a sweet wrapper on a sports field in comparison. Such a small square on which to build a life.

She had a sudden urge to go back to Harvest. It had been almost twelve years since she had. She'd gone to watch Joe's coffin lowered into the earth alongside their parents. Where Pa's lungs had been weak from asthma, Joe's had found another kind of weakness – a lesion Grace imagined as black as tar and probably caused by the same thing. At least they'd been laid to rest in the correct order: the child last.

She'd like to visit their graves – they'd be in a state. She figured Pa and Joe wouldn't mind that the dandelions and clover had been allowed to grow wild above their bones. Mother would prefer that hers be well-kept, the edges neatly trimmed and fresh flowers placed in a jam jar resting against the headstone, just once in a while, to show those in the town that someone still cared.

Maybe she could make amends with those hills that once held her, spend some time watching their colours change and see the beauty of them through different eyes. The old farmhouse might even be still standing, the rooms they once slept in, ate in, used as a store for hay or grain perhaps, with the eating and sleeping done in a smart new house across the way. She thought it more likely her family home had fallen down by now – smashed to the ground by a wind that wouldn't let up on her nail-rusted sides, or dropped gracefully one still evening, like an old lady's curtsy taken on knees too tired to push her up again. If the old barn still stood, she might hold her eye to a knot hole in the wood. Time might lend her a new vision in the dim light.

ACKNOWLEDGMENTS

A novel springs first from the mind of its author, but is then touched by many others, each of whom leave their mark, if not necessarily on the final work, most certainly on the life of the author.

Of those people, special thanks must go to friend and mentor Kris Olsson. Your gentle wisdom, subtle questions and well-timed silences helped me to pause, think and find confidence, and your humour and friendship kept me grounded in the real world.

Heartfelt thanks to Caroline and Lynda who have been with me since the first word; Alison and Julie for never losing faith even when mine was lagging; and Jane and Christine for helping keep the dream alive. Thanks also to Jocelyn, Louise, David, Sue, Michael, Sarah, Mick, and my Tuesday friends for your support and encouragement; and to Wayne, Janina, Martin, Andrew, and the enviably younger Grissie cohort − for your friendship and laughter.

Thanks to Varuna, The Writers' House in Katoomba, NSW. The publishing fellowship I was awarded at this unique and invaluable place came at a crucial time in the novel's progress.

Gratitude and thanks to Judith Lukin-Amundsen – your relaxed and generous conversations were as important to me as your insightful editorial notes. Thanks also to the professional and supportive team at UQP: Madonna Duffy, Jacqueline Blanchard and Meredene Hill – your enthusiasm and energy for books is boundless.

Finally, thanks to my family – to John for never questioning the purpose of it, and to my sons, Aaron and Liam, your curiosity about the ways of the world is ever contagious, as is the humour you bring to our table.